LIVE
THROUGH
THIS

KRISTEN McGUINESS

LIVE THROUGH THIS

A NOVEL

RISE
BOOKS

Rise Books

Jacket design by TK
Interior design by Aubrey Khan, Neuwirth & Associates, Inc.

Library of Congress Cataloging-in-Publication Data
Available Upon Request

ISBN 978-1-959524-00-7 (hardcover)
ISBN TK (eBook)

Printed in the United States of America

First Edition
10 9 8 7 6 5 4 3 2 1

To Tere . . . this was always a love story.

Gigantic,

Gigantic,

Gigantic,

A big, big love.

THE PIXIES

LIVE THROUGH THIS

ONE

I don't know. Maybe marriage is just a bad idea," I confess, as my husband and I drive through the little suburb we now call home.

Montrose is surrounded by mountains and sunshine, a series of tree-lined streets where six-year-old girls ride their bicycles unaccompanied, pigtails fluttering behind them as neighbors greet each other by name. Even though it is mere miles from the beating, bleeding heart of downtown Los Angeles, the suburb is wrapped in an Americana usually lost on big cities, its town center dotted with the type of shops that filled main streets back when housewives took their buggies for midday walks and husbands came home tired, some with shiny black briefcases, others with stained uniforms, their names stitched onto the pocket. The only indication that it is 2016 is the dueling Starbucks and Coffee Bean, which sit across from each other in permanent repose at the town's main intersection.

We turn left at the Starbucks as I continue, "It's just too much. I mean, three days with my best friends and I'm pickled. But somehow, I'm supposed to spend every day with you, and deal with finances and this fucked-up shit and then what, I'm still supposed to put your dick in my mouth? It's just all too much."

Theo and I have been driving in silence since he told me his news. After three months working at yet another drug and alcohol rehab, he's been fired.

"I'll get another job, Jane," he replies, way too quickly, ignoring that this isn't the first time we've had this conversation, knowing that it likely won't be the last. But then he looks over at me with that quick smile, the one that made him so inviting to begin with. "But you still want to suck my dick, right?"

"Not really," I reply, laughing though his easy good looks now rarely charm me, his wide shoulders and head of brown curls, the green eyes that once reminded me of the deep end of the ocean. We didn't have a smoldering love affair but we had enough fire to attract each other in the dark, warmed by the knowledge that out of the people who had failed us, we could, at the very least, trust each other. But then the responsibilities of life moved in, with bills to pay and jobs to lose and all the fears that come when you're dancing with debt and sleeping with financial insecurity. And though we were once a couple who always fought a lot, we also fucked. Now, we just fight.

We moved to Montrose the year before, having found ourselves and met each other in the hipster neighborhood of Silver Lake. Of course, we lived there when it was still rough around the edges and cheap, wearing tight jeans and striped T-shirts, Wayfarers on. We rented a one-bedroom bungalow on a street with a babbling brook running under it. But when we could no longer afford it, we headed north to the suburbs where we found Montrose—the towns of Los Angeles as distinct as though they were in different states, not just right up the street.

I don't think either of us thought we'd end up here, eating at Panda Express and pining for a Target to open in the neighborhood.

"It's just exhausting," I finally say as we pull up to our house.

"But it's also that." Theo points to the ballast of pink balloons attached to the front of our house, an announcement to anyone passing by, to our now shared and suburban hearts, which trip and flutter at the reminder, that our sweet little girl is turning one.

We get out of the car and walk into our house carrying cake and food and more balloons, preparing for one of the few rites of passage in modern life: the first birthday party. The celebration of surviving sleep regressions and breastfeeding struggles and the trauma that occurs when you go from being carefree to caring for someone for the rest of your life.

At the last minute, we changed the festivities from Sunday to Saturday, telling everyone it was because of a rainy forecast. But the real reason was that I was obsessed with booking a children's musician who played the ukulele and went by the name Peanut. Peanut was booked on Sunday, but she could do an hour in the afternoon on Saturday and so, three days before the party, I sent out the text, lost some guests, and got fucking Peanut.

"Of course, you did," Theo laughed when I told him about the change. "You always get what you want, don't you, Jane Ambrose?"

That was true once. Back when I walked with the hard swagger of someone who was going to become something. Bold and determined, oozing sex and ambition, watch out, you lucky bastards, here I come. Back then, my blonde hair was long and wild, a wavy mess that in college led my friends to call me a hunter, known for my voracious appetite in school and in love. My full lips and wide nose only adding to the metaphor. As someone once told me, I wasn't the marrying type, and though it broke my heart to hear the words, I couldn't help but agree. It's as much of a surprise to me that I ended up here, tamed beyond recognition.

I pull my hair back up into a bun and wipe off a dash of frosting that has oozed out of the cake box onto my denim shirt. I thought the husband and the kid and the house in the burbs would swallow the ghost of that other woman. But when you pop a balloon, you can still hear it cry.

"Where's Zoe?" I ask, putting the cake down on the table.

"Outside," Andrea's lips turn downward. "Your friends are here."

My mom and uncle Dennis have come into town for the celebration. They don't like LA, though they both only live twenty miles south in the South Bay, blocks from each other in Redondo Beach.

"The streets are so narrow here," my mom Andrea often remarks, after driving to our house, as though the city of LA doesn't have enough cement.

My mother doesn't approve of our friends either, most of whom are other recovered alcoholics who Theo and I met in AA, having gotten sober and grown up together, exchanging methamphetamines for Montessori and one-night stands for mid-century nightstands.

"Just so many tattoos," she frequently remarks after meeting any of them, ranking tattoos just below bangs as one of the worst decisions a woman can make for her life.

I look over to where Theo opens the door to Peanut, the musician in question. I welcome her in but can tell Theo is frustrated.

"What's going on?" I ask.

"My parents." He shakes his head. "They should be here by now."

"Have you called them?" I ask, looking out the front door as though they might be pulling up.

"I tried the house phone but it's not like they would have brought their cell."

"Yeah, why would they do that?" I can't help but scoff.

Theo's parents are both immigrants from Greece. But whereas some people came to America and left their identities in the towns and villages from which they departed, Theo's parents lugged theirs like heavy trunks onto the plane. I have the grace of distance from my ancestors' shores, but Theo's parents were far closer to the source of their twentieth-century pain, remembering grandparents who lived in caves, hiding from the Nazis, and a version of the 1970s that was steeped in poverty and desperation and not the idealized decade of Theo's and my youth. And like many first-generation Americans, Theo carried portions of that load, both in the promise he once held for them, and the disillusionment he felt compelled to repeat.

"They'll be here," I offer, trying to find the kindness that can be the formaldehyde to marriage.

Theo and I both knew what it was like to betray a dream. Theo was given a contract with the Dodgers when he was just seventeen years old. A high school dropout with a golden arm, everyone expected he would be the kind of name to go down in history, but what Theo's managers and coaches and agents didn't know was that Theo was also a drug addict.

By the time he was eighteen, the contract was gone, he was smoking meth on the streets, and unless you were a Dodgers buff, no one remembered the short-lived career of Golden Arm Karras.

Theo goes to close the door just as my friend Rose walks in. Rose with the pretty face and reckless curls, her style a marriage of

Stevie Nicks and Morrissey, wearing long flowing skirts with punk patches on her jean jacket and the same dirty Docs she's had since high school. I've known Rose since then too, back when we were both outsiders, along with our friend Maggie. Three girls who couldn't find a way to fit in. I was the ambitious one, Rose was the artist, and Maggie was the romantic. After dropping out of Julliard, Rose came back west even before I did, playing bass in a couple early aught indie bands at the kind of bars that served up PBR on draft by mustached men in deep V-neck shirts. By time 2012 rolled around, Rose quit the stage and instead became a music booker for one of those same bars, the Mojave Saloon, a honky-tonk venue out in the desert.

I go to greet my friend, never knowing that her appearance will forever alter the course of this story. But maybe that's just how life works. Maybe there are a million different choices a person can make every moment of every day, playing chess with God, moving the pawn, jumping the knight, hitting the timer in a game where, in the moment, the stakes never seem as high as they are.

"John Thomas will be playing at the Mojave next week," Rose announces. "You guys should come out."

John Thomas is a famous LA punk rocker from the eighties, who settled into a retro country vibe as he got older, blending his old persona with a Johnny Mathis suit. When I first got sober, I went to see him perform with Rose. It was the first time I realized I could listen to music without a drink in my hand, that going out at night didn't require complete obliteration.

"When?" I ask as I put out the chips and guacamole for the party, pulling out the drinks as Theo unloads the ice into a bowl. How I wish our duties were always this equally split.

"Friday night," Rose replies, stacking the cans of LaCroix as she jokes, "LaCroix darling."

"The only drink that no one ever finishes," I reply. We are opening the boxes of pizza as I realize, "Shit, my mom will still be here."

"What do you mean?" Rose asks.

"We can go, without Zoe."

"Are you sure?" Theo interjects.

"You can bring Zoe, if you want," Rose offers.

"Really, you two? One night, John Thomas, the Mojave Saloon, do we really want to bring the baby? I mean, look, Theo, if you want to stay home with Andrea, by all means."

We look over to where my mom is sweeping the floor in the middle of the party, determined that our house could be cleaner.

He shakes his head and smiles at Rose, "We'll see you Friday night, I guess."

In some ways, Theo is the more committed parent. Though I love Zoe with every proton and electron buzzing through my body, there is something in me that still aches for independence, for a dream I never realized. Theo's dream is achieved: he has a family.

As though on cue, the door opens, and Theo's brother enters the party, followed by his father George. When Theo and I first started dating, I became fast friends with his sibling, Peter, who then still identified as his sister. Because at the time, Peter was a butch lesbian who wore leather jackets and rode motorcycles. But by the time Zoe was born five years later, Peter had begun to transition, becoming the man he always knew himself to be. Though Lydia in all her conservative Christianity didn't know how to accept that her daughter was a lesbian, she knew Peter was a boy since the day she found out she was pregnant.

"Where's Mom?" Theo asks, nearly barricading his brother and father in our foyer.

The same year they realized Theo had ADHD, Lydia was diagnosed with bipolar 1. In the early eighties, less was known about the disorder than even now, leaving his small Greek family adrift in a sea of psychiatric hospitals and electrotherapy and calls to 911 that never seemed to solve the problem. But as Theo got older, it became harder for him to tweeze apart the disorder from the woman suffering from it, to understand why she just couldn't show up.

"She wasn't feeling well," his father replies, pushing past as Zoe toddles up to him, beginning to realize that this party is indeed for her. As Zoe arches toward her grandpa, already so determined after a single year of life, we see the confidence that blooms when a child isn't raised in trauma.

As the party moves into full swing, Theo and I watch from the corner of the room as our child, this incredible combination of DNA and the belief that this time we would do it better, stands in front of the musician I was determined to hire. Peanut is in the middle of singing "Itsy Bitsy Spider" in English, Spanish, and Hebrew. She has bright red lips and thick black bangs and a ukulele framed with just enough cleavage to make the dads pay attention.

Theo puts his arm around me, trying to connect. "It would be fun to see John Thomas."

I want to give in, want to ignore that Theo has been fired again, and that I will now have to figure out the consequences. I feel trapped between the desire to have fun—to celebrate my daughter, to love my husband, to get away for one night to the desert—and the responsibilities of being an adult whose rent is due in a matter of weeks, and who needs to pay her Honda lease by Friday.

"It would be more fun if you could just grow up," I reply, unable to soften even in the soft moments.

"Jane, I'll figure it out," Theo promises, but it's the same promise he's been making since we met, and five years later, it still hasn't happened.

My uncle Dennis walks over, and I can tell he sees the tension as he smiles and nods toward Zoe. "I can't believe we're doing this again."

I laugh. "Dennis, I'm thirty-five years old. It's about time someone around here finally reproduced."

Dennis has been single for so long, people have stopped asking him why. My grandmother was a Hungarian immigrant, emigrating to Los Angeles in the hopes of becoming a star herself. Like Andrea, she believed beauty would solve everything. Maybe it was Dennis's golden boy looks that had skewed life for him, imprisoning him in an all-American-ness that never allowed for the messier parts of life, like love or marriage or reproduction. Instead, he became a pilot for American Airlines, spending most of the year flying international routes, pretending he was living in a different era, when the job was still sexy. He would sometimes tell people that he would have married the right person, but that person never showed up. I now wonder whether Theo was the one who showed up or if maybe, there is a part of me that inherited my uncle's inability to settle down.

Andrea walks over and whispers to me, "Are we ready for the cake?"

"I sure am," I reply. We walk into the kitchen where Dennis is already pulling the cake out of the box. Since Zoe is too young to choose her favorite cake, I bought mine, a strawberry cream cake from a small bakery in Chinatown. Dennis notices the Mandarin writing on the side and jabs, "What? Is American cake not great enough for you?"

We've managed to ignore the looming 2016 election until this point, and the disturbing fact that my charming, kind, and generous uncle has swiftly gone from being an economic conservative to someone who is now parroting the presidential candidate Donald Trump.

I turn, hoping Theo hasn't heard him but it's too late, "There's not space for any of that here, Dennis."

"Well, you're really crazy if you think old man Bernie is going to win," Dennis replies, as Andrea and I hurry to get the cake out, suddenly afraid of the political debate that sits on the edge of every conversation between my uncle and husband.

"I don't care about that," Theo continues. "You don't mention that racist shit in our house, and certainly not at my daughter's party."

I know Dennis wants to reply, wants to say something about it being my house or Theo not paying for our life, but he also knows who he's up against, and you don't fuck with Theo Karras.

I smile, remembering that this is what drew me to Theo in the first place, his willingness to make people uncomfortable. He wasn't afraid to stand up, to the police, to my uncle, to the managers at the Dodgers. And though he had paid the price for it in all kinds of ways, as had I, his intensity was what had made me fall in love with him in the first place. And like that, Theo shifts gears, wiping the now dried whipped cream off my shirt, "Yum."

"Gross," I say, even as I ruffle his hair, wishing I could hold on to this feeling.

He smiles. "Happy one year, Mama."

And maybe this is what it means to be the marrying type, to not just accept that I have become a caregiver, but to celebrate it, to break out the cake and candles in its honor. I look over to where Zoe sits in front of Peanut, busy shaking the rice-filled eggs carried by all children's musicians.

Shake, shake, shake. Zoe grins for her audience.

Shake, shake, shake. Theo takes a picture.

Shake, shake, shake. This is our life.

TWO

My boots hit the dirt in the dark, the bright desert sky stretching above our heads as Rose and I move across the sand, nimbly navigating the cactus caught in our shadows. We are running over to a nearby barn where the musicians hang out before the show, smoking and drinking whiskey, like it's a different decade altogether.

Rose slows down, lighting a cigarette, stopping before we walk into the barn.

"So how are you guys?" she asks, referring to my marriage with the nonchalance of someone who doesn't really believe in love. I want to take the cigarette from her hand and join her.

In many ways, Rose is not so different from Dennis. Though she never seemed to be disappointed by the choices in her life, I felt like something was missing in the space where we reach out to find one another.

"I don't know if I can keep doing it," I finally reply, catching a glimpse of myself in the barn's window, always slightly surprised by the reflection—the safe blonde highlights, my hair hanging anonymously past my shoulders, the wild mane now trimmed into something far more manageable. Everything about me feels like a betrayal.

"He got fired again?" she asks.

"Yeah, did I tell you at the party?"

"No, he did. You know, Jane. We all have our shit. It doesn't make Theo a bad guy."

"But doesn't it make him a bad husband?"

"Depends how you define husband."

"I'm not sure I can let go of the standard definition," I admit.

"But can you let go of him?" she asks.

The minute I met Theo, I was mesmerized. He walked up to me in an AA meeting, looking like a young Bob Dylan, blood on the tracks. As he approached, all I could think was, "Who is *that*?"

His strong shoulders and easy frame sloped even while he somehow bounced, as though he had never been quite tethered well enough to earth. By the time he shook my hand, I knew my life was about to change, and not just because I was sober. A few weeks later, when I needed help with the pilot light on my heater, Theo came over and never left. Within the space of a year, we moved in together and got married as I found a job working for a nonprofit and Theo tried to parlay the brief baseball career into helping other athletes get sober. In theory, it seemed to make sense, both of us getting a second chance, only the second chance couldn't help but remind me of the first one, of the shot I didn't make.

I look at Rose, this friend who adopted Theo as a brother, watching as we fell in love, got married, struggled to have a baby.

And she also knew, that despite Theo's flaws, he was the antidote to my years of being with men who didn't know how to love me.

"Jane," she tries again. "I know you want more, but maybe that doesn't have anything to do with Theo. Maybe that's just about you."

When I was growing up, Andrea would make me watch Robert Redford movies the way some parents make their kids practice the piano. I wasn't sure if she wanted me to follow in the family foot-steps of attempted stardom or if she just wanted me to fall in love with Robert Redford. We would watch *The Way We Were* and cry at the same scenes, aching with Streisand's words as she pleads, "I want, I want, I want."

I wanted and for a long time, I allowed the want to drive me, but then it seemed my wanting only hurt me. That the wants were bigger than I was capable of achieving, they were bigger than the world would allow. And I decided instead that wanting was for other people. The train had passed me by, and I found myself standing alone on the platform, wondering where all the promise and passion had gone. But it wasn't always that way.

In the late nineties, I left my strange little South Bay world for NYU. It was a boom-time economy and boom-time fun—no wars, no terrorist attacks, just a slew of young pop stars and platform shoes. It felt like the world was only going up from there, a sure and steady place, and I was determined to play a role in it. It's no wonder the term *irony* became the calling card for my generation, trapped between the theory and practice of what was and what might have been.

It wasn't like I was the head of my class, but I was a part of something, of a movement of bright and able college grads who believed we were going to change the world. I graduated right before 9/11, caught in the straddle of the old world and the new. The baby boomers held all the reins to power, but we were building a better bridle, it was called the internet, and we were going to harness it for good. I found myself producing one of the biggest news shows in the world. I traveled from Kansas to Kabul. I wasn't going to be somebody—I *was* somebody. In just a few short years, I was already making the lists, thirty under thirty and all that jazz.

Yet here I am, ten years later, moored from those old dreams, working every day as a grant writer in foster care, sitting in an anonymous office at the children's courthouse, hitting save, and driving home. The worst part is I come from a long line of people who failed to meet their potential. Dreams as big as grapefruit have died on the vines of my lineage. My father risked it all to make it and lost it all when he failed, and my mother gave up so long ago, I'm not even sure she put up a fight.

As we drove out that afternoon, bitter and quiet along the I-10, I felt like one of those celebrity couples who goes to Bermuda for a week to decide if they want to stay married.

"I don't know." I look up at the night sky. "I've never been married before. I don't know if I should leave or if this is just what it's supposed to feel like."

"You'll know when you know, Janey," Rose inhales her last drag, before dropping it on the ground and heading into the barn.

I linger for a moment and look out at the mountains. I sometimes wonder what Theo and I would have been like in an alternate dimension. Who would we be if we didn't have to worry about the money and jobs and Theo's ADHD and the frustrating disappointments that seemed to leaden our love? Who would we be in a space where all the hard facts of life didn't wrench themselves between that first night and the one we are in right now? Who would we be if it was all just easier?

Because ever since Zoe was born, Theo and I have become once-extraordinary people now living ordinary lives, blending in with the other hip playground parents with their CRVs and Subarus, vinyl collections, and "meaningful" tattoos. But maybe that's just part of getting older—you give up on the Oscar speech, the broadcasting career, the World Series, and you settle for lesser awards, for being unique among your peers, but not among the world.

O ver here," Theo calls to me as I search for him in the slowly gathering audience. He's close to the front of the stage. Theo knows I hate being in front, trapped between obnoxious guys pushing the crowd forward and girls with sweaty makeup screaming the wrong lyrics, but that doesn't stop him, because he loves it. I immediately get annoyed. And this is the awkward dance of marriage, moving from tenderness to rage in the space of minutes.

"Where were you?" Theo asks. The first band is busy breaking down their set before John Thomas arrives.

"We went to meet John," I reply, trying to reclaim the hope that bloomed inside me only moments before. "He was really nice. Rose said you'll definitely meet him after."

"Oh, no worries," Theo leans in to kiss my cheek. "I'm glad you got some alone time with Rose. Where is she?"

"She's over at the office, dealing with management and some paperwork."

Theo turns back to the stage, waiting for John to walk out.

"Theo," I say, unsure of how to reply:

"*I love you.*"

"*I'm sorry.*"

"*I don't know if I can do this anymore.*"

But he doesn't let me finish. Pulling me in, he whispers, "I'm glad Zoe's not here."

I laugh and pull away, checking my phone to see if my mother has responded to my text asking whether Zoe has gone to bed. She writes that the baby is fast asleep.

I look at the time. I will remember it later: 9:42 p.m. The odd collection of numbers and letters that are meaningless on their own, but married together in the right way, become history.

"Yeah, we wouldn't be here if she was," I reply, letting go of the more important thing I want to say. "There is no way we would have been able to keep her up for this."

"No way," Theo repeats. With no great fanfare, John Thomas's band takes the stage, everyone setting up their instruments like dental technicians, efficient and friendly.

Years ago, right after we got married, Theo and I visited the Mojave to see another friend of Rose's perform, the folk singer Victoria Williams.

When I was in sixth grade, my father died. The year after, Victoria Williams was diagnosed with multiple sclerosis. To help pay for her medical bills, musicians came together to do a benefit album covering some of her greatest songs—including Pearl Jam, who sang Victoria's "Crazy Mary." I was obsessed with the song. It was part of the mix tape of my adolescence, when I would walk around Redondo smoking cigarettes and listening to music that I believed no one else could possibly understand. Of course, I hadn't met Rose yet.

When we came out to hear Victoria play, Theo and I drove around the desert all afternoon before the show, listening to Victoria's version of "Crazy Mary" as I sang along. Most friends would turn up the radio whenever I sang, but not Theo. He liked to hear me howl.

I looked out the window at the desert that day and shared with Theo, "It's like, all those plans you have when you're a kid finally came true. I moved to the big city. I went to cool places. I married you."

"It's been a good life," he replied.

"It ain't over yet, Theo." I rolled down the window, letting in the hot desert air. "It ain't over yet."

The music starts and Theo takes my hand, giving me space to dance. Because for every piece of me he appears to forget, he still knows the parts that really matter. John Thomas's grizzled voice fills the Mojave Saloon, and suddenly I don't want to leave. I want to stand there and dance and hold my husband's hand forever.

Theo moves up to take photos as I close my eyes, and let the music take over, reaching past the lack of sleep and the undistinguished life, lighting me on fire, and reminding me of everything I thought we would be, back when I loved my husband in ways I believed would last. I can feel Theo approach and I open my eyes to see him smiling at me. Some of the girls in the crowd glance in his direction, his slugger's shoulders still such a draw for the female gaze.

And I want to sing, "Naw, naw, ladies, that shit is mine, I just wish I wanted it all the time."

Theo puts his hand to my cheek, and I see the look in his eyes, the one that usually makes me shy away. Instead, I begin to return the smile.

I don't hear anything. Don't see the man enter the bar behind the stage. No one screams or says "Run!" or "Hide!" or "Fight!" All I see is Theo's smile freeze, the look of joy in his eyes twisting into shock before the weight of his body pours down on me.

There are some things that we can never truly imagine as they are. Moments that no matter what you think you might do when they happen, you will come unprepared for reality.

Caught between the overwhelming pops of the gun, I lay there under Theo. I feel like I'm in a tunnel, dark and miserable, and I just want the bullets to stop so I can hear his breath.

I look at the tin roof above me. I feel something warm on my face, but I can't tell what it is; I wonder if I'm bleeding. I know that there is no safer space for me right now than under my husband. I know that if I try to get up, I will become a moving target. Theo feels like he is moving on top of me, but he isn't saying anything. All I hear is my own breath, heavy and terrified, deafened by the ringing in my ears. Maybe that's why no one is screaming. Maybe that's why it's so quiet. There are thoughts. I think of running. I think about how I can't move. I think about Zoe. I think how utterly pointless and priceless this whole business of living is as I feel the bullets hit Theo's body.

Someone screams but it's cut short. Another round of shots goes off. I hear glass breaking and then a bigger blast, loud and definitive.

Finally, someone begins to yell, "He's dead. He's dead. He's dead!"

It goes quiet again. Like everyone just wants to go to sleep and pretend nothing has happened. It's like a lump in the breast or a car swerving into the wrong lane, sentencing us to a fate we didn't choose. I lay there in the silence, my eyes half-open, waiting for Theo's breath to return, to feel his chest expand with life. But I know my prayer is hollow, a perjury of hope, even as I make it.

Sirens whirl in the distance.

Theo's body gets heavier, but I don't want to leave. I want to feel his skin. I want to smell his warm and cedar scent. I want to lie there and never let go.

I hear someone near me whisper, "Is that it?"

I wonder the same thing. Is that it? We wait for what feels like a lifetime to meet the person who completes us—we have their child, we create a family. We build tree houses of our dreams, inching up the ladder while holding on to their perilous frame, knowing that each rung is made of equal parts magic and excrement. And then without warning or warm-up, the whole fucking mess falls apart.

Outside, the sirens blare, as people begin to stand. Wood scrapes the ground and moans rise through the air.

People begin to call out, "I've got someone over here!"

I slowly move my hand up to Theo's face. I reach to hold the back of his head, but there is nothing there. It's just wet and soft and I want to take my hand away, yet I also want to touch his hair, remember the shape of his head. I feel something hard in my hand and I pull back. It feels like a small rock in my palm, like a pebble Zoe might find on our walks. I tighten my hand around it. I can feel my nervous system as if it's in real time—ventral vagus, amygdala, cortisone. My bladder releases and my chest heaves.

And then I hear them; the police and medics have arrived.

I know they're coming for us. I know they'll take him from me. I know he'll just become "someone." When he was never just someone. He is Theo Karras.

I can see someone standing above us, looking down at my husband and the blood-stained woman beneath him. I know what they're about to do, but I stop them.

"We're fine," I say. "We're fine."

The man says something into his radio, even as I continue to repeat the words. He bends down to me, his face close to mine, practically whispering in my ear, "Ma'am. My name is Ben. I am an EMT. We're going to need to lift this man off you to make sure you're okay. Can we do that please?"

I feel like Zoe when she grabs at my legs in the morning as I leave for work. I circle my arms around Theo's back. I try to make my voice strong, like I wish I had so many times before when I was too afraid to ask for what was mine.

"My husband and I are fine."

I hear him stand up and murmur something to someone else.

He comes back over, leaning in again, "Ma'am. I am very, very sorry. But we are going to remove your husband so we can check you. We need to check you now."

I know I scream because I can hear it. I hold on to the pebble in my hand, even as I feel it dig into my skin. I can't stop screaming. I'm not sure I'll ever be able to stop.

I feel everything I ever wanted to feel toward Theo. I want to say *I love you and I'm sorry and I can't do this*. I don't know how to do any of this. I want to scream until there is no voice left. I stare at Ben who is kneeling in front of me, checking me for injuries and taking my pulse. He puts a silver blanket around my shoulders and explains that I am to be taken somewhere for further evaluation. I think he says *evaluation*, but I can't hear him above the screaming. And I wonder why he can't hear me. My mouth is open, but nothing is coming out. He puts his arms under my shoulders and lifts me to my feet.

I look around and there are other people, too. I see a man in a wheelchair and a woman yelling someone's name. I see a couple cowered in the corner, there is a medic tending to the man as his wife pleads with him. I cannot hear her, but I can see her lips, "Stay with us."

I turn back to Theo. He is still on his stomach. I can't see his face. I have to see him. I rush to Theo's body, using everything in me to turn him over, and there he is. He has blood on his face but he's still there. The jaw, the brow, the lips that I kept forgetting to kiss. I press mine to his. I hear someone behind me say, "Wait."

I lay my head on his chest, hoping his breath might still return, confused by how quickly we can be extinguished.

I always thought if there were a shooting, Theo would save us. He would be the guy to wrestle the gun out of the shooter's hand. A hero searching for a crisis.

I can hear the EMT step closer to me.

"Jane?" he says, though I don't know how he knows my name. Did I say my name? "We need to get you out of here."

Ben lifts me back up; another medic begins to cover Theo with a sheet. I know he will never look the same again. The next time I see him, he will be a corpse. But in that last fleeting moment, he is my husband.

THREE

"M a'am, I'm sorry, but your name?" The police officer sits in front of me, but I can barely hear her, like the words are being called out over a canyon, faintly audible from across the divide. I'm on the edge of a medical chaise, the silver blanket has fallen to the floor. The piece of bone I have been holding in my hand has dug itself into my skin like a splinter that won't budge.

"Ma'am?" the police officer leans forward, her words finally becoming distinct. "A counselor will be here to talk to you in a bit, okay? I just need your name."

"Jane," I finally sputter, though the word feels strange. My face burns for a second as if I'm lying but then my name comes into focus, "Jane Ambrose."

I never took Theo's last name of Karras. It wasn't that I didn't like it, but Ambrose had been my name for so long, I felt weird abandoning it. Theo didn't mind. We were both the last of our lines, holding on to our surnames like sinking rafters in a sea of ancestry. Theo's uncles all had girls. Theo's father, at least, had him.

"If we have two boys," Theo once told me. "One of them will be Karras, and the other will be Ambrose. That way both names will live on."

Instead, we had Zoe. Our dear, sweet Zoe, whose face now haunts me, with her full lips and perfect nose, her dark blonde curls and pink cheeks that crinkle with laughter and shrill with tears. It's almost as though she was there with us, as though she, too, is lost. I finally look around, past the woman who is telling me her name (I think it's Patty), as though this is a normal exchange. The room is a cold off-white, like no one really cared what color to paint it. And then in an attempt to make it look like someone gave a shit, they threw a painting on the wall, a desert landscape. I finally notice the stack of bloodied paper towels on the counter and close my eyes. This is what they don't tell you about trauma; it's embarrassing. I don't know what to say, trapped by the thoughts in my head. The bargain already beginning: *Please God, I take it all back. Make time reverse, perform a magic trick and bring him back.*

"Ma'am?" Patty asks again, but I've returned to the painting, staring at the bright yellow sun depicted at its center, exploding across the canvas. I don't even look up when Patty leaves the room.

Instead, I lean back and listen to the officer's voice outside the door, picking up bits and pieces, muffled by what I am beginning to realize is a slight deafness in my ears, as though I have been to a loud concert, only one that barely began.

"Husband."

"Alone."

"No ID."

I try to remember how I got here, and it's not an existential concern. I really don't remember how I got to this clinic. Was it in an ambulance? I rub the bone in my palm with my finger as I stand up, wanting to feel my legs beneath me. Wanting to know that I'm still here. I feel like I got drunk and blacked out. I wasn't really a drunk who did that, but I found the process mesmerizing. One minute you're there, and then, poof, you're gone.

People really don't honor the vanishing act enough.

I touch my head, and my hair is hard. So is my face, which feels sticky and burnt. I can hear Patty walking toward the door, and I sit back down, like I've been doing something wrong, stealing a prescription pad or maybe too many tongue depressors. Patty walks in, and I know she knows. I want to tell her it's okay, but all I can say is the one word that still has meaning and shape.

"Zoe," I announce. "My daughter. She's at home in LA."

"Okay," Patty's face lights up. She pulls out her notepad again, like she just scooped me. "Where is she? Who is she with?"

"She's with my mother. I can call her. I need to . . ."

But I can't continue. I can't say the horrible truth just yet.

The announcement of my daughter sends Patty right back out of the room. I am pretty sure she's never done this before, sort of like a bomb raid drill you might have prepared for in the eighties, crouching under your desk and giggling at the boy across the way.

Fuck. It all used to be so simple, and now Patty is gone and I don't know what else to do. I feel kind of angry but not my usual anger. It feels hard and lumpy, and I just want it all to go away. I don't even notice that Patty has returned, but she is looking at me, waiting for me to answer another question I haven't heard. It's a shitty situation for us both.

"There's a therapist coming," she explains. "We're a little short staffed."

She frowns like this is her fault.

"It's okay," I reply.

But then Patty looks up, trying to make it right. "But I'm going to get you that phone call, okay? I have two little girls . . ."

I nod, happy for the information. *I have children, too* is the secret handshake between half the world. I don't know anything else about you or your life or why you're covered in blood sitting in a medical clinic with no meaning, but I know what it's like to love a child.

"I'm not sure you can make a phone call just yet," Patty warns. "I don't know how they're doing this, so I'm going to go back out and check, okay?"

"Okay," I reply, shocked by the quietness of my voice. She walks out the door, and I lay my head down on the chaise and falling asleep.

Out of all the memories over all the years, I'm not sure there is a more perfect day than the first time Theo took me to Topanga Beach, the spot he had been surfing since he was a kid growing up in LA. We had just started dating and so I pulled out my phone to take pictures, still attracted to the life of a surfer's wife.

I stood up and walked into the shallow part of the ocean to watch him do the one thing he loved most, Theo's self-defining act. The water picked up speed as the swell moved toward him, chasing him down as he maneuvered the board onto its crest. Negotiating with gravity and the velocity below, he got up into a low lunge and found his balance on the break. His board slid down the line, cutting against the wave. And then Theo stood up, confident in his ability to walk on water, to dance upon the sea.

Later, as we were sitting on the beach, I asked him if the surf was good.

"Yeah. There's not a lot of swell but it doesn't matter. Just getting to be here is important. You can feel the waves even if they're not breaking right now."

"You can feel them?"

"Yeah, it's like you can feel a force within the ocean. Even if the water is perfectly still, you know it can kick your ass."

"I guess I never realized how much surfing is really about holding your own against the tide," I told him, watching the glassy waves break against the shore. "It's not about going with the flow, it's about resisting it."

"Sometimes." Theo put his warm, tan arm around me, and I wished we could stay like that forever. He kissed me on the neck and took the camera from me and began to look through the photos as the sun set in the California sky.

"But other times, it's too strong to resist. Once you make the commitment, you're locked in. You either dance with the water . . ." He cocked an eyebrow at me and smiled. "Or you die."

Jane." I can feel a hand on my shoulder.

I don't open my eyes. I know it's the first time I will wake up to this truth.

And I don't want these first times. This grief feels familiar and yet so distant, the moment that the world comes crashing down, but you don't hear the crack before the fall. Because I don't know

if I know how to do this without Theo. He would know how to
guide us, demanding to call home, asking that we get a trauma
therapist in here right now, yelling in the hallway, never knowing
the difference between advocacy and agitation. Instead, I apologize
to Patty, "I'm sorry. I fell asleep."

"Of course, honey," she keeps her hand on my shoulder. "I'm
here to take you to a phone where you can call your mama."

"Okay." I sit up, but I don't want to move. I just want to stay
here, in this alternate universe, because once I step outside that
door, there is no going back. I am already tempted by the story-
book version of our lives, the one with the happy home and the kid
and the dog, the life you think you're supposed to build, the picture
you believe you're supposed to take.

We walk down the hallway of the urgent care, passing rooms
with other people, bloodied but otherwise intact. Patty brings me
to the front desk, "Wait here, honey. Another officer will help you."

She starts to walk away, and then turns around, "I'm really
sorry, Jane."

I smile, which feels like a weird contortion on my face. "It's not
your fault."

In fact, I'm not even sure whose fault it is. Maybe it's mine.
Maybe it was always mine. And then I see her.

A woman stands there in the mirror. She is wearing overalls,
smeared with clotty streaks of brown, her hair matted with blood
and sweat. She is me and yet, I immediately want to go back to the
woman I was, just hours before, standing in front of the bathroom
mirror at the Mojave Saloon. When I was in my twenties and inse-
cure about everything, Rose told me, "Don't worry, because one
day, none of this will matter. Once we reach a certain age, we won't
care what we look like anymore. We'll know how beautiful we are."

I applied a swipe of coral lipstick in the honky-tonk restroom and looked at myself, knowing Rose was right. But also, that I cheated a bit. Theo's love was the foundation of that confidence. He believed in me, and because of that, I believed in me, too. I thought to myself, *I'll tell him that*.

But then I walked out onto the dance floor and here we are.

I don't want to replace that moment with this one. I want to hold on to that image of me in the mirror, on the way to greet my husband, made right by his love.

I hear a commotion behind me as another woman runs out of one of the rooms.

"Nooooo!" she screams, and I turn. She is around my age, maybe even a little younger. She is Latina and pretty. She is younger than me, but I can tell she is tired, too, even before this moment, as I watch her break down across the room from me. "Call the hospital. He's there. He wasn't at the restaurant. I looked. I looked."

"Ma'am," a large police offer tries to calm her. "They found your husband, the manager IDed him. Alfonso Ramirez. That is your husband?"

"No, no," her voice cracks. She sobs and I don't even know what reality I am in. It's like I am watching a movie about our lives, and then I remember the woman, searching the bar after the shooting, calling someone's name.

A nurse comes out and collects the woman as her cries echo down the hall, repeating the same thing over and over, "My husband."

My husband. The police officer now lumbers over to me. He has close-cropped hair, and his eyes are bloodshot. I can tell he's been crying. I haven't cried yet, and it registers like a failure to breathe. I thought it was an autonomic response, but maybe it's more manufactured than we think. I can hear every scuffle along the floor. I can feel every molecule in the air, detecting barely imperceptible sound and movement. But I feel nothing. What the fuck is wrong with me?

"Ma'am, you need to call your mother?" the officer asks.

I'm pretty sure I nod.

The officer gestures toward the phone, but I can only stare at it. And then the man softens, as though he has been through this before, quietly offering, "Take your time."

A clock ticks somewhere in the room and I can hear the officer breathing. I reach forward and pick up the receiver. Suddenly, I remember my cell phone. It had been in my purse, which I lost as soon as Theo and I hit the ground. I don't care about the phone except for what it contains: texts, pictures, memories. I wonder whether I used the iCloud right. Despite all the adrenaline, my fingers move deliberately around the keypad of the phone, dialing the ten digits to my mother's cell phone with dread. The phone rings only twice before Andrea answers, her voice heavy with concern at the call's late hour.

"Mom," I try to steady myself, keeping my voice tight as I grip the reception desk.

"Jane, what's going on? Is everything okay?"

"There's been a shooting . . ."

"What? What shooting? Janey? Are you okay?"

"Yeah," I hesitate, trying to choose precise words. "I'm not injured."

I can hear the relief on the other end of the line, "Oh my God. Honey, thank God."

There is a moment of silence, that silence.

"But Theo . . ." The officer looks away. I know that I can let go right here, go deep under the water, and let it all out, tumble against the reef and rocks of this unimaginable grief. I remember

Theo that day in Topanga, standing on the edge of his board, the sun glinting at his back. I close my eyes, and decide to stay above, surfing instead across the wave of glassy loss.

When I call my mom from the urgent care, I tell her just to send Theo's brother, Peter, but she's adamant, "You're my baby, too, Jane."

And for the first time in years, I believe her.

As I wait in the urgent care for Andrea and Peter, I look down at the palm of my hand, which is encrusted in blood, that small piece of bone embedded in my skin. I don't know why I do it, maybe because the minutes are moving by slowly, maybe I just want to go home. Maybe because I can tell that the night is changing into day and I can't imagine ever having to see the sun again, so instead, I stare into the palm of my hand, and pick out the hard sliver of Theo's skull.

I move it between my fingers like a diamond, examining it in the light, knowing that this is all we are. Just vulnerable pieces of tissue and bone and spleens and hearts and the idea that we're so much more than the basic mechanics of human anatomy.

The last few hours have been filled with professionals—doctors and detectives, therapists, and Patty—all trying to gently squeeze the details out of me. Finally, there's a knock at the door, "Jane?"

Patty pops her head in. "Your mom is here."

She leads me out to the waiting room; the first thing I see in my mother's eyes is fear.

"Janey." My mom runs to me, then hesitates. I know she doesn't want to get blood on her, but how can she not? Tragedy is forcing us all into roles we don't want to play.

She grabs me in an awkward hug, but then again, my mother's hugs have always been awkward. She is thin and flimsy, made up of sinewy muscle and blonde highlights, smelling like new car leather and Chanel perfume. Her hair is pulled back into a bun. Her tan skin is now taut around her face, making her look even younger than she usually does.

There is no greater conflict of interest than the relationship between a single mother and her only child. And for Andrea, I was the last shot she had—investing in me like an IPO, intent on living off the dividends. And there was a time when I led her to believe that her hard work paid off. I got the scholarship to NYU, I landed the big job, and then I turned twenty-seven and let it all go.

Andrea pulls back, looking down to see if she has been stained by the blood. Lucky for her, it's dry. Patty tries again, "Jane, we have clothes you can change into. I would really recommend getting more . . . fresh before your drive home."

My mom nods excitedly, as though a change of clothes will fix everything, "Yes, honey. Let's get you out of those—"

"I'm fine," I repeat, as though Patty hasn't suggested this numerous times throughout the night. I can't change yet; I can't reconcile what just happened in some borrowed sweats from a policewoman's closet. "Where's Zoe?"

"Rose called, she came back to LA right away. She's with Zoe now, she's still sleeping . . ."

Both women stare at me as I begin to realize that I have no idea how I'll share this with a one-year-old baby. I don't even understand it myself; how could Zoe possibly comprehend?

Patty begins to explain to my mother that I will need to sign a number of releases, which I do after Andrea reads them, trying to explain what I am signing. But it's all meaningless to me. Finally,

Patty leads us to the back door. She explains that the media have already begun to crowd at the entrance.

"Someone must have tipped them off." Patty shakes her head and I feel like I am suddenly two places at once, remembering a time when I was once one of "them."

While I was still in college, I found a job working as an underpaid intern for one of the biggest journalists in the world, Blake Edwards. Blake was Texan, handsome, and controversial. For most of the Clinton and Bush administrations, he was everywhere, saying what he wanted and angering many, though a lot of what he said was also true. It's hard to write nice things about him now. It's hard to remember that we were once in love.

My mother was beside herself when I got the job, having sent him the handwritten note that landed me the first interview. Over the next four years, I made us both proud. I became the heir apparent to Blake's brand. By the age of twenty-four, I was ready to launch. CNN, NBC, the networks were calling. Blake taught me that the truth is like heat, it rises to the top. And with Blake, I was on fire.

I loved getting those calls. The quick texts that would follow as we grabbed our coats and laptops and ran downstairs to the truck.

Andrea and I walk out the back door of the urgent care as I am blinded by the rising sun. My mom clutches my hand as she searches for Peter.

"We took your car," my mom explains as we walk away from the urgent care. "How Petra rides a motorcycle every day is beyond me. Where is she?"

"He," I correct.

When I first met Theo, his family felt like my chosen home. Peter was the brother I never had, and though Theo's parents came with their own traumas and mental health diagnoses, they also took care of me. They fed me soup when I was sick, and Theo's mother stood by me in those first days after Zoe's birth, high from her mania, yet channeling it into fettucine alfredo and knitting a misshapen blanket for Zoe. Theo loved that crocheted mess, and as I stand there in the morning light, I wonder how we will survive this.

Andrea starts to move toward the lot that has been fenced off. I can see the media in the distance, waiting at the front of the wall. And then I see my CRV, driving toward us. As Andrea and I begin to walk toward the car, a police officer stops Peter. I can see him in the front seat, explaining who he is picking up. My mother and I are caught in the parking lot. My head turns and something deep within me shifts. They see me, and I see them. I know what a media pit looks like—the crush of hair spray and body odor, the microphones shoved forward as the voices clamor, the questions toppling over one another like an avalanche. The only difference is that I've always been on the other side of the mic, pushing alongside my boss for the quote, hoping that there might be enough familiarity that they will turn our way and take the question.

Even from my first days on the job, Blake would bring me along to events like this, because he said no matter what, a young blonde was more likely to grab someone's eye than just another cock in a suit, even if he was a famous one.

But Blake would remind us that our privilege came with a responsibility, "Use your power for the person who can't."

That was the part of Blake that made him so attractive. Because underneath the bright lights and big contracts, even in his worst moments, I believed he wanted to change the world. And back then, so did I.

But now, so many years later, I am the one standing in front of the media, ignoring my mom as she pulls on my shirt.

The reporters start running slowly toward me across the quickly heating pavement, and their energy meets mine long before they reach the barricade, long before I walk toward them, holding out my hand. A young reporter reaches me first. She is young and pretty, a brunette with a fresh blowout. I imagine her curling her hair in the back of the van, racing toward the scene.

"Ma'am," she calls out as we close in on each other, her voice softening as she sees that I'm not wearing a brown outfit, that I am caked in blood. "Oh my God, are you okay?"

I feel my mother rushing up behind me, her hand on my elbow, "Honey, we have to go. Peter's here; we can go now."

I stand there, staring at the reporter as her cameraman joins her, the rest of the reporters quick on their heels. My mother tries to pull me back, but I step toward the first woman, seeing her eyes, scared and hungry at once, shocked by the sight of me.

The reporter's voice is quiet, maybe even too quiet for the cameraman to pick up, "What happened to you?"

I open my palm.

"My husband," I tell her. She doesn't understand, as she nudges her cameraman to get a close-up. "This is his skull. This is what happened."

I don't know why I say it. I haven't even thought about all the words and arguments and memes that will soon follow, but I declare, "This is what guns do."

I hear the snapping of cameras, the quick rush of voices and questions as my mother quickly pulls me away, admonishing me, "Why did you just do that?"

I remember when I worked for Blake, he once said to me, "Janey, I know the thoughts in your head are brilliant. I'm just not sure you know how to get them out."

I knew how to make the witty comment, and say the right thing, I just didn't know how to do it at the right time. Maybe that was why I struggled to command an audience, the way that Blake was so good at doing, attracting the attention even when the story wasn't about him. My mother shelters me as I get in the passenger side of the car.

I look at Peter and I don't know what else to say but, "Hi."

"Hi," Peter smiles sadly as he puts the car in drive and follows the cop, who is now instructing us out onto the cleared road. It's already hot outside and though the air-conditioning is on in the car, it doesn't matter. I feel like a fever is coming on, or the stomach flu. My nervous system aches.

Andrea begins to dispense information from the back seat, "Patty said we'll have to come back tomorrow or the next day to," she pauses, "to identify Theo."

Peter and I don't reply as my mother continues, "I guess they'll have some sort of meeting then for the families to explain what happens now. They're hoping to have that this week, but they'll call me. I gave them your number, too, Peter."

I look over at Peter, who I can tell has been crying. His cheeks are red and puffy, and though he's wearing sunglasses, I know there are tears under there.

"I'm so sorry, Peter," I say, my vision getting blurry in the sun.

"Jesus, Jane," he replies, handing me his sunglasses. "What the fuck happened?"

I know we've all seen this before on TV, we've watched the images of the shootings, we've feared these same moments, all while believing dumbly that it was someone else's story, but as I look over at Peter, his pain so real, I can see we are now in the show.

"I called Dennis," I hear my mother talking from the back seat. "He's driving up now. I've been coordinating with the police."

I stop listening, as my mother likes nothing more than scheduling, coordinating, planning, problem-solving. She lives for paperwork.

I look out the window as we move onto the I-10, away from the desert. I have been out here so many times over the years. The wind turbines and mountains rise in the distance, reminding me of long brunches and relaxing by the pool. But now it has been replaced with something else. Something so long and tragic it feels like a whip lashing out across the rest of my life.

My mother sits back in her seat. I pull down my visor to block the sun, which offers me a view of Zoe's empty car seat. I imagine her sleeping in her crib, so sweet and unaware. At least, when the police arrived at our front door, my father had been missing from our lives for years. I knew he was a complicated man who borrowed love and money. I knew that it was okay to feel relief. What will Zoe know when she wakes up?

I wonder what time it is as the sun begins to climb, worried if we will make it back home before she wakes. I check the clock and see it's 6:45, the exhaustion finally taking over. I clutch the bone and close my eyes as the smooth highway moves us toward a home that I will no longer know.

FOUR

The first device identified as a gun was a bamboo tube that used gunpowder to fire a spear, appearing in China around AD 1000. The Chinese had only just invented gunpowder the century before. By 1336–1350, breech-loading guns called cet-bangs were being used by the Majapahit Empire, but around the late fourteenth century in Europe, smaller, portable handheld cannons were developed, creating the first smooth-bore personal firearm. By the late fifteenth century, the Ottoman Empire was using firearms as part of its regular infantry.

The first successful rapid-fire firearm was the Gatling, which was fielded by the Union forces during the American Civil War in the 1860s. Following its success, Theodor Bergmann invented the world's first submachine gun (a fully automatic firearm with pistol cartridges). It was introduced into service by the German Army during World War I. By World War II, the Germans introduced the first assault rifle, known as the StG 44, bridging the gap between long-range rifles, machine guns, and short-range submachine guns.

On September 30, 1959, Colt sold its first AR-15s to Malaysia, marketing the rifle to various militaries around the world, including the US Navy, Air Force, Army, and Marine Corps.

Thanks, Wikipedia. I haven't slept in our bed since the shooting, taking to the couch instead, which sits right outside Zoe's room. When she wakes in the middle of the night, she joins me and our dog Rocky, all three of us huddled together in the storm of our own confusion. But at night, when it's quiet, and I'm alone, I find myself googling AR-15s, unable to look at my previous late-night searches—vacations and shoes and celebrity gossip and articles on *Mother Jones*—which all feel moot at this point. Sometimes I can hear a gun in the distance like an off-screen boom, but otherwise, I'm not sure what happened that night. I can't remember the details or the sounds or the fact that I was trapped under Theo while he died. I can't remember seeing the shooter or knowing what was happening, even as the details are being reported in excruciating detail on every news network, which my mother and uncle watch only on their phones, tucking them away when I enter the room. They have been renting an Airbnb around the corner though Andrea has explained to me no less than five times how very, very expensive it is.

The morning after the shooting, I sat with Rose, showered and clean, knowing as the blood circled down the drain of our shower that I was never going to really understand what happened that night, no matter how many times people told me the story.

"I was in the barn," Rose explained. "I was just doing some paperwork for the venue, after John took the stage. I didn't know Jane . . . I didn't know."

She cried as I held her, unable to cry myself, unable to feel anything except for that dull boom echoing through my now-quiet days.

"Rose." I pet her head. "How would any of us had known?"

I didn't blame Rose. I didn't even know how to blame the shooter, Martin Montgomery. Though I recognized he was the trigger, he wasn't the gun. The more I read about the weapon that murdered Theo, the less I understand about how someone like Martin Montgomery could have legally purchased it, how it was even permissible to produce an instrument that served no other purpose than mass murder.

I peek out my tightly drawn shades to see if there are any trucks yet. I see one down the street, attempting to gain access before I call the police and they are forced to disperse again. It didn't take them long to find out who we were: "Jane Ambrose, a former producer for the critically acclaimed news program *Tonight with Blake Edwards*, and Theo Karras, the LA Dodger who lost his career to addiction."

According to most sources, and a couple extreme religious sects, it was a miracle I survived the shooting. Eleven bullets pierced my husband's body yet none of them managed to penetrate mine. When I received the autopsy report, I couldn't reconcile it with the events of the night. I stared down at the outline on the report, bullet marks noted across the outline of a body: 1, 2, 3, 5, 7, 8, 9, 11.

Sometimes, I just want to turn to Theo and say, "Man. This shit is heavy."

I don't understand it any more than I understand the strange fervor around the internet suddenly interested in the life and death of this former Dodger most had long forgotten. And then there was the photo on Facebook. Maybe if we hadn't looked so lovely and normal in that picture, they would have tired of us more quickly. But the media is now trying to merge that image with one I offered them the morning after the shooting, covered in blood, holding a piece of my husband's skull out to their greedy lens.

Of course, they would want more. I did when I was one of them.

But what could I possibly say? He's dead. Our marriage was hard. And yes, I survived because his body protected mine, but everything feels so cruel in the aftermath, I'm not sure I know how to translate it. They say grief is a neurochemical dance—hormones and neurotransmitters moshing around the confines of your cerebral cortex, your limbic system popping and zinging like a 1990s club. It's the Limelight in here, and the ecstasy's wearing off.

"I haven't cried yet," I tell my mom as I sit in my and Theo's bedroom. Though it's been less than two weeks since I last slept in the room, it already feels like a mausoleum.

Andrea stops and looks at me. I see compassion in her eyes, but she doesn't know how to respond to any of this. She has been so focused on funeral arrangements, it's as though she's planning a wedding. A part of me wonders if she almost prefers this to our actual wedding where she watched all her decades of hard work and grooming go down the tubes with my one auspicious choice. I keep wanting to remember the best of Theo, but as Andrea begins to riffle through the documents of our life, I can't ignore how hard it all was.

"Janey," she asks me that morning. "Did he not pay his car registration?"

"We couldn't," I try to explain. "There were so many parking tickets."

"Parking tickets?" my mother asks, not understanding or knowing that you can't register your car unless you've also paid off all your parking tickets from that year, and we simply couldn't afford all the ones Theo had accumulated. My mom doesn't get parking tickets.

"There were a lot of them," I admit guiltily, as though somehow it was my fault, as though I should have been able to take care of it.

"Why you got him that truck is beyond me," she scoffs. Andrea was livid when we leased Theo a brand-new Toyota Tacoma, but his previous pickup didn't have a back seat and we needed another car when Zoe was born. We couldn't afford to buy anything; it was easier to lease something new.

I kept my old Honda and Theo got the new truck.

Blake used to tell me that marriage was for the lonely. That if you were truly whole, you wouldn't need a partner to complete you. I saw that truth echoed in Dennis and to a lesser degree Andrea. That somehow, we were better off on our own.

I close my eyes. And I try to remember what it was like when Theo was here, beneath the arguments that once lived in this room, beyond the fears of what we couldn't be to each other, between all the parking tickets that stood between us. I try to find him under the loneliness that I feel now in ways I never have before.

Andrea walks over and puts her hand on my cheek, "You'll find your way through it, Janey." For a moment, I remember what our relationship was like when I was young, when we held hands and were best friends and all I wanted to do was please her. I look around at the details of our life as though it's someone else's. The portraits of us in childhood, me, hand-drawn at the fair in Pomona only months after my father left, and the rare photo of Theo as a child, wearing a cowboy costume on horseback. I am sitting on the rocking chair where I struggled to nurse Zoe in those first hard weeks after her birth.

Meanwhile, Dennis plays with the baby in the next room as my mother smooths the black dress she has ironed for me, laying it on the bed. I don't even know how she found an iron. I haven't used one in years.

I stare numbly at the dress, knowing we have to leave soon.

I used to quip to my mother that a thousand people would show up for Theo's funeral. She didn't argue the point, simply reasoning, "It would be nicer if they showed up for his life."

After loading into Dennis's car, we drive to the church where four years ago I married Theo Karras. The same church where we christened Zoe only six months before. Draped in gold and gilded icons, St. Sophia's was one of Theo's great gifts, a jewel box in the middle of Pico-Union, a neighborhood that had long welcomed immigrants from all over the world, from the Greeks and Armenians who once settled with their shared Mediterranean culture, to the Central American communities that now flourished there. The memorial is flooded. Church security surrounds the car, ushering us in.

Zoe looks around, bewildered. I am grateful she doesn't understand any of this. I remember being twelve at my own father's memorial—a small and awkward affair. Theo's is a circus in comparison. I keep thinking if he was just here, I would be able to process it better. It's such a shame that the person most needed at a funeral is the one being grieved. Andrea, Dennis, and I take our seats at the front of the church. I sit down and begin to bounce Zoe in my lap. Her unawareness is all the more heartbreaking as we sit right in front of the altar where Theo and I performed our wedding rites. I loved our wedding day, the ritual of the Orthodoxia. The hand-painted icons, the golden robes, the deep guttural sounds of Modern Greek, touched by the Middle East, because you can't go back to Constantinople.

"You okay?" Dennis asks as I stare at the blank space where we once stood. I shake my head.

"I know you didn't want me to marry Theo," I begin to tell him.

"That's not—" he tries to argue.

"Jane?" Theo's father George interrupts. Theo's mother clings to him, too weak to walk. Andrea takes Zoe from me as I try to help my husband's mother, buoying her as she collapses next to me in the pew.

"Lydia." I grasp her hand as George and Peter take their seats next to her.

"Janey-Mu, Janey-Mu," she repeats my name breathlessly. "My Theo . . ."

Her voice lowers into a deep wail as I hold on to her hand, hoping that somehow I can help her even though no one ever could.

From Theo's telling, his first years of life were the beginning of an immigrant success story. George had come to America at the age of sixteen from a small island between Italy and Greece. George and his father had left behind the rest of their family to join an uncle who had made it in America. And they soon followed suit, opening restaurants not far from this church in the heart of Los Angeles. But as George reached his twenties, his father noticed his young son's fast love for women and booze, deciding it was time for him to marry. Because even today, marriages are arranged to benefit the arrangers, George was sold to a wealthier family, whose youngest daughter had yet to be promised to a local man.

"She's a good girl," George's father asserted when his son protested the marriage. Against the long, tan legs of the California girls with whom George had become entangled, the short, stubborn villager in a black dress, still mourning a brother who had died two years before in South Africa (another Greek diaspora), cast a long and committed shadow across his sunny American dream. A month after their wedding, Lydia announced she was pregnant. Eight months later, Theo was born, and seven years beyond that, after being found naked on a beach because the Virgin Mary promised she would find Jesus on its shore, their little family began to learn what it meant to live with a mother who was mentally unstable.

Theo and I knew there were plenty of people who lived harder childhoods than us. We heard enough stories from the podiums of AA about cigarette burns and fathers sneaking into beds where they didn't belong. But we also knew that like most childhoods, ours had their own sadness. Theo lost his mother around the same time I lost my father, and in their absence, something went missing in us both.

Lydia's moans grow louder as I try to calm her. Peter gently rolls his eyes in my direction. Now, as the whole church looks in her direction, I am reminded of the stories Theo used to tell me about how his mother would claim she was having a heart attack in the middle of one of his baseball games, the paramedics being called in just as he was walking up to bat. He got so used to it, he could hit a double as she was hoisted into the ambulance, running the bases as the sirens whirred in the background.

I can hear the waves of condolences swelling up behind us as more people fill the seats, but I can't look back now. I don't want to have to lock eyes with every missed call since Theo's death. I don't want their tender nods or genuflections. It's not that I don't understand. I've attended my own share of memorials and funerals for people I knew and loved from a distance. Even if we hadn't spoken in a while, I still wanted the chance to say good-bye, passing through the deep grief that for others had become a permanent condition.

I clutch Lydia tighter, trying to find the words that I hope might calm her. "He's still here, Lydia," I say. "He's still here."

But we both know he's gone.

I am alive today because of Theo Karras," Darren Lopez begins to speak. Darren was a professional skater in the nineties when street skating was still the rage. He was nine months sober when he met Theo, both recovering athletes who watched addiction destroy their careers. I feel like we are all lost in a silence that used to be filled with Theo's voice, always talking, always opining, always connecting to people in ways I never could.

Darren finally gets it together to share, "Fuckin' Theo, man. There was no one else like him."

Fuckin' Theo, man.

And then Peter takes the stage.

"My brother," Peter begins. But then he also stops, closing his eyes. He can't go on. He shakes his head at me. "We shouldn't be here right now . . . We shouldn't be going through this. He should be here. Theo . . ."

I know I should break. I can feel the pain flooding my body, pushing at the dam of my restraint. But I nod lightly, my breath growing fast under the weight of the day. I turn to where Zoe fusses in my mother's arms and I take my baby. I bounce her on my lap, trying to find distraction in the softness of her skin. And there she is. My soft place to land. No matter how many times Theo would be late to pick Zoe up or go surfing when he was supposed to be working, or pretend he was going to do something and fail to do it, for every time he made me bristle, Zoe reminded me of the reason we were brought together, the purpose of our meeting. If bloodlines were made to commingle, I believed in ours, and the result of those ancestries, of those old stories of Hungarian actors and Greek cave dwellers and the long unspooling DNA of our family histories being born into this child who though she is just learning to talk, moves the mountains of my love inside. I never knew if I wanted to have a child, but I knew I wanted to have her. As soon as I met Theo, I knew that we were supposed to mate.

As Peter sits down, the priest rises to deliver the final words, but I can't hear him. *Death, Jesus, Holy Spirit, Jesus, Jesus, Jesus, come back, this Church is your home, who the hell is going to help pay for all this gold?*

He offers a sad smile along with the condolences, but I hope he keeps going. I know what comes next: Lydia and I will sit here as everyone pays their respects. Some will be the ritual friends (attending weddings, baptisms, and funerals), some I will be meeting for the first time, some I will love dearly.

Those are the hardest. My actual friends. The people I'm supposed to rely on. Over the last two weeks, my voicemail has been filled with messages from the friends Theo and I got sober with, celebrating marriage and welcoming children within years of one another.

But I can't call them back. I can't see the life I've lost so suddenly mirrored in their own. Instead, I've been ignoring their texts and goodwill, and I am now confronted with their awkward questions. They all hold their partners' hands, clutching on to the lives they once took for granted and probably still do.

With each one that approaches, my voice catches in my throat. I don't even know how to be me—the girl with the witty one-liners, the star of karaoke night, the one who should have been up there offering tears and laughter for a husband she could have loved better.

I've started lying to my friends, telling them, "I'll call you soon," when I know I won't.

And then I see her: Maggie. The other member of Rose's and my trio, finding each other at the private high school where our parents sent us, gravitating to one another through the throngs of the privileged and plastic girls. Rose was too weird, I was too smart, and Maggie was too perfect. As the only Black girl at Sacred Heart, she was an outlier not in personality or looks, but simply by virtue of not trusting her other options. Maggie waltzed through our school looking like a young Beverly Johnson with her movie star skin and silk pressed hair, but she never trusted the easier path in life; the other girls didn't know what to make of her. Instead, she became friends with us weirdos, though our prom photos looked like they came from three different schools, with me in a tux and cowboy boots, Maggie in hot pink couture, and Rose in some Betsey Johnson number with high Doc Martens.

After Sacred Heart, Maggie left the West Coast for Howard University, the alma mater of her own overbearing parents, both doctors.

But when she started dating Chris in her junior year of college, it seemed as though she had found her prince. Chris had been all the things that my mother had wanted for me; from a wealthy Palos Verdes family, he and Maggie were part of the South Bay's Black elite, a small but formidable group of families who had grown up in the area, building their wealth after their own grandparents came to California during the Great Migration.

Though Chris went on to get his JD at Harvard, he came back to the South Bay to be with Maggie and started practicing corporate law. By day he was all Savile Row suits and the perfect fade; at night, he was the life of the party.

Back in our twenties, Chris would take Maggie and me out to the best restaurants and bars. We would do the best coke. We would stay up late smoking cigarettes and talking politics, and then I'd go home with one of Chris's friends. Years later, when Maggie and Chris got pregnant with their first child, buying a four-bedroom McMansion in Costa Mesa, I felt nothing but joy for them, even as the cracks in my own life were widening. Four years later, Maggie's did the same. All it took was one sloppy email for Maggie to realize she wasn't the only woman in Chris's fairy tale. She hired a top lawyer, determined to bring down the man who she once joked was too perfect to be true.

"I guess we all ended up spoiled," Maggie told me once, after realizing that what had felt like an arranged marriage was becoming a failed one. Maggie and Chris were in the middle of what their lawyers deemed a "high-conflict divorce" when I met Theo. And he seemed like everything Chris wasn't. Despite the hardships of Maggie's life, and the faint but sad lines around her eyes, she is still able to stop a room with just her smile. The divorce money bought her a small condo in a nice neighborhood in Orange County, and ultimately, Maggie found work in a plastic surgeon's office, where she gets free touch-ups.

She looks tired, but then again, we all look tired today, the grief feeling like a fog the sun just can't burn off. Maggie grabs my hand and tells me, "You will get through this."

I nod obediently, even though I know Maggie never really did.

"You will. You have Zoe." Then she looks around. "Where is she? Andrea? Dennis?"

She's known them for decades, as though they are extended family.

"They already left . . . with Zoe. Don't ask."

"You need a ride?"

"We both do," Rose remarks as she walks up, and I watch as my two best friends see each other for the first time in years, pulling me into a group hug, just as we used to do when we were young and silly and had no idea what lay ahead.

'm so sorry I've been so out of touch," Maggie remarks as soon as we walk to her car after the service.

"Oh Mags, we've all been busy with our own lives." I reply.

"I mean, at least you'll still give us a ride." Rose laughs.

"That's cause Maggie always has the nicest car," I add.

"Fuck y'all." Maggie laughs as we walk up to her Lexus.

"See," I add. "Probably even has leather seats."

"It's a Lexus, Janey," Rose chimes in. "They only come with leather seats."

"Yeah, Rosie," Maggie replies. "And I hate to break it to you, but it's not going to smell like patchouli and sage, like yours probably does."

"You think I have a car," Rose laughs. "That's why you're driving us back."

"It's my pleasure." My beautiful friend smiles, before asking me, "Why did Andrea and Dennis leave, though?"

"You know my family," I share. "They're just fucking weirdos." Andrea practically rushed out of the funeral, explaining that it was better for Zoe to get home, leaving me alone to deal with Lydia and the hordes of well-wishers.

"Yeah, they were really up one today," Rose adds. I realize that we are now all single again, alone in our different ways.

"What did they do now?" I sigh.

"Dennis was fine, even though I'm pretty sure he tried to convince me to vote for Trump . . ."

"Sounds like Dennis." I laugh.

Maggie looks back at me. "We're going to your house?"

"I guess," I reply, finally relaxing into the back seat, relieved of pretending I am some traditional widow wearing black and wondering how I'm going to go on, even as I wonder how I'm going to go on.

"God, Maggie. I can't believe it's been so long. When did we last see each other, the wedding?" Rose asks from the front seat. Though Maggie and I stayed in touch, Rose's parents moved out of the South Bay years ago, leaving her little reason to visit. Once I became a mom, Maggie and I started to see and talk to each other more, but she and Rose had little left in common, as Rose ambled into her post–rock star existence and Maggie retreated to the safety of Costa Mesa, miles away in travel time and light-years away in culture from Rose's nomadic life bouncing between LA and the desert.

"Yeah, wow. What a blur that day was," Maggie replies, her divorce finalizing just as my marriage was beginning.

Only four years before, Theo and I drove out of this same church parking lot the day we got married. We were also left without a ride, another unfortunate consequence of both of our families. Our friends drove us to the reception in the back of their used Prius. That was back when I didn't mind the mayhem of our lives, when the surprises didn't feel so insulting.

"How are you doing?" Maggie asks Rose. "I tried to call. "

"I know. I'm sorry, I just," Rose pauses. I look over to see Maggie take Rose's hand; Rose grasps back. I know that Rose has had her own complicated dance with this, standing outside the club, hearing the shots, and not knowing what to do or how to help. Later, she told me the only person she could think about was Zoe, not knowing if either of us would emerge. I look out the window. There are some days when LA looks so bleached it doesn't even feel real, like it's being filmed for a nineties rap video. I don't say it, but I wish Maggie would take the streets. I want the longer route home. In a rare moment, I pray for traffic.

Maggie rolls down her window and tries to keep the conversation alive. "Someone told me that you guys are meeting the president next week?"

"Yeah. Peter is, at least," I reply.

Rose looks back at me, "You're not? I thought he was meeting with all the families."

"Under other circumstances, sure," I admit, remembering the email sent by a contact at one of the advocacy groups, explaining the procedures and protocols of life after a mass shooting: the interviews, the briefings, the meet and greet with the president, like it was some sort of consolation prize. "Anyway, Zoe and I are going to Big Sur next week."

Every year, Theo and I went on vacation to Big Sur, staying at a cabin in the redwoods, imagining a life where all the stresses of modern life would magically disappear.

"Big Sur is kind of remote," Maggie warns, echoing Andrea and Dennis. But I've engaged in this debate too many times now not to know the answer.

"We already scheduled it, and I just . . . need to get away, from my family, from everything. I need to prove to myself that I can. Plus, I can't go back to work yet. I . . ."

I don't know how to say that I'm not sure I'll be able to go back. When I first got sober, I started working in temp agencies across Los Angeles until I was finally placed at a nonprofit that provided social services to teens transitioning out of foster care. I loved the kids, but I didn't love the organization, frustrated by the throngs of white social workers who thought they were leading with the best of intentions, but who often failed to get our kids where they needed to go. My first job with the agency was as the assistant to the CEO, but over time, I moved up, becoming a fundraiser and then their lead grant writer, making just enough money to pay our rent and the bills and provide healthcare and all the things that a woman must do when she has a child with a husband who can't provide.

But it never felt like a fit.

Rose moves the conversation to the national election. I hear her telling Maggie that Nate Silver has predicted that Hillary Clinton has an 80 percent chance of winning, but Maggie doesn't appear to be listening. As we finally turn in to my neighborhood, the trucks are waiting for me to emerge in the black dress, hoping I will give them another fiery speech after saying farewell to my husband. I know there is a space for me in that conversation. I know that the girl I once was wouldn't have kept her mouth shut.

I let the sun hit my face and I hear the boom again, the scent of iron and gunpowder in the air, but I also don't know what weight my voice should carry. Me, just another girl who didn't get what she wanted, who lost something she didn't know how to love. I don't want to trot out and show them this, because I don't even know what this is. I don't know how to describe the marriage I just lost nor the grief I'm not sure how to feel. All I know is that my daughter just lost her father, and in another week, they'll forget this story entirely.

Rose is wearing her Misfits jacket, with a picture of a skeleton on the back, its middle finger out, and she covers us with the coat as we rush inside the house. A reporter calls from the sidewalk, "Jane Ambrose, can you give us a statement?"

I don't look up. As soon as we get in, I see a man sitting on our couch. He is tall and handsome, wearing a pinstripe suit and a sad smile.

My mother sees Maggie, whom she quickly embraces. Maggie, with her blown-out hair and biweekly manicure, was one of my mom's favorite friends. Andrea would have done better with Maggie as her child, so focused on keeping things in order. I only knew how to be messy.

Then Andrea turns back to the stranger in our living room, "Jane, this is James Toobin."

She doesn't need to tell me who he is. James reached out two days after the shooting. He is part of a gun control network called Families United, an elite force of survivors, bonded together through grief and propelled to advocacy. He lost his daughter Rachel in the Dear Valley shooting, outside Austin, and like many surviving parents and spouses and children and friends, he has channeled the metal of pain into some version of gold.

James stands up and shakes my hand. "I thank you for meeting me."

By the look on his face, I know he has been here, too. Fresh off tragedy, shaking hands like we're at a business interview. The fucked-up thing is I agreed to this. I just didn't realize my mother scheduled it for today. After James left me that first message, he ended up connecting with Andrea, telling her about the groups of families that had been built over the years, starting with Columbine up through the Mojave Saloon, the names of the shootings echoing through our cultural consciousness like the titles of movies we've all watched—*Star Wars*, *The Shining*, Columbine, Dear Valley.

But some of us were in the film.

My appearance that morning before the camera crews—with Theo's skull in my hand—had lit off another firestorm in the debate. Most shooting victims were cleaned up by the time they appeared on camera. I am sure Patty took the brunt of it after the footage emerged, but what else was she to do? Hold me down and change me like a child?

"I know this is a strange day to meet," James says. His suit is black, and I realize that he has just attended Theo's funeral.

"All days are strange lately," I reply, remembering my friends who stand behind me like hired heavies.

I turn to them, "You guys want to wait for me in the backyard?"

"Dennis is out there with Zoe," my mother adds.

I sit down but only because I know that James Toobin deserves my respect. As he shared in our first phone call, his daughter was only twelve years old, and as I look outside to see Zoe pushing past the window in her little pink Cozy Coupe, I say the silent prayer offered by Maggie, "At least I have her."

"I've been sitting where you are, Jane," James begins his pitch. "And I get that being an advocate isn't what you're thinking about right now."

My mother leans forward as though James Toobin is about to pull out a movie contract, her old ambitions being resurrected by his presence.

"Mom," I interrupt James. "Would you mind checking on Zoe?"

"I'm sure she's fine."

"I'm sure she is, too, but I think I just want to spend some time with James alone."

My mother slowly gets up and leaves. I turn to James and smile as gently as I can. "I can't even imagine what you went through, what you're going through."

James looks down, before replying, "There comes a time when you realize your life will never be the same. That no day will ever be ordinary again."

I look around our living room, the photos of our little family sitting like religious icons. James continues, "There are lots of roles for people in the movement."

"I'm sure there are." I smile. "I actually donate to your organization. You have to know, though, I've been close to that world before. I just feel like it isn't right to suddenly take some public stage."

"It's okay, Jane. I'm not here to pressure you," James replies warmly. I look up at him and though he is older than me, formal in his funeral attire and corporate posture, he is also unmistakably handsome, with thick brown hair, which is graying at the temples so perfectly that I almost wonder if he gets them colored that way.

"You need to grieve," he adds, his eyes crinkling up at the corners like he means what he says.

"I don't even know what that looks like yet," I admit to someone for the first time, realizing I don't know how I will describe Theo to others, his goodness often lost in the fears and frustrations that clouded our marriage. I don't know how I'll explain any of this—to James, to the media, and certainly not to our baby, who still can't grasp that her daddy isn't coming home. "I think I might be a terribly awkward widow for your work."

I smile and the way James smiles back at me almost reminds me of who I am, my blonde hair pinned back by Andrea's determined styling, my full lips and sad eyes creating their own offering, but I'm a lot like my dear friend Maggie. I refuse the easier route.

"Plus." I smile sadly. "I gave up fighting a long time ago, unless it was in my marriage."

"There's no such thing as a marriage without fighting." James shares his own sad smile. "But remember this, you don't know how this might change you. Sometimes, pain drives something up from deep inside us that we never knew we had. Don't be afraid of that."

I hear the back door open, as though my mother has been standing outside with a glass to the door. James stands up to leave, and I know my mother is disappointed. It's clear we didn't have enough time to make plans or commitments.

James and I hug, and he says good-bye to my mother.

After he leaves, my mom can't help but ask, "Well?"

"Not yet, Mom," I reply, walking out the back door to see my daughter who now plays between her two aunties, my oldest friends and the only people I feel I can trust in this desert I have yet to escape.

FIVE

We were like any other slightly hipster couple living in Southern California in the early 2010s—living in Silver Lake, and vacationing in the trifecta of California locales: Joshua Tree, Ojai, and Big Sur. All haunts of people who believed there was something lost when we traded in our typewriters for the iPhone.

Maybe that's why we loved Big Sur so much. Because we also loved Jack Kerouac, and as Jack himself once wrote, "At the bottom of the sea, lives a very sad turtle." Big Sur was the sad turtle. Even in all its glory, it wasn't light and fun like Cabo or Hilton Head. There was a sorrow in its redwoods, a weeping to its willow. Theo loved surfing the cruel and untamed waves of the central Pacific. Because surfing is a lot like love, fear is part of the high.

I take Highway 1 up the coast, moving across our well-tread path, reminded of so many other trips along this road, postcards from a lost history, and, for a moment, I almost forget. I know it's dangerous to play that game, to pretend nothing is changed, that Theo is merely waiting for us somewhere. Then I reach Big Sur.

Miraculously, Zoe is asleep when we arrive. The entire drive, I have been anticipating the inevitable unloading of the car with fear, picturing a barking dog and a screaming toddler as I struggle into the cabin alone, dragging the cooler and the pack and play, the luggage and the lanterns, the firewood, and the groceries. Unloading the car has always been Theo's job. He would get the bags to the cabin, start the fire for dinner, and take the dog for a walk as I would organize the kitchen, prep the food, and set up the pack and play, which I now pull from my car. In a rare instance, our roles would split down traditional gender lines.

I carry our bags quietly to the cabin. And then finally, it hits. But it's not the wave I expected. It feels like I'm going over a waterfall, gravity betraying me as the ground bails beneath my feet. I know I am still in a three-dimensional room, but a fourth dimension has been added and it's a terrifying void. I hear the bags drop with a heavy thud as the truth engulfs me. I stumble forward, grabbing on to the rocking chair in the corner of the room, managing to sit down on its edge before I fall—unable to breathe, unable to scream, felled by the smell of the place, the dust wafting through the air, the piercing desperation of life without Theo. And then I am no longer here, in this room. I am somewhere else, I hear the loud bang of a gun, the sound overwhelming my ears, and I can feel someone on top of me. I hear my breath. I hear the one word I want to say, and yet am terrified to speak, "Theo."

I try to wake up, opening my eyes. But the room is now moving. I can hear Theo swearing over the fire pit as he tries to light the kindling, his heavy footsteps echoing just outside the front door. I grip the arms of the chair, waiting for the door to open, waiting for him to walk through. Oh God, please, please, please. The neurons of past and present become jangled as I look around the room, the cabin suddenly foreign and threatening.

"Make it stop," I begin to call out, unsure of who can help me now. My baby is in the car outside. I think I hear Rocky barking, but I can't move. Years ago, when I first quit smoking, I would get panic attacks on the freeway, convinced I was going to veer into head-on traffic, or hit the median on the freeway. But there is no easy way out of this terror, and I know that, too.

Just like that, the attack passes. A tornado twisting quickly through my psyche before dissipating on the horizon. My hands relax on the wood. I find my breath. Inhaling until I think I am going to choke, I come back to life just as someone knocks on the door; I scream a weird, contorted gurgle in response. In any other circumstance, I might have laughed at the sound.

"Are you okay?" a voice calls out, my blood pressure dropping at its familiarity.

Theo and I met Debra when we first began dating and came to stay at the campground. The three of us became fast friends. With her short, naturally gray hair, worn-out sweatshirts, and raspy voice, Debra looks like she belongs in a mountain town. That same voice now pulls me across the final threshold into reality. I shake my head, hearing something else. Zoe is crying.

"Zoe," I shout as I move past Debra and run to the car, the adrenaline that just paralyzed me pushing me toward my daughter's voice.

"She's okay," Debra says, walking casually behind me. "I think she's just wondering where her Mama and Papa are."

Debra looks around. "Theo down at the store?"

I don't reply right away, instead pulling Zoe out of the car and bringing her back up to the cabin's deck where Debra is standing. Bouncing the baby in my arms, Zoe begins to calm, taking in the redwood trees and our little cabin in the woods.

"Jane, is everything okay?"

"I guess you don't watch the news," I finally say.

"Not many people up here do." Debra laughs. "Kind of the point."

It's the first time since Theo's death that I am recounting what happened. I'm not sure if I'm ready to give the explanation I will repeat for the rest of my life, the same one Zoe will repeat for hers. The same one I have had to repeat for my own father. But I know if I'm going to experience another attack, I will need someone who understands.

"He died last month," I say slowly.

"Good God," Debra exclaims, reaching out to grip my arm tightly.

"The shooting in the desert."

Debra's hand crosses her heart. "That one at the bar?"

"Almost three weeks ago."

Debra slowly begins to nod her head, as though she knows without asking why I've made this trip. "Whatever you need. Anything, Jane, okay? Anything. You need me to stay with Zoe, walk Rocky, I'm here."

I look up. "There is one thing."

Memory's a motherfucker. I guess I knew that before now. I remember waking up the morning after it ended with Blake. I was hungover and hurting, my clock radio was blaring some old Mike and the Mechanics song, and, for a moment, I thought everything was okay. The night before was erased, the shots of whiskey at the midtown bar, the call to Blake in the middle of the night, begging for everything to go back the way it was, the long walk up to my fifth-floor apartment, aching at every step.

And though I now have no way to dull the pain, the sensation is the same. As though every morning I wake up, there is a chance that everything will go back to the way it was, even if I'm not sure that's what I wanted in the first place.

But sensations get shattered, and reality swiftly returns. When I was one year sober, I was introduced to a therapist who also moonlighted as a shamanic healer. It sounded shoddy and so very Californian, but Elissa was the real deal, filled with the truth I needed to hear when I needed it most. She asked me if I thought that Blake was just a stand-in for my father.

I shook my head and explained, "Michael's been gone from my life for so long, I wouldn't have even known what to look for."

She leaned forward and quietly suggested, "Close your eyes, Jane. Maybe we can find him together."

I was newly sober and like anybody who is newly sober, I tried meditation a few times, but this was different. Elissa led me into a valley in my mind I didn't know existed. She beat a drum and led me into a trance that was more than meditation, it was a journey into another time, a time of my ancestors, of the many lives that live in all of us, the ones of our grandmother's grandmothers, and even those before them. The original tribes of all our peoples. I felt the warrior in me rise, wanting to find what now stood at the source of my wound: the father who could never be found. As Elissa guided me into the eclipse of my meditation, I felt myself wandering through an empty desert.

Michael had come from Sicilian immigrants, filled with a failed reckoning of their own ancestry. I walked along the sand, the sun burning down on me when I saw an image ahead. A man standing along the ridge of the horizon, a tan scarf wrapped around his head. He turned around and I saw the face of my father, weathered as he was at the end of his life, but still handsome. I stood there in the vision, afraid to approach. He walked toward me and smiled, finally saying the words I had waited all of reality for him to share: "I'm sorry, Jane."

I don't know why he killed himself. Whether it was because he lost all his money, because he was facing jail time from the 1990s S&L crisis, because he was an alcoholic who didn't know how to stop for the people who loved him. Because he didn't know how to love us back. But that day in the darkened room of Elissa's home, I felt the release that I had been hoping for my whole life, the forgiveness extending across that desert, as I began to realize that I could find him here, in the space beyond the veil, and even if it only existed in my mind, that was enough.

"I'm sorry," he repeated that day, and I knew he was. I knew he was sorry for all the grief, both before and after his death.

A week before the shooting, I booked a couples massage for Theo and me at Esalen, the famed retreat center along the Big Sur coast. I know for every bill that went unpaid, there were these luxuries, too. The travel that confused people, that made me reach the end of the month and wonder, *where did it all go*, spending money with the imperiousness of people who had made it, refusing to give up the lives we once thought would be ours, even if we didn't have the cash to afford them. It just became so hard balancing all the caretaking with the fact that I was someone who also loved to have fun. And we didn't want to deny ourselves the adventures that stood at the heart of our love.

After I decided to make the trip alone, I decide to still go to Esalen.

"Please turn over, Jane," the masseuse says, tearing me out of the fever dream that is now my life.

I open my eyes and am overwhelmed by the sudden brightness of the massage room. As I lie back down, the masseuse rests a compress across my eyes. It sounds as though the waves rushing outside the room might suddenly rise and pull me out to sea.

"How are you doing?" the masseuse asks, the predictability of her words soothing my panic.

"I'm fine," I reply, knowing the words are just a scab for a wound I have yet to clean.

After the massage, I lie alone on the table listening to the waves crash. There is no Theo waiting for me outside. For the first time, I finally ask myself the unthinkable, *will I be able to do this alone?* For so many decades it was just me, the only child, the terminally single girl. But in six short years, I've become dependent on this man, suddenly unable to breathe without him.

I get up and go to the outdoor showers, which stretch out over the Pacific Ocean. Esalen was built in the 1960s as a place for acid-induced thinkers like Alan Watts and Aldous Huxley to look out at the sea and envision a better world. And they did, imagining a place where war machines were reduced to rubble and the unity of humankind was a reasonable option for the future. They would be ashamed with what we did with their hope. At the end of *Mad*

Men, Don Draper heads to Esalen to find himself. Wealthy techies would later follow, but nature never fails to disappoint. I stand in the shower and stare out over the open ledge.

There are people out at the baths, relaxing naked in the hot springs overlooking the sea. Their laughter and easy conversation drifts into the shower area like a foreign language.

Theo's great waves crash below, past all the cluttered details that I thought once made up our life. With sudden clarity, I see the first dance at our wedding to Bob Marley's "Chances Are," my jewel-encrusted flats moving next to Theo's sockless shoes. I see our first home in Silver Lake, where we could pick avocados from our bedroom window. I see us on ferries to Greece, on planes to New York, on road trips through Kauai and across Italy, and driving up the coast to Big Sur. I see us making love, I see us screaming horrible words, I see us giving birth. I see us on that first morning after Theo came over to my apartment, lying in his arms, the light dawning outside my bedroom window as I knew, finally, that I was home.

And then I am somewhere else again. I am on the ground; I am staring up at the corrugated ceiling of the Mojave Saloon. I hear other people screaming, and the sound of chairs scraping, I feel Theo's body on top of me but then he moves. He says my name, "Jane."

I don't hear myself begin to scream. I think it's a silent sound coming out of my mouth, like what happened after the shooting. As the first person rushes toward me in the shower, I wonder what she's doing here, and why she's getting so close. But then I see the look of fear in her eyes, as she clutches a towel to her chest, and I know that it's coming from me. I can hear the terrible sound emanating from my mouth, but I don't know how to stop it. There are no tears, just the brutal scream, refusing to remain silent. The woman tries to reach out for me.

Then the others come, a sea of naked bodies moving toward me, like a wave of flesh. I wish I could laugh, I want to laugh, but I can't stop screaming. The nude horde engulfs me. I can hear some whispering, "Shhhhh . . ." even as others call for help. They wrap their arms around me and then the light goes out.

I wake up in our cabin. Zoe sleeps in the crook of my arm, which has long gone numb. I remember being taken into an office; towels wrapped around me like a swaddled baby. Debra quickly arrived, leaving Zoe with a yoga group when she heard the wailing from across the campus, knowing it was me. I remember driving back to the campground, unable to speak, horrified that Zoe saw me like this, when I have fought every day to stay strong. When I wake up from the nap with my sweet baby next to me, we take the dog for a walk and eat dinner and thank Debra for her help and I promise myself that one day I'll apologize to all those naked people at Esalen.

Good god, it should be easier than this.

I open my emails, which I haven't looked at since we arrived in Big Sur, and I am shocked by the name on top: Yvette Morales.

Yvette was Blake's production assistant in my last year with him. She was five feet tall and one of the most beautiful women I had ever met, and even at the age of twenty-two, she was also one of the cockiest, acting like she owned the place from her first day. In the nineties, a lot of lesbians weren't out professionally, but Yvette was pretty confirmed in her status, and Blake respected her for that. There was something about a woman he couldn't sleep with that made Blake behave.

Together, Yvette and I traveled the world. Humvees in Kabul. Scooters in Mumbai. Traveling across Israel in the back of a pickup truck, the night hanging above us while we enjoyed the wild adventures of being Blake Edwards's crew.

And then there is her name in my inbox, as stark as the sun rising on a Big Sur morning.

Dear Jane. Jesus girl how long has it been? I couldn't believe when I saw your picture in the news but I think you and I now share the same story. Two years ago, my wife died from cancer. I was pregnant with our second babe. For the longest time I was fucking frozen. A robot in my own life. I don't know if that's where you are. Don't be fucking strangled by that shit. I'm still with Blake and I talked to him about it. We want to give your pain a voice. Come on the show. Tell your truth.

Yvette

There is a moment where I hesitate, but only a moment, before I move my finger over the trash icon, and delete her message. After getting breakfast ready, I load Zoe and Rocky in the car, and drive half a mile up the road to where Theo's and my favorite hike begins.

I arrange Zoe in the baby carrier before slipping a small sandwich baggie of ash into the pocket of the carrier, tucking a part of Theo against Zoe's back. I breathe in deep and lead them into the state park. Though dogs aren't allowed, Theo and I found a secret entrance a few years back, hiking our way up to the cliffs overlooking the ocean, and ultimately sneaking down into a private beach next to the park. I make our way through the hike until we reach the trailhead, peeling off to where a broken trellis protects a portion of private land from intruders. I slide under the loosened boundary of the fence before cautiously making my way down the rocky boulder to the beach, grasping Zoe in the Ergobaby and Rocky's leash with the other hand. After the funeral, Peter brought the bulk of Theo's ashes to the paddle out, shaking them across the water among Theo's friends and fellow surfers.

Peter and I sat on our patio after the ceremony, eating In-N-Out as he told me about the event. "You could see the ashes bobbing there for a moment. It was like Theo was talking, giving a final speech, trying to say good-bye, and then, they were gone."

It wasn't right that Theo died in the desert. He would have much preferred to be taken out by the sea.

Zoe and Rocky walk along the beach, the same one where, only two years before, Theo and I made Zoe, traipsing across the hot sand until we found a large enough piece of driftwood to anchor Rocky. Theo wrapped a sheet around his body like a toga and we had sex on the beach, Rocky barking the whole time. Two weeks later, I got sick after lunch, and knew that after two years of trying, I was, at last, pregnant. I bring Zoe down out of the sack, pulling out the Ziploc bag in the process. I close my eyes and smile, as Zoe plays at my feet. A wind picks up across the Pacific as I shake the bag out, watching the ashes skim the surface of the wave. Like a surfer going the wrong way, they head to the horizon.

"I love you, Theo," I whisper, picking up Zoe. I begin to tell her, "Say good-bye to . . ."

But I stop myself. Zoe will one day have the chance to say good-bye, when she understands what just happened to our lives. And though there is a part of me that wishes I could grieve with her, share this pain with the only other person on the planet who could possibly understand what we have lost, she can only respond to our days and often long nights with the cries and coos of a one-year old, a baby who still expects her father to return home. As I look down at her, sitting on the beach where only two years before, we brought her into being, I am shocked that I am now here, doing this alone. As much as I wished for my time with my baby, hanging Theo on my resentments that I had to work so much because he failed to hold a job, I wonder what it will mean for us to do this life without him. Because for Zoe, the man who was once her rock has now turned to ash. We walk back to the car in silence. Even Rocky is calm on his leash. I load Rocky into the back of the Honda and put Zoe in her car seat. That morning, as Debra helped me pack up the car, she offered me a job at the campground, the chance at a new life. But as I direct us home, moving south along Highway 1, I know that Big Sur is just another fragile memory, faded by our loss.

SIX

I get into Theo's truck and try to steel myself. After the shooting, Peter asked if he could take over the lease for the Tacoma. Since it was in my name, they wouldn't let me turn the lease in early without a fine, so it made sense, even if it also meant that every time Peter drives up to the house, Zoe calls for daddy.

One month after the shooting, we are driving to the San Bernardino County Sheriff's Department where the families of the victims and survivors of the shooting have been invited to learn the truth of their tragedy. According to Peter, it's a standard briefing. They received one when Peter went out and met with the president, but this meeting is expected to be more detailed. As I was quickly realizing, more work went into investigating the shootings than went into preventing them. Afterward, the ambulances fled in and the police and the detectives and federal agents came next, followed by lawyers, always the lawyers. And there were so many talking points, twisting through the anguish that seemed almost pedestrian to those who weren't inside it. But on the inside, it was hell.

"How was your presidential reception?" I ask Peter as he drives, watching the strip malls pass by us along I-10.

Peter laughs. "Honestly, it was pretty formal. He said all the right things, seemed like he cared, but I don't know. I thought he'd actually do something, like pass a law or something."

"I don't think presidents pass laws," I reply.

But it was also one of the reasons why I didn't want to go. I didn't want to be a meet and greet on a politician's trail. Theo used to say that politics were personal. That who you believed in echoed who you were. We once believed in the president, but we weren't so sure anymore.

"Hillary won't become president," Theo threatened the week she won the primaries, defeating Bernie, our chosen candidate.

"You're being sexist," I accused him.

"I'm being honest." He stood over Zoe's changing table, negotiating a dirty diaper off our now mobile one-year old. "And, really, I blame the president."

"The president?" I asked, as I organized the clothes in her baby drawer, annoyed that as the stay-at-home dad, Theo was incapable of throwing out six-month-old onesies and making sure her leggings were neatly stacked, all the details I knew I would have gotten right if only I had more time.

"Yeah." Theo secured the diaper. "They all look the same now. They're zombies and no one wants to vote for a zombie."

"Well, they're not going to vote for fucking Trump." I could feel myself getting angry at the mere thought. I didn't have much faith in my country, but I still believed in it, like a God you pray to even as you doubt its existence.

"How are your parents?" I ask Peter, looking out the window, trying to forget the last time I drove out on this road, in this truck, arguing with Theo about his mother and her demands that we have a second child.

"They'd like for you to visit," Peter replies, but I don't know how to respond. After our last visit to the house, filled with dead flowers and pictures of Theo at every turn, I didn't know how I could go back. As much as I love Lydia, I also saw her as Theo's great wound. How could he ever grow up when all she wanted was for him to come home?

"It's just hard," I reply.

"It's hard on all of us," Peter offers flatly as we drive. We don't listen to music, sitting hard in the silence. I haven't been able to turn on the radio since the shooting. It's all too sentimental.

"Yvette Morales wrote me," I finally tell Peter as we make our way across the Inland Empire.

"Yvette Morales?" Peter asks, not recognizing the name, and I am reminded how little Peter and I know about each other's lives. We spent so much of our time together with Theo, that telling personal histories seemed moot. Most of the private time we did share was usually spent talking about Theo or whatever woman Peter was dating at the time.

"She was one of the assistants when I worked for Blake Edwards. She runs everything now," I explain. "But then, we were friends, back before everything fell apart."

Peter glances at me. "You dated Blake Edwards or something?"

I look out the window before I admit, "Or something."

t's been almost ten years, and still the memory nauseates me, like I've jumped into the deep end of a pool and my equilibrium is thrown. I can never forget that last day with Blake, the other moment when everything changed. I would have never known waking up that morning how my day would end, that I would be someone different within twelve hours, that the identity I had cherished for years would be obliterated in minutes.

I don't even remember now where I read the *Times* announcement. Sometimes, I think it was on the subway in the morning, scrolling through the headlines on my BlackBerry, just a few quaint years before the iPhone. Or maybe it was once I got into the office. The sign for *The Blake Edwards Show* hanging behind the receptionist's desk, surprising me every morning, even as I arrived straight from Blake's bed. Maybe it was at my desk, a colleague dropping the paper down in front of me, the engagement section reflecting my shock.

But I will never forget reading the words, "World-famous correspondent Blake Edwards to marry model Victoria Sarkisian."

Maybe it wasn't even the *Times*, maybe it was the *Post*'s "Page Six." Only they would be crass enough to describe Blake Edwards as "world-famous," a title he would have eschewed in public but would have made his ego grin.

I do know I spent the whole day with it, feeling my colleague's furtive glances. And I remember that the only person who said anything to me about it was Yvette Morales.

"Fuck him, Jane. Honestly, fuck him." But ten years later, my career would be long gone, and Yvette would be his executive producer.

It wasn't until late that night that he returned to the office, acting surprised to see me. Although he knew that if I wasn't with him, I was always there, writing the next segment, researching the pitches that would magically come to air, my ideas adopted as his own. But I didn't mind. Where else would a twenty-something associate get to broadcast her wildest beliefs to the world? Did it matter that Blake was my microphone?

I watched him from my cube. Suddenly, he wasn't my lover, or boyfriend, or best friend—all roles he openly claimed—he was my boss. I swallowed hard and walked into his office, dropping the copy of the announcement on his desk.

"When were you going to tell me?"

Blake looked up at me with the cool smile I'd come to know—the slight curl at the corner, the promise of a kinder man than he was. Except to me. Where Blake could be cruel to others, he treated me with kid gloves. His Janey, light of his life.

"Janey." He barely glanced down. "They scooped me. Can you believe it? The assholes."

"Fuck you, Blake. It's an announcement, not a blind item."

He shrugged. "It's my life, sweetheart."

I moved toward him. "It's my life, too."

"Not quite, Janey."

I ignored his meanness, struggling to make sense of it all. "I mean, I knew you were fucking her. I didn't want to admit it, but marry her? Who the fuck is she, I don't even understand?"

Blake finally looked down at the announcement, his eyes flashing a sad recognition, like he wasn't as excited by the news as he should be. A part of me still hoped it wasn't real.

He soldiered back up. "We're a good match."

"Then what are we?" I felt the tears rise in my voice. "Jesus, Blake—I was just with you last night."

Blake stood up and walked to the window, overlooking midtown, the last time I would ever see the view that had been the backdrop to our life together.

"Remember when we saw the Fellini retrospective in Rome?" Blake asked, his back turned to me. I sighed, recalling how Blake failed to tell me that there would be no subtitles. He spoke Italian, but I spent the three-movie event guessing at the plot. "Blake, you're not Marcello Mastroianni."

He tensed at the insult because of course he was.

Ignoring me, he continued, "Guido in 8 ½, he is surrounded by all these women. The wife, the muse, the whore."

I moved quickly across the room, my anger taking over. "And what? I've been the whore? Blake—are you forgetting what we've been through together? Are you forgetting everything you've ever said to me?"

"No, Janey." He turned around to me and replied earnestly, "You were the muse. But you don't marry the muse . . . Jesus, sweetheart, you've been my light over the last couple of years. And I see so much for you."

He walked back to his desk, suddenly official, like a lawyer preparing a brief. "But you're not the marrying type."

Blake slowed, recognizing his own callousness, "Don't get me wrong, Jane, you're a gem. You are. Just, maybe, slow down on the drinking, okay?" he offered, his voice suddenly distant and fatherly. "I know it can be fun in this business, but you're never going to get what you want if you keep drinking like you do."

"Is that what this is about?" I asked, hoping I could still salvage the life that was dissolving in front of me.

Blake looked genuinely sad, like he might be losing something, too. He sighed, twisting the Rolex on his wrist. "Jane, sometimes life just serves us a nonnegotiable. How we accept it is what matters."

As Blake walked to the door, I watched everything I had worked for begin to slide through my hands. He smiled at me coldly. "But I've already talked to HR. I think it's time we move on."

In that moment, I couldn't even respond, suddenly realizing, I wasn't just losing a lover or a boyfriend, as I had been naïvely calling Blake for years, I was losing my job.

I panicked. "Move on? From the relationship? Or from my job? What would you talk to HR about?"

He smiles gently, "They've put together a very nice package for you."

"Package? What did you tell them? That you've been fucking me for three years, but you're done? That you're paying me off?"

"Janey, consider your options here."

"Fuck you, Blake. You can't break my heart and take my job too. I'll go to HR myself . . . I'll tell them everything."

"This can either be a footnote in your life, honey, or it can be a chapter."

"It's the whole fucking book, Blake," I sputtered as he walked out the door. I was left standing alone in his office, having woken up that morning in one life and ending it in another. I picked up the remaining whiskey in his glass, gulped it down, and never went back.

The next day, HR called me in and offered me $20,000 to sign an NDA. My hand signed the agreement, but my heart took the hit. For the next two months, I tried to find another job in New York, but despite all the friends I had made, word got back that

Blake had begun to describe me as difficult to work with. He raised the drawbridge, and I found myself on the outside of the career he once promised to help me build.

My heart was cremated. I moved back home to Dennis's house, blazing through the cash until I found bottom.

Peter and I walk into the conference room of the Sheriff's county headquarters and find our seats in the packed auditorium filled with family members and the agencies investigating the shooting. The agents share that Martin Montgomery had been plotting the massacre for three months. The sheriff shares from the podium that the motives were both personal and political. "According to comments found on 4chan," he says, "Montgomery apparently referred to the current administration's continued occupation of the Middle East as manslaughter against the remaining troops."

I wonder whether the president knew this information at the time of his visit, that Montgomery wasn't just a lunatic with a gun but also one with a vendetta against him and his administration—these faraway decisions suddenly coming home to roost, imploding our otherwise naïve lives with their consequences. We sit patiently as the various agents and officers and coroners and medical examiners give their summations on the case, the CliffsNotes version of the lived event. They talk about witnesses and emails, text messages and timelines. They share what happened during the space of the two minutes and twenty-eight seconds that changed everything. From the first shot that entered Theo's skull to the last shot that entered Martin Montgomery's. They offer us a schedule of briefings and ask for our contact information so we can stay informed as the investigation develops, passing around a clipboard like we're signing up for Girl Scout cookies. Finally, they open it up for questions, but I am no longer listening. I know what happened; I was there.

As we get up to leave, I see James Toobin, the man my mother invited to the funeral. He is no longer in his black suit, but he still looks formal in pressed khakis and a button-down shirt.

He notices me and walks over, smiling warmly. "I thought I'd see you here."

"You come to these things often?" I ask, a little surprised by his appearance.

"I know, funerals and briefings." He laughs awkwardly. "I really don't, but it's part of my job to track the cases, see what we can do to intervene."

After our last meeting, I read a bit more into Families United, how they are known to show up in the aftermath of a shooting, offering a fellowship of grief but also an opportunity for advocacy. I smile, knowing James has the best intentions though I'm not sure how I feel about making a job out of a loved one's death.

"Are you here to recruit?" I ask him, trying not to sound snarky.

"It's not as tasteless as it sounds," he replies before adding, "but I've come to accept that it's the only thing I can do to make it right. I'm here so she knows how much I loved her."

There is a pause before James adds, "I wasn't a great father, Jane. I didn't show up at the school performances or the big games. I failed her so many times, and then I wasn't even there that last morning." His voice catches. "I never even said good-bye."

I'm not sure if this is a story he tells often, but I haven't seen it in any of the footage I've watched late at night, the interviews on CNN and MSNBC, even *The Blake Edwards Show*.

I smile. "I wasn't a great wife. I think that's what makes this all so weird."

"You can love the wrong way and still miss them," James offers.

I nod, knowing this is when the tears should come, but they've been delayed so long, I'm not sure they'll ever arrive. "I'm trying to figure that out."

"You will," James says, seeing someone he knows over my shoulder. He waves them off for a moment. "When you're ready, you let me know."

"If I'm ready," I correct him.

He smiles knowingly. "Sure."

He hugs me as though we've known each other longer than we have. Even though James looks and acts like the politician he's been forced to become, there is something about him that feels real. Or maybe he just feels raw. He looks at me and the room quiets around me. He lingers for a moment, whispering just above my ear, "Take care of yourself, Jane."

I watch as he walks off and Peter approaches.

"Who was that?" Peter asks.

"One of us," I reply but then I see someone else, the woman from the urgent care. I remember her immediately, crying in the hallway, believing her husband was still alive. She is standing alone against the wall, and I realize I am not the only awkward widow here.

"Give me a second," I tell Peter as I walk over to her. I can see her eyes are swollen as though she has been crying the whole time.

"Hi." I reach out my hand. "I'm Jane. I was in the urgent care with you that night, when you found out about your husband."

I can tell she doesn't recognize me, likely didn't even notice that anyone was sitting there that night.

"I'm sorry. I don't remember," she says quietly.

"I saw you. I wanted to say something, but it was too hard. I was so confused. But I lost my husband, too," I explain.

"Wait?" She recognized me. "You're the lady from outside that morning. They got you on TV."

"Yeah, I didn't mean to be there, I just . . ." I look down, realizing I haven't even introduced myself. "I'm Jane."

"I'm Gisselle, Gigi, everyone calls me Gigi."

"It's nice to meet you, Gigi. I'm so sorry. I mean, for both of us. I'm so sorry we're here."

She smiles. "I wasn't going to come. It's all been so hard. My children . . ."

Gigi begins to cry, and I reach out to her. She begins to sob as I awkwardly hold her, unsure how comfortable either of us are in this grief. "We just don't know how to live without him. He was our world, our whole world."

I offer the only thing I can think of, because even in my own grief, I don't know what to say, "We're going to get through this."

"You might." She pulls back, her eyes clear and wet and righteous. "But I don't know how to feed my children without him. That monster took everything from us, our home, our life. I don't know how to make it here alone without Al. I don't know that we will."

"I'm so sorry," I mutter even as we know the words are meaningless, but I don't know what else to say. The idea of being the head of household doesn't terrify me; I've been checking that box on our last four tax returns, and yet I see the fear in this woman's eyes, the desperate confusion of what lies ahead, and I want to fix it, for both of us. Because Gigi's husband and mine died for the same reasons: the gun that killed them is legal.

"Me too," she replies before turning and walking away.

P eter and I pull over at a Ruby Tuesday on the way home. Andrea has come back to help for another month, taking time off work while I return to my own job. When my father died, she was the sole beneficiary of his modest life insurance policy, using the money to buy a condominium where she still lives today.

She's agreed to stay with us and watch Zoe while I try to figure out who will take care of the baby once Andrea heads home and I am back to working full-time, but now there is no Theo to help. I was raised by a single mother and I remember the way it felt like we lived our whole lives bone against bone.

"I can help out," Peter tells me as we sit down.

"Oh, I know," I tell him. "But I still have to find a day care."

I don't know what to do next. There is $600 in our checking account, and we haven't had anything in savings for months.

I can't tell Andrea because I know her reply will be to question the trip to Big Sur, to question every expense in what has become an increasingly expensive life. Every day, it feels like another bill arrives that I'm not sure how to pay. And I have a job. I can't even imagine what it's like for the untold number of families who just lost their breadwinner, for mothers like Gigi who still have mouths to feed but no money to do so, all the families with no life insurance policy in their back pocket. I am grateful that we at least have that coming, though my company tells me it will take a couple months to get it sorted and paid. In the meantime, they have approved my disability request, giving me more paid time off, which I know is more than other companies would offer, and yet I also know there is nothing in me that wants to go back. I didn't even want to be there in the first place. And it wasn't that I didn't care about the kids at the heart of our work, but I was so tired of pushing paper and pretending that it was going to help. And the marriage and the job had become so intertwined that one felt like prison and the other parole.

I look over at my brother-in-law and smile, "We'll figure it out, I'm sure."

When Peter told me he was planning to transition, I was thrilled for him. I knew how hard it had been for him, pretending to be someone he wasn't, binding his heavy breasts with tape and sports bras. For a while, Theo referred to Peter as his sis-bro, because he just wasn't ready yet to give up the little sister he had known and loved and protected since he was three. I'm not sure whether it's from Theo's death, or from a boost in confidence since regulating his t-shots, but now, more than ever, Peter is becoming the person he was meant to be. I wonder if when no one has any memory of the people we were before, we're finally free to be ourselves. Maybe it's why I stayed away from friends like Yvette. I didn't want her reflection to remind me of who I once was, someone who believed that there was no middle road in politics, who thought that the only way change could be achieved was through permanent revolution, building a new economic and political system that benefitted the hundreds of millions of people like me and Gigi and everyone in between.

In college, I wrote my thesis on the power of daytime television to inspire revolution. I jokingly imagined a world in which soap operas comingled story lines of economic liberation and workers' rights alongside dangerous affairs and deathbed confessions. Blake read it as part of my application process. In my first interview, he laughed. "Are you really a radical or just young?"

But it wasn't just youth. I didn't know injustice the way some people did, but I met it through the death of my father. I saw it in the years where my mother worked for a boss who kept her late whenever he wanted. Though he was married with young children, he told my mom their relationship was part of the job, and though she knew better, she also didn't know enough to leave.

Years later, I would find myself in the same relationship, but I believed Blake was different. There was no wife, there were no children, there was just me and this man who told me that the revolution I wanted was ours to create. In the end, my mother retired with a watch. I at least came home with a check. But I believed in the work, that the words I wrote and the things I believed and the dreams I held for this world weren't just fancies of youth; that with Blake's power, we would make the change real.

I was radical for a reason. And so was Theo. It was our politics that had made that first morning in bed so easy, so aligned in how we saw the world and what we wanted for it. But for every charge Theo leveled against the world, it felt like he was incapable of seeing where change was also required of him.

"Are you dating anyone?" I ask Peter as I bite into my burger.

Peter smiles. "Yeah, a woman I met at the gym."

"That's great. Who is she?"

"She's a teacher and a mom, actually. She was married before. I guess, it's time for me to settle down, too. I'll bring her over soon."

"You better." I hesitate before asking, "Is she open about your relationship?"

Peter has had a habit of dating straight girls who preferred to keep their relationship with him in the closet, "Yeah, she knows who she is. She's a grown-up."

"That's awesome. You deserve a grown-up."

"He was working on it, Jane." Peter takes a bite of his burger before adding, "I grew up with him, remember? I know how hard he could be. But don't forget, he was a good guy, too. He was one of a kind."

I remember back to Gigi at the briefing. Her husband was her world and I'm not so different. As much as I was tired of being his gravitational pull, Theo, from the moment I met him, floated firmly in the middle of my orbit.

SEVEN

I once believed New York would save me. Growing up, I imagined myself walking through Manhattan snowdrifts with a big fur coat, adopting that old American accent that got lost after the early 1970s. *Hello gorgeous.* Before everything ended, I would step out of work after sharing a cocktail with Blake, the dream sanctioned by his attention. I would pull my wool coat around my shoulders, slip on my Walkman headphones, and light up a Marlboro to the sounds of Ella Fitzgerald. The city would glisten under the glaring headlights and white snow of winter in Manhattan, a grand and boisterous musical. And I was going to be one of its stars.

As the plane descends into JFK, I'm still not sure why I agreed to come here, but after the briefing in the desert, I keep thinking back to Gigi. I know it's easy to blame Martin Montgomery, but I also know there is more to what happened that night than just an angry man with a gun.

I was in New York during 9/11. I stood next to Blake as his intern, as we watched the second tower fall, melting in real time like a candle in fast-forward. I saw how easy it was to blame monsters and not the systems that enabled them. The long, wiry threads of history that made violence inevitable.

And all the people who lost their worlds because of it. When I got home from the desert that night, I opened the trash file in my inbox, and I found the email from Yvette, hitting reply before I could think twice.

Of course, coming to New York means leaving LA. It means leaving Zoe. It means leaving Theo's memory, our history now a warm vapor drifting through my days. I see him standing in the kitchen, making Zoe's oatmeal. I go out to dinner with Zoe, teaching her how to say *doggie* and *milk* and *happy*, and feel him watching across the table, smiling as our daughter discovers new words. As I was leaving for New York, I clung to Zoe, terrified to say good-bye. I am now her only parent and though I know the statistics on plane crashes, the idea that she might ever have to live without me brings a terror I cannot even taste. And yet, I am drawn to this city I once called home, Yvette's words reaching out like a life preserver. Because she isn't wrong. I am being strangled, and I've been strangled for long enough.

M s. Ambrose," the receptionist calls out as I sit in reception area, waiting for Yvette.

The same sign for *The Blake Edwards Show* still hangs there, evidence that some things don't change. But I have. The Jane Ambrose that worked here was a different woman. She began to fade away that night in the office when Blake left her for Victoria Sarkisian. And she all but vanished when over the following weeks and months, despite her contacts and media connections, no one would hire her. I know at some point in the story, I've got to make a comeback. I need to listen to some Beyoncé or Eminem and hit a punching bag, preparing to rise like a phoenix and return to life. I know I've become too comfortable with defeat.

The receptionist offers me a sad-eyed smile as I hear Yvette approaching down the hall. How such a slight woman can have such a heavy gait is beyond me. She enters the lobby with the confidence of the New York power player she has become. Starting only a year before I left, Yvette ended up running *The Blake Edwards Show*. Then, when he created his own digital network, she ran that, too.

"My God, Janey," Yvette whispers into my hair as she hugs me. "What did they do to you?"

The question is so intimate, a part of me crumbles in response. Yvette was a firebrand, short and slender with jet black hair and, as I used to tell her, a "trophy wife" profile—pert nose, full lips, soft forehead. By contrast, I felt like the masculine one, my nose jutting too far off my face, my features too broad, my voice too brash, yet despite her photogenic beauty, Yvette never wanted to step in front of the camera. Another reason Blake loved her. As her small arms hold me tight, she reminds me for a moment that I can be buoyed in this grief.

"I don't know, Yves," I shudder. "I don't know."

And it's true. I know what happened to me. I just don't know why I didn't avoid it. I don't know why I can't just be the woman I believed I once was. The woman Theo fell in love with years ago. The one Blake loved long before that.

Yvette and I pull back from the hug to get a better look at one another, suddenly reminded of the friendship we once shared, when we dreamed of changing the world. Yvette was first generation Mexican American, growing up in El Paso, watching as her parents worked in the back of a cousin's restaurant, never able to rise above poverty, but like Andrea, they put everything they had into their honor roll daughter, watching as she earned scholarships to camps and academies and finally Fordham, where she studied pre-law until one night watching *The Blake Edwards Show* with friends, she sent in her résumé and landed a production assistant gig, the same job I had been promoted out of three years earlier.

By the end of her first month, as I showed her the ropes, she asked me about Blake.

Naïvely, I told her with a smile, "We're in love."

I saw the flash of disbelief in her eyes, a familiar response, but even Yvette gave in after a while, seeing how Blake would hold my hand while we were all out to dinner, how I was invited as his date to black-tie events, although not onto the red carpet. She once asked me about the exclusion, but my answer was the same, "It's not time. I just need a few more years."

I thought once I was older, twenty-nine or thirty, the age difference wouldn't draw so much attention. People would forget how long I had been by his side, and by then, I would have a career of my own, reporting for Blake's show or even, as he often promised, for my own.

Yvette is wearing cowboy boots and tight jeans, her uniform since her early days with Blake. The day before I went out and bought myself a vintage gold dress, soft enough to not look flashy, but bold. We walk to the elevator to head downstairs. Before Yvette presses the down arrow, she stops. "The girl I used to know never fucking held back. She said whatever she wanted, and she did whatever she wanted. Please, Janey, I don't want your grief. I want your truth."

"What if I don't know how to tell the truth anymore?"

"You did that first morning after the shooting, didn't you? That's why we're here, right? No one had ever really seen what that shit looks like, but you showed them."

Yvette punches the elevator button, "Show them again." She continues talking, but I am barely listening. In all the days that followed the shooting, I could barely return myself to that moment that brought the media flocking in the first place, the image of me drenched in dried blood, holding out the piece of my husband's skull, demanding answers to questions I had barely begun to ask, questions I've managed to avoid the last two months.

"And Blake? What does he want from me?" I finally inquire, knowing that the miles between us have now turned into yards, feet, mere inches.

"I don't fucking care what he wants." Yvette laughs. "Look, he's the old guard. And I respect him, I do. But he doesn't understand where any of this is going. Things are changing, Janey. Trump, Hillary, we are standing on the precipice of history. And either we rise up to it, or we fall in."

We exit the elevator as Yvette picks up the pace. "Shit, we better get down there. Remember, we're live."

I stop in the hallway, knowing what's next—the hair and makeup, the rundown with an associate producer before I'm led to the stage.

"Yves?" I ask, as my old friend stops and turns back to me. "Can you use the last name Karras on the show?"

"What do you mean?" Yvette asked.

"I mean, as in Jane Karras. I never took Theo's name, but . . ." I don't know what else to say. That I should have?

"Sure," Yvette replies. "Jane Karras. You got this."

The smell of the soundstage—of plywood and dust—reminds me of those long nights on set. Even Yvette, as safe and loving as she might be, harkens back to those days, coaxing the guest into an anxious comfort, working to build an immediate and intimate rapport. I am about to sit down when the soundstage door opens. I hear Blake before I see him. I know how his body moves through the atmosphere though it's been years since we were last in a room together.

"Janey . . ." His voice is quiet as he says my name like he used to, stretching the syllables out into a sigh.

I turn and prepare myself for the old feeling, our energy rushing to meet each other's, colliding to the point of whiplash. But what I see surprises me. In ten years, Blake Edwards looks like an old man. When I would see him on TV, he seemed to have aged well, but before we can even say hello, I realize it's the makeup. All this time I imagined him striking and strong and handsome, but the man in front of me is short and slight, with thin gray skin pulled taut along his cheekbones. How memory distorts.

"Blake," I reply with a smile, but not with the sadness I was anticipating. Yvette might have wondered what happened to me, but I could ask the same of Blake. He pulls me in for a hug and I can smell the booze underneath the $300 cologne. He has already had a morning cocktail. When I pull back, I see his ring finger is bare.

"I'm so sorry, Jane. Honestly." He stops. "How's your daughter?"

I knew that he and Victoria had three children in the last decade, but I don't remember reading anything about a divorce.

"She just turned one. It'll take its time."

"Are you okay to do this here?"

I am surprised by the question, but, then again, that is part of Blake's charm, being honest when you least expect it. I remember my journalist's smile, bright and quiet at the same time, like Blake taught me, on the verge of a laugh, but never leaning in.

I reply, "How could I do it anywhere else?"

I mean it. In that moment, I realize that I couldn't have sat down on another soundstage. It had to be with Blake. We take our seats, ignoring that the energy is gone. Instead, we just get comfortable in our chairs and prepare for the conversation we are here to have. Before I know it, the requisite hand gestures are being made across the stage as the grips move the cameras into place, and "Action" is called. Blake introduces me, though I've gotten good at not listening to certain parts of my new story.

"June twenty-seventh . . . Jane and Theo Karras . . . Mojave Desert . . . The shooter came in through the back door . . . US Army . . . eleven killed . . . shot ten times. But the one thing most people don't know is that Jane Ambrose, I mean Karras, used to work on our show. She was one of our best producers. And we all feel her loss."

Yvette signals that the cameras are on, as the world suddenly slows, the facts of that night coming into view again. I hear the first pops of Martin's gun, I see Theo's face, and then I see Blake's.

Surviving one man only to be destroyed by another. I can smell Theo dying on top of me when all he ever wanted to do was live.

Run, hide, fight. Sandy Hook. San Bernardino. Mojave Saloon. Blake Edwards. The injustice. The wars. The lies. The bullshit. The TV sets and smart dresses and blowouts and compassion. The centuries of being told that this is just how it is. Being told that there is nothing anyone can do. The fucking hell of it all. And then I feel the small stuff, too. The work. The child. The exhaustion. The nights crying by Zoe's bathtub before Theo was even dead. The soul-sucking, unfair fight that I just don't know how to do anymore. And then this one stupid chance to say something about it.

Blake smiles at me, reaching across the couch to squeeze my hand. "How are you?"

I stare into the darkness where the cameras watch me, waiting.

"I don't really know, Blake. To be honest . . ." I pause, remembering Yvette's directive, "I can't even cry. I can't even understand how to feel."

"It's just horrible, Jane. It is." Blake nods, full of sympathy.

"He was shot eleven times, not ten. And . . . I kept waiting to hear him breathe."

"These shootings, they are all so senseless . . ." Blake starts.

"Yes, they are." I look down as I speak, unable to stare into the studio's abyss, but then I remember Yvette's words. If I don't speak my truth now, how long before I am strangled by it? I look up. "I didn't even really mean to come here."

"Then why are you here?"

The question is simple and straightforward yet there is a cruelty in it. At first, I want to say, *I don't know*, but I do know.

"Because . . ." I pause, realizing that I have yet to admit this truth even to myself. "Because I realized I'm not alone. There are so many of us. So many of us who loved someone who's now dead because a bullet, a tiny little piece of metal, made their big, beautiful life disappear in a second. But I'm the anomaly. You know. The media, they show up at my door but they ignore entire communities who taste this grief way too often."

Blake tightens. "Jane, I know many people, myself included, who report on gun violence in this country. Certainly, these shootings hit different . . ."

"Why do they hit differently?" I find myself pushing him, not knowing if I'm angry about Martin Montgomery, Theo Karras, or Blake Edwards, but I feel angry.

Blake offers that famous half-smile again. "Well, people, they're not used to seeing what it looks like after, you know . . ."

"After your husband is shot and dies on top of you? Yeah, they're not."

"But also, your words in that moment, right? What made you say, 'This is what guns do?'"

I stop, having asked myself that question a hundred times. Why did I say anything? I might not have known then but I do know now.

"Because what else are they supposed to do, Blake? What is the point of a semi-automatic if not to tear into flesh and destroy the living entity on the other side of those bullets? It's not for defense or survival. We keep them legal simply for chaos."

"There are a lot of people working to change that, Jane. A lot of good work is taking place right now, as we speak."

I smile, "Then why is the AR-15 still legal?"

"You know how hard it would be to change that," Blake begins to admonish me.

"Really? Hard? See, here's the thing, Blake. Every time one of these shootings happens, you show up, right? You get the media hits and the outpouring of grief. People want to know how many people died and were there kids involved, and oh my fucking God, he was a baseball player. But then when we say, this is what is takes to stop it, the shooting doesn't really matter does it? I mean, it's not complicated math here. It is seriously two plus two."

"It is, Jane. And it's an epidemic."

"No, Blake," I start to laugh. "It's not a disease. It's not something we can't control or don't understand. I don't think we want to control it. I think it's a choice to allow these guns to take over our world. Because this isn't cancer or a flood." I feel my pulse speeding up as my hand grips the arm of the chair, my nails digging in. "Violence doesn't have to be inevitable."

"You're talking gun control?"

I lean in, nearly hissing the words, "No. I'm talking about all of it. About who makes the decisions and who has power and who gets the attention and why people keep dying and no one fucking stops it—"

"Janey, it's not as easy as you think . . ."

"Yes, it is." I feel tears in my eyes for the first time. "We need to make it stop. Theo . . ."

His name is the levy in my dam, finally giving way to the pressure of everything I've been holding inside since that first explosion in the Mojave Saloon.

"Theo," I whisper. The man who changed everything. I feel the room begin to spin, the bottom of the floor dropping out as I reach out and grab Blake's arm to steady myself. I can hear myself, like I'm watching from above, begging in a broken craw. "Make it stop."

The wave breaks over my head, crashing down, filling my mouth and eyes and ears with pain. I am in the Mojave Saloon, I feel the shots hitting Theo's body, I feel him grabbing at me even in the horror, I feel myself go under, my head hitting the reef as I lose myself in the words, repeating over and over, "Make it stop. Make it stop. Make it stop. Make it stop."

Blake looks toward Yvette, knowing we're live.

"What do we do?" He searches for his producer's face in the dark, breaking the fourth wall, asking Yvette as much as the audience watching. "What do we do?"

On the live program, that same audience hears Yvette's voice as she replies, "We cut."

Yvette comes on the stage, and without saying a word she leads me off. We walk back to the greenroom, as I clutch my old friend's arm. She puts me on the couch and sits down in a chair opposite me.

Finally, I open my eyes. "I'm sorry."

"For what?"

I finally sit up. The room feels normal again, just another three-dimensional space in a world that has lost all dimension. "For losing my shit?"

"No, Jane. You did something way bigger than that. You gave grief a voice. You're not wrong. We need to make it stop. All of it." She grabs my hand and looks me hard in the eyes. "All of it."

Blake enters before we can say anything else. He pulls me up from the couch and into a deep hug, the kind I remember from when we were together, safe, and all-consuming. And then I hear his voice cold in my ear. "I guess I put you in the wrong seat. You make a better guest than a host."

I realize then why I gave up. Why I walked away. And it didn't have anything to do with a broken heart or a bruised ego. The truth was, I was perfectly fine speaking up for everyone else, but I didn't know how to speak up for me. I wanted to be the hero for my mom, I wanted to right all the hurts and injustices of our little middle-class life through the platform Blake was offering me, only to find out there was a trap door under me the whole time. I move toward Blake, and without even thinking, I pull my fist back as far as I can and sling it across his cheek.

"What the fuck, Jane?" Blake spits, holding on to the side of his face.

I don't know what to say. My first instinct is to apologize, but for what? This man single-handedly destroyed my career, the one thing I loved more than anything else—a love so big, my marriage paled in comparison.

Blake rubs his cheek. "Did you just punch me?"

As I look at Blake, I realize he stands for everything I want to fight in this world, building his career on controversy but never creating change. I once believed that we could use the media to inspire people to act, to make progress, but as I look at this small and angry man before me, I realize he lives in a world where gold-plated awards and points on the back end are the evidence of his victory, not justice and certainly not revolution.

I finally feel like myself again, back in my body, in this present moment as Blake turns to me, waiting for an answer. I feel the blood drain from my face as the words I have been waiting for years finally escape. "You took everything from me."

"Is that why you came back here, for this?" he barks.

"No, I came back here because I'm broken, Blake. But I was broken long before Martin Montgomery burst through that door."

"Jane, you don't have to . . ." Yvette tries to comfort me, but I have come here for this.

"I loved this job, I loved this work, I loved the stories and the travel and the adventure and the truth, and when it was all over, it was like a part of me was dead and I couldn't get it back. Theo didn't get the person you knew. He got someone who was half-dead. Even my baby, she's had a mother who's been half-dead, and you were the one who killed me."

Blake's eyes go cold. "You did it to yourself, Jane."

"No Blake, you did it to me. You made sure that no one would reply to my emails or answer my calls. You made sure I couldn't find work. I loved it so much and you knew that. More than any-one, you knew that."

He doesn't even shudder and I wonder what has happened to him over the last ten years. The man I knew was passionate about this job, about telling the stories of the world, and not just from our privileged perspectives. He was the one who showed me that the truth was everything. It was why we were here, to seek justice, not to betray it.

"Well, you're not going back out there," he threatens.

"I don't need to." I pick up my bag as Yvette follows me out the door. She grabs my hand and pulls me into an embrace, whisper-ing, "Call me," before I step out onto the hot streets of a New York day in August. I stand there, the mad life of the city I once called home rushes around me, wrapping me in the force that fed my dreams, and for the first time in years, I feel alive.

EIGHT

've never experienced a troll but then again, I've never fucked
with the NRA before. I left my job with Blake right before the
explosion of social media—in the badlands between Myspace
and Twitter—and though I started a couple blogs over the years
which some friends liked and commented, there were no angry
clapbacks, no one telling me to "get a life," no one threatening the
one I have.

"Don't read the comments," Yvette warns after the onslaught
begins, before Rose helps me to set my social media accounts to
private, as the anger gathers in the digital universe.

My phone rings from an unknown number, likely just another
reporter looking for the scoop, wanting to know more about me,
about Theo, and—for those savvy enough to pick up on the tension between Blake and me—about my time working for the
famed journalist. I turn off the ringer on my phone and spoon

another bite of yogurt into Zoe's mouth, trying to feed my baby before heading to work. My mother does the dishes while Dennis watches me. He came up to visit yesterday; Andrea probably called him. We've been running on empty for weeks, yet we're not quite sure where to go. I'm scheduled to sign all the paperwork for Theo's life insurance today, and Dennis's surprise visit feels like an ambush.

"You could come home, to my home," my uncle proposes. "With the insurance, you could build a fresh start. Maybe even buy a house. You know you can still get deals in Torrance, Cerritos."

I can tell Dennis and Andrea have discussed this already, trying to approach the topic like it's a casual offer. It was my father's life insurance policy that bought Andrea's condo after all, giving her the financial freedom to be here with me now.

"Dennis, that's not an option."

Andrea's hands tense on the dish she's washing. "How many options do you have, Jane?"

I know the money isn't significant. I know $180,000 after taxes looks like a couple years of living, but that's all I need. Just a year to breathe and be with Zoe. Just a year where I'm not feeding her oatmeal in the morning so I can be out of the door by eight. Andrea and I have been visiting day cares over the last week. Despite her optimism over a few of them, I know they will only add to the financial burden while deepening my heartbreak.

Theo and I had worked so hard to keep Zoe at home, with Theo taking graveyard shifts and me taking on freelance grant writing jobs so he could work less hours. We knew that daycare was a common enough solution, but we wanted Zoe at home with us. Theo would always remind me that we could just move to his parents' island in Greece and live off the land.

"Then we can be with Zoe all the time," he would promise, but it was one of those ideas that never felt like a real option until you find out that life is a finite timeline with infinite choice.

"Just let me get through the benefit tonight, then we can figure it all out," I offer, rising to get ready for work.

John Thomas has scheduled a benefit concert for victims and their families on the two-month anniversary of the shooting: August 27. The numbers etched like hieroglyphs into my life.

Rocky barks at the back door, a welcome respite.

"Dennis, would you mind taking him for a walk?"

"No problem, Moose," he ruffles my hair. For years, Dennis and I had a family pastime of debating politics. Since the 1980s, Dennis had been a Reagan Republican, although Theo and I used to laugh that Dennis's politics were a ruse, hiding a closeted liberal. Because Dennis was so compassionate, he would frequently rent the extra rooms in his house to people who had hit hard times, barely charging them so they could get back on their feet. Much to Andrea's chagrin, there had been a long list of newly divorced dads, newly sober women, and people who didn't know how they were going to pay rent who Dennis would invite into his home.

"Someone's going to refuse to leave one of these days," Andrea would warn, but they never did, grateful for this man who had so kindly offered them grace.

And he offered me the same grace when I came home from New York, giving me a room in the house, even though all I could do was drink and lick my wounds.

Together, Dennis and I would go to a local bar and drink boilermakers until our laughter became louder than my pain, heading home to drink whiskey and watch *South Park* until Dennis passed out. I would drag myself back to the guest room, falling asleep to the sound of my uncle snoring down the hall. We never agreed politically but that was part of our relationship, sparring about different ideas and still ending on the common ground of love. But that was then, before Trump, when I still naïvely believed that we wanted the same things for this world.

And now, I am once again the walking wounded. Dennis hesitates before asking, "Are you going to be okay at that concert?"

"Of course, I'll be fine."

My mother interjects, "Jane's a rock now, Dennis."

"That's not true," I shoot back, both of us knowing that we can't live together for much longer. "I just don't have a choice, do I?"

"Janey," Dennis says, rubbing my hand, "you can be sad."

I get up to put my lunch in a bag for work, not wanting to start the day with this conversation. "I'll be fine. Really."

"The benefit's in a bar, though?" he asks cautiously.

I begin to laugh, not even thinking about that until this moment. "That's what you're afraid of?"

"Shouldn't we be?" A look passes between Andrea and Dennis.

"No. I could never do that to Theo." But even as I say the words, I wonder if they're true. My sobriety feels like such an immutable truth of my life, like the color of my skin or my birth date. For some people, they think of sobriety as this perilous struggle, but Theo and I saw it as a core part of our identities. Zoe looks up from her oatmeal, innocently rejoining, "Dada."

Even as she learns more words, *dada* stands at the heart of Zoe's vocabulary. She points to the family pictures across our house, landing on Theo's image with a joyful "Dada." If Theo's name is said, Zoe replies, "Dada."

I nod and smile. "Yes, monkey," I say. "Dada."

I grab my purse, fill my water bottle, and kiss Zoe, heading to the office I resented even before Theo's death.

Dennis follows me to the door, "No one doubts you're sad, Janey."

"That's nice of you to say." I kiss my uncle on the cheek, the closest thing to a father I've ever had. "But sometimes I don't even know what I am."

"You're not supposed to, Moose," he replies. "Grief is supposed to be complicated."

I nod, grabbing at my uncle in a surprise hug. He pulls me in, but I break away, offering numbly, "I need to get to work. I won't be home too late."

I drive to work, pulling off the SR-2, frustrated by rush hour's concrete casket, exiting onto LA's grid of congested streets, the city's common language. Despite everything that has been irrevocably changed, this is my one constant, driving through the city alone.

I park in the courthouse garage, pulling down my mirror to quickly do my makeup, just as I have for years.

The Edmund D. Edelman Children's Courthouse is where children get sent into foster care. Every day, I would try to walk in without being noticed, staving the break in my heart as I watched babies teeter by, many not much older than Zoe, not knowing myself how I ended up here.

After everything blew up with Blake, I didn't know what else to do but move to Dennis's house. Until one morning, Dennis found me passed out in the bathroom, covered in my own vomit. He told me that he knew the difference between a party and a problem.

"And you, my love, have a problem." Somehow his words were the spark against my desperation's flint.

What happened after that? Sobriety, odd jobs, I think I might have considered becoming an actress. I didn't know what else to do but focus on sobriety, and then a temp agency placed me at a non-profit. Those who can't make money, fundraise.

The upside was when people ask you what you do, they don't say, "What happened to your career, man? You were such a rock star."

They just say, "How good of you," and they mean it, kind of.

I arrive just in time to prepare for a site visit scheduled that day with a funder. But before I can sit down, my boss walks up to my desk.

"Jane," Adam asks me quietly. "Can we talk?"

Adam came up in fundraising during the AIDS epidemic, working for the Gay Men's Health Crisis at its height. After years in celebrity-studded AIDS fundraising, he has now also found himself working in foster care, which struggles to attract the same Hollywood crowd.

I follow Adam to a conference room where our HR director awaits. I presume it's about the media presence that now lurks outside the courthouse, adding an extra burden to the families coming into the building. It is exactly what I didn't want. I know we don't have enough time to go through the life insurance policy. I assume instead they're going to relieve me, tired of the circus that has become my life.

I never liked Debbie, the woman from HR. She is overly tanned with frizzy blonde hair and an undying love for the New England Patriots. Rumor has it she supports Trump.

"Hi Jane." She doesn't even stand to greet me.

Adam sits next to her, and I can't help but get excited. I am going to be free. I won't have to come to this office anymore. I won't have to pretend that this is the life I wanted.

"Go ahead and sit down," Debbie advises.

I listen as Debbie pulls out a folder.

"So, we received your claim for the life insurance benefit," she begins.

I look to Adam. Why is she acting like we've just started the process?

"It appears your husband didn't complete the medical examination," Debbie continues, as she slides the folder over to me.

I look at the paperwork. My life has been filled with paperwork over the last two months, reams of white paper with black letters and demands for my signature. I notice Theo's familiar scrawl on the page, and I swallow my saliva.

"They asked him to go to a lab to provide a fresh urine sample, and he never completed the process," Debbie explains.

I finally look up, questioning Adam with my eyes, but it is Debbie who is here to deliver the news. "They are denying the claim."

"You can of course appeal," Adam offers gently. He looks so sad, but I don't want him to feel bad. One of the main reasons I have stayed here is because of Adam, even when the job was hard, the stories brutal, the hope slim. He showed me that the most important work you can do is pay attention to the stories others ignore.

"Our eleven o'clock will be here soon," I tell them, sliding the paperwork back to Debbie. "I'll figure it out."

I walk back to my desk, unsure whether I am more upset over the insurance company or the fact that such a stupid mistake has now left Zoe and me with nothing. Andrea reminds me every day that this job has done so much to take care of me, giving me as much leave as their policies would allow, offering me an additional month through some creative disability. I returned the week after going to New York, and, up until this moment, I've been pretending I can still do it.

The receptionist calls me, and I know our funders have arrived.

I go to greet them, knowing that the meeting will initially be highjacked by my story and not by the work we do, but I do my best to keep the meeting on track, as Adam joins me, quieter than usual. Years before, when I was still seeing my therapist Elissa, she asked me what kind of life I wanted, and I told her that I imagined standing on a cliff in Greece with my two children, looking out at the sea. I told her I couldn't survive without the adventure; I just didn't know anymore how to find it. I had looked for it in marriage, but it wasn't there, and then in parenthood, but it wasn't there either. And though the baby made it worth it, she still couldn't make it right.

And now Theo is dead and here I am, back in the same life and the same office. Everyone is concerned but no one understands, except perhaps Yvette, who I now speak to almost every night after Zoe is in bed, just as Yvette gets home from working on the show.

"Does it get easier?" I ask her one night as I lay on the couch in the living room, still unable to return to our room.

"No," she tells me. "I don't know. When I was in high school, I once spent a year in Seattle for some gifted kids' program. At first, all I could do was complain about the rain, but after a while you get used to it. The rain, the gray. You don't like it any more than when you moved there. But then it becomes part of your life. Grief is learning to live with the rain."

After the funders leave in a flurry of promises and goodwill, I know what will happen next: I will send the thank-you emails and write the grant request for the suggested $50,000 donation. Then I will scan the document before sending it off, save it to my database, and set a calendar reminder to follow up in three weeks. I will make the follow-up calls and write thank-you notes when the grant is announced. Adam will send an email congratulating me on my work, and Theo will still be dead.

I start to walk back to my desk, but then I remember the moment of relief I had only an hour before when I thought this job was over, and I know that, finally, it is. I turn around and walk back to Adam's desk where he sits composing an email.

"I can't do this anymore," I say, my voice clear and sure. The sunlight streams into our open office where LA looks surprisingly green and lush outside.

"Do what?" Adam looks up from his computer.

"Work. Come here," I admit. "Pretend."

Adam sits back in his chair, before asking quietly, "Are you sure you can do that?"

Adam is thirty years sober, and maybe because of that, I feel the need to be honest with him. He knows what that life insurance would have meant for Zoe and me.

"I have to do something," I say, suddenly realizing it was my inaction that kept me here, turning me into a woman I could no longer recognize. I was defined by roles I never quite learned how to play.

"Okay," Adam agrees. "But we're going to want to pay you through the end of the month."

"Oh Adam, you don't need to do that," I begin, the guilt returning. I don't deserve this place. They have been so kind to me when all I wanted to do was leave.

"We do. And we will."

I walk back to my desk, which I never really decorated, pretending the job was temporary when it had been nearly six years. My only personal effect is the same photo that the media pulled from Facebook—that picture of Zoe and Theo and me, the perfect family living an imperfect life. I get in my car and begin to drive home, but I know what the conversation will look like there. Instead, I head east on the I-10, driving to Theo's parents. As I move slowly down the trapped freeway, I remember that drive with Theo out to the desert. He had been forty minutes late to pick me up, after a visit to his parents had turned into a fight. Lydia had torn into him because we hadn't gotten pregnant again, warning him of the dangers of only children.

"Jane is an only child," he argued.

"Exactly," she replied.

The words stung as much on that drive as they do on this one, but I don't know where else to go. I want to run to Theo, but there is no Theo. I remember looking over at him that day and wishing he would die. I thought about the life insurance policy and how I would move on with Zoe, how it was better that we didn't have another child, so it might be easier to leave. And then, I remember him smiling sweetly at me.

"I told her," Theo grabbed my hand, "that you were perfect."

I felt the tears sting my eyes as I looked out the window at the passing towns, wishing I could return the sentiment, wishing that I didn't see every flaw in this human who refused to see any in me. But I never had the chance. The traffic begins to move as I exit into El Monte, driving to the family that delayed Theo every day of his life. My phone rings and I look down, recognizing the number. James Toobin. Out of all the people asking for my attention, he is the one I like most, but I don't know how to be his cheerleader either. I feel his pain, I fear his pain, but does a man like James Toobin really need me as his sidekick? It reminds me of how Blake would push me out into a media pit, hoping my blonde hair and big eyes would catch the attention of our subject.

"This is your chance to go after the career Blake stole from you," Yvette lectures me one night before I'm even considering quitting the job I have now just left, continuing the conversation that started between us in New York.

"I'm not doing that to Theo" is my default reply.

"Don't you think that is exactly what Theo would want you to do?" Yvette pushes me, having heard enough about my husband to know both his personality and politics.

I could have said no to the interview with Blake, but I thought if I said my peace, I would feel better. Instead, I walked into a war. The comments and memes don't bother me as much as they bother my mother. I know they're empty anger from people who weren't there that night. I guess I should be afraid for me or for Zoe, but as I told my mother the week before, "No one's going to do anything."

"These are different times," she warns me. And I understand they are. Hillary Clinton and Donald Trump are edging closer to election day, and America gets to choose between the lesser of two evils, as Theo would have said. I can hear him ranting at the TV right now.

I look out my car window at Theo's parents' house. Theo's truck is parked in front of me, which means Peter is visiting. He kept Theo's "Bernie" sticker on the back, which is beginning to fade in the sun. For a moment, I imagine the driver's door opening, and my husband's frame bounding into the light.

I get out of my car into the brutally hot day and knock on the front door. George answers, his face brightening. Lydia hasn't come to our house since Theo's death, and George has stayed with her in the measure of her mourning.

George hugs me quickly, ushering me into the living room. Their house isn't much cooler inside. The air-conditioner is turned off, leaving the temperature and cigarette smoke to mate in the sticky heat. Then I see her. Lydia sits on the couch in the dark. Peter is next to her, holding her hand, but I can tell by the energy in the room that she is having a manic episode.

"What's going on?" I ask. "Is everything okay?"

"Is everything okay?" Lydia mutters.

Peter explains, "My mom just had a little scare this morning. Her heart. We had to go to the hospital."

I move to where Lydia sits, "Lydia, what happened? Are you okay?"

She doesn't speak. Instead, Peter begins to fill in the details before George interrupts, "She's fine. She's just sad. The sadness, you know Janey-Mu."

I wipe away the line of sweat furrowing at my brow. "Should we turn the AC on least? I'm sure this heat isn't good for anyone's heart."

Lydia finally speaks, "What? Is the temperature not good enough for you?"

"No, I just—"

"You just what?" Lydia's eyes narrow. "You never come visit us. Never bring the baby. And now you come here and insult us."

"Lydia, you know you're always welcome at our house." I look around at Lydia and George's house, filled with dead flowers from Theo's funeral, now over two months old. The coffee table is covered in lit candles and scattered pills. And then there's Lydia, her sorrow so jagged, I fear Zoe might cut herself on it.

"Does this disgust you?" Lydia continues, her voice beginning to rise. "Huh, big-time television lady?!" This accusation would make me laugh on any other day but right now, it lands like a bull's-eye.

"Mom, please," Peter tries.

"No, Lydia," I begin. "It's just with Zoe, it's hard to . . ."

"What? Your precious little daughter is too good for us, too? You poison everyone for us, Janey-Mu. You poison your daughter. You poison my son.

"You use him to become famous," Lydia spits.

"Mom," Peter tries again to put out the fire.

But I can feel my own blood beginning to boil, the red curtain flitting at the corners of my calm. "I lost him, too, Lydia."

Despite her thick belly and sick heart, Lydia suddenly moves with the grace of a gazelle, leaping up to push me off the couch. I crash into a full tray of cigarettes, landing in the ash, trying to make sure none of them are lit.

Lydia is now standing over me, screaming, "You ruined him! Every day, you chip away at that boy. Until there is nothing left."

I don't want to be angry, but I am. I am so angry. I am angry at Lydia for not raising Theo right. I am angry at me for not loving him right. I am angry at the world for taking away his life.

"I took care of him," I hear myself screaming, quickly getting to my feet. "More than you ever did."

"You killed him!" Lydia shrieks.

I don't even feel myself do it. Instinct prevailing, I shove Lydia down on the couch. Peter suddenly jumps in, pushing me back.

"You should have died!" I scream over Peter's shoulder as he tries to move me toward the door. "It should have been you!"

"That's enough, that's enough," Peter keeps repeating as George moves to hold his wife back as she begins cursing at me in her native tongue. I don't need to understand the words to feel their venom.

In an instant, I am back outside in the heat, my eyes burning with tears and rage.

"She did that," I try to argue, but Peter just shakes his head slowly. We both know that Lydia is unstable. The world expects more from me. I'm not Lydia or even Theo. I don't have a diagnosis that crushes me. This calcified pain has left me incapable of compassion, replacing it with rage.

I get in my car and drive away, refusing to watch Peter fade in my rearview mirror.

NINE

"Fuck," I cough lightly into the cloud of smoke that now fills the alleyway.

"Is it okay?" Rose asks, watching me like a nervous teenager as I try to take a drag off the cigarette she has just given me. I lean my head against the stucco building in Echo Park where the John Thomas benefit is being held. Once upon a time, I used to dance at this same club. I was newly sober, hanging out with my sober friends and Rose, meeting cute boys, and believing my second chance at life was finally about to begin.

I look down at the American Spirit, softly shaking my head, knowing how angry Theo would be if he saw me indulging in this habit he hated so much.

"I don't think I've ever needed a cigarette more in my life." I finally laugh, slowly inhaling the tobacco, working my way around the need to cough.

"We can go," Rose suggests.

"No," I stare dimly at the cigarette, "I should stay."

"You hanging in there?" Rose asks, finally lighting up a cigarette herself.

I shake my head, leaning it back again, one foot on the wall, staring up at a starless sky. "Nope."

"You wanna talk about it?"

"Not really." I know Rose deserves more than that. Few people knew Theo and me more intimately than this friend who once regularly crashed on our couch, who was the only friend we allowed to visit us in the hospital on the day that Zoe was born. Even now, she and Maggie are the only people I feel I can trust outside of Yvette. Rose doesn't say anything. Doesn't try to fill the air with words like so many other people around me. She just leans her own head back as though there might be something interesting in the blackened carpet above our heads, the bright lights of LA blocking out the starry night above.

I take another drag, breaking from our reverie. "I just don't know how to do this."

"Janey, I don't think anybody knows how to do this. What happened, none of this is natural. It's not how we should be existing at this point on the planet."

"Maybe not." I finish the last drag and look up just in time to see Maggie approaching.

"You girls partying without me?" she calls out as I look to Rose.

"Thought we both could use some extra moral support . . ." I explain. Maggie grabs me in an overwhelming embrace before breaking into exaggerated coughing.

"Shit, don't tell me Rosie got you smoking again," she jeers.

"It was just one," I try to reply.

"Yeah, that's what you said when you were fifteen."

I put my arm around Maggie's waist and smile at Rose. I'm not sure what any of this means, but after years of marriage and divorce and distance, I'm glad to be back with my friends. The door to the back of the club opens. Someone is taking the stage, the sound from within sucking us into the club and back into the memory of the last time I walked into a bar to hear John Thomas perform.

Two months, and time has become an inexplicable ghost, weeks flashing by, seconds dragging on, disappearing, and emerging without reason. In yet another blink of an eye, I am standing in the audience as John Thomas and the band set up with the same methodical calm as the night of the shooting. The audience moves toward the stage. The energy is building, the back door opening, the first shots exploding.

"We can leave," Maggie offers, grabbing my hand.

"I quit my job," I announce as Maggie tightens her grip.

I sway slightly, remembering Theo's face that night, his arms around me, the heavy weight of his hand as it held my own, and the universe suddenly feels fast and loose again, like a slack rubber band.

I close my eyes and wish him back. Wish for him in the bed that I still refuse to sleep in. Wish for him to hold Zoe, smothering her in kisses as she giggles, pushing away his rough face and overwhelming love. Wish that we never went on that trip to the desert, never went to see John Thomas. I wish we were home right now, watching an episode of *Narcos*, and falling asleep with Rocky between us.

I can see a cold beer sitting on the table only feet away from me. I want to pick it up and down it in one gulp, let the relief slide down

my throat, and feel my brain explode, curling into the memory of
Theo's flesh and building a wall of booze to keep me there. Maybe
I'll find him in that old cocoon, lurking in the hazy realm that lies
beyond the first drink.

John Thomas finishes up and clears his throat. "We're here
tonight because we shouldn't be here tonight. And I am so truly
sorry for that."

I hear the first bars of the next song and the hard cement floor
of the club drops out from beneath me. John launches into Dylan's
"Forever Young," the song I sing to Zoe every night when she goes
to bed, since she was a little babe nursing, and here, here, is Theo's
great message. In that song is the love that I failed to accept, that I
twisted from at every turn, and the room goes dark again. I am
lying on the ground, and the only thing I can see is the tin roof
above me, watching like an unfair God, refusing to intervene when
we need a miracle the most. I stare up into the roof, which turns
into the sky, and I feel Theo on top of me, but he is no longer dead
weight, he is alive, he is protecting me.

"You can fix this, Janey," he whispers into my ear. "You can
fix this."

I reach up and feel the back of his head, but it's not wet, it's not
the soft loss I felt that night. He is there, and he is breathing, and
we are back together and the music plays in some distant space,
John Thomas singing Dylan's famous tome to his own children.

"Theo," I cry but he shushes me, the sound more like a whistle,
a call to something else, to whom we might have been, not the
fractured pieces we became. And then he is gone. I am lying there,
and the sky above is filled with the desert's sun, baring down on
me with all its weight until I can no longer breathe. And then suddenly, it's all gone, the vision, the sun, the tin roof. I am standing

in the middle of the benefit and all I can do is suck in the air, one deep, immense gulp after another, the breath I kept waiting for Theo to take.

However good the beer looks, I am thrust back into the sharp reality of the life Theo and I worked so hard to create. Because for every hard memory, there were other moments, singing our baby to sleep, walking the dog at sunset, knowing we were building the kind of family we never got as kids, and somehow together, however imperfectly, we were trying to fix the broken parts. I look past the stage, my mouth moving wordlessly with the lyrics and my heart erupting as the blood once again remembers to rush through my veins.

Two hours later, we walk out of the club, my friends acting as though they haven't spent a day apart when the three of us haven't been together in years.

"What are you doing next weekend?" Rose asks Maggie.

"I don't know, hanging with William. His dad is out of town, so I have him the whole weekend. Thought we might go to an A's game."

"I'd be down for the that," Rose interjects, and I realize how lonely she must be in all this. I have Zoe and Andrea, but after her own parents moved to Idaho, she is alone here.

"What about you?" Rose asks me.

I think about it but realize this might be the largest crowd I can handle for a while. The idea of being in a large stadium with all those people immediately overwhelms me.

"Not sure I can handle many more people than The Echo at this point." I turn to Maggie, "But I really want to see William. I want to see you."

"Great," Maggie decides. "You come down for the pre-party with Zoe and then we'll head to the game. I mean, how else is Miss Carless going to get down to me. Deal?"

"Deal," I reply, as Rose puts her hand in the center of the circle, and Maggie and I place our own on top of hers just as we did when we were all in high school, repeating the one-word chant from our adolescence, "Bitches."

I laugh and remember when Rose and I tried to offer this to Maggie as everything was falling apart with Chris, but she couldn't allow for it. She wanted to hide in her hurt, and I wonder if maybe that's why she's here now. She knows that's not how we heal.

Rose and I head to my car as she argues, "You don't have to drive me home. I can catch the bus."

"No, it's cool. I want to."

We begin to drive down Sunset Boulevard. Though Rose and I met in the South Bay, we both share an abiding love for this town. A place so rich and complex, most people just don't get it, only seeing its flash and sizzle and not its smoke and burn. I used to tell people, judging Los Angeles on the two square miles between Doheny and Highland and Hollywood and Wilshire, was like judging New York by Times Square. There was a side of town that was locals only, and for a long time, Rose and Theo and I had prided ourselves on being from those parts of town.

Even as we move through the now gentrified landscapes of Echo Park and Silver Lake, I still remember when it felt like we were in the sweet spot of gentrification, when the middle-class artists and the long-standing Latine population lived side by side, eating empanadas on the street and winding our way through the hills.

I look over and see tears streaming down Rose's face.

"You okay?"

She chokes out the words, "Janey, I know I should be . . . over it. Or something. But I go to bed every night hearing the shots, I go to bed every night running toward that building and then stopping, knowing what was happening. I hear the screams, I hear the screams."

She stops, and I realize how much my own erasure has saved me, how much not being able to remember has become a boundary I cannot blur, but then again, didn't I just do it tonight? The pieces seeping in, the border becoming more porous with each passing day.

"Rose, there is nothing we can do to change it." But even as I say the words, I wonder if that's true. Is there a space where I can go back? Is there a space where I can heal what happened that night?

"But I can't stop living in it," Rose tells me. "Every day, Janey, I wake up in it. Fuck. I feel so bad complaining to you, but I feel like no one else understands, they don't understand what happened . . ."

We're at a stoplight but I put the car in park and turn to my friend, "No one can understand what happened. Because it shouldn't have happened."

I look at my eternally optimistic friend, the one who could shoulder any challenge with a snarky laugh, but I can see she is more broken than she has let on.

"You okay, Rosie?" I ask. "Do you want to start seeing someone?"

I realize how hypocritical the question is since I have refused any therapy or help since the shooting, even ignoring the calls from my old therapist Elissa.

Rose shakes her head, "I started. I found a really good group, you should come . . . but they've all lost wives or children or a sister. What the fuck did I lose?"

She begins to cry harder, "I don't have anything to lose."

Ever since we were in high school, being cool was all that mattered to Rose. It was about how she dressed and what music she listened to and who she was willing to fuck and where she lived. Though she never would have admitted it, she had given up everything for this sense of coolness she felt she had to uphold—including the idea that being settled wasn't half bad.

"Rose, hey buddy, hey. That's not true." I rub her back. "You lost a friend, you lost your safety. Fuck, we all lost something that night, even if we're not grieving a husband or child. We lost a piece of who we were."

The light turns green and I continue down Sunset Boulevard. "We're going to figure it out," I say determinedly.

"You don't need to fix this," Rose replies, but I don't know that I agree.

"Can we go somewhere?" I finally ask.

"Sure." Rose wipes away the tears.

I look out the window as we drive through LA and I turn on the radio for the first time since Theo's death. A Michael Jackson song fills the car as we drive down Sunset and up Nichols Canyon, making our way into the sleepy neighborhood at its top. From the lookout, Universal City sparkles below. I tell Rose, "This was Theo's favorite spot."

We check for cops before running across the street to the closed park, which overlooks the city. I sit down with my legs crossed as Rose dangles hers over the edge of the hillside. I pause for a moment before making my own confession. "I shoved Lydia today. I mean she came at me first, but I know better. I can't even imagine how I would feel if it was Zoe. And I know it's easy to blame me, but I'm just so pissed. I don't know how to make it stop."

"Did you just meme yourself?" Rose asks, and for a moment, this all feels like one big cosmic joke, where even death becomes a viral moment.

"You got another cigarette?" I ask.

"Are you sure?" Rose hesitates.

"Dude, just give me one. I didn't get drunk tonight, did I?"

Rose slips two out of her pack before lighting them. She's quiet for a moment before asking, "You're not going to drink, are you?"

I've never been a Big Book thumper like Theo, proselytizing the twelve steps to anyone with a drinking problem, but I also know that for those who came in after me, I offered hope. And I get it. I came in nearly dead and in the space of seven years, I got married, had a kid, and built a career, even if it wasn't the one I wanted.

I smile, firm in my answer. "No. I'm not going to drink."

We sit for a minute. In that silence, all I need is her friendship. Never mind that I quit my job or pushed Lydia or left myself with little room for what's next, I still have Rose, and now again, Maggie.

"Have you talked to Blake?" Rose asks, finally breaking the silence.

"No, God no. But I talk to Yvette a lot."

"So, there wasn't anything there with him?" Rose asks, gently prying into an area even I have been afraid to touch.

"Not after I hit him." I laugh. "Jesus, I'm a mess."

I take a drag off my cigarette. "I don't know. I think a part of me judged Theo by him. Like Theo was no Blake Edwards. I mean,

how could he be? But the minute I saw him, I realized Blake
Edwards was no Theo Karras."

I can't speak, the words hitting.

"I just fucked it all up, Rose."

She puts her arm around me. "No, you didn't, Jane. Theo knew
how much you loved him. Maybe even more than you did."

I wonder if she's right. Maybe love doesn't define our grief;
maybe it's grief that defines our love. I put out my cigarette. "We
better get going, before my mom calls the cops."

As we run back across the street, I turn around just as the lights
surge below.

I walk into the backyard to find Dennis waiting for me, drinking
a screwdriver out of his red Solo cup with the baby monitor sta-
tioned in front of him.

"Hey, Moose," he calls quietly as I walk up, checking the screen
before sitting down. Zoe sleeps peacefully, her body spread across
the crib.

I eye the pack of cigarettes resting next to Dennis's feet.

"How was the show?" he asks me as I lean forward and grab the
Marlboros.

Dennis tries to stop me, "Hey, hey. Janey, no."

"It's okay."

Dennis begrudgingly pulls out his lighter as I lean in with my
cigarette.

"You okay?" Dennis asks, as though that's the only question
people know to ask me. With his beachy brown hair and wide,

white smile, Dennis has that easy American look that makes people trust him before he even buys them the first drink.

You okay? The whole day begins to engulf me as a horrible
choking sob finally escapes from my throat. Dennis moves forward
to grab me, leaning his head into mine as I stare down at the cigarette, wanting desperately to cry into his arms. Instead, I tell him,
"I quit my job."

I wait for the lecture, but Dennis just kisses my forehead, keeping his arms wrapped around me as though to ward off some evil
spell. He whispers into our circle, "Good."

And for the first time since Theo's death, I am okay with being
held.

"Come home," he whispers. "You can stay in the house for free,
you and Zoe and Rocky. You can figure out what you want to do.
Take a break, Janey. And if you want to come back up here, we'll
figure that out, but right now . . . right now, I think you need to
come home."

I know this is the easiest solution, even as the thought of leaving
the house I shared with Theo, and all the dreams we built during
our short but fractured marriage, make me feel like I am ripping
yet another wide gash in the fabric of the universe.

I whisper back in reply, "Okay."

TEN

walk up the street, on a Saturday morning in September, pushing Zoe in her BOB stroller, headed to Starbucks to meet James
Toobin. Theo and I used to always go to Starbucks on the
weekends, walking Rocky while we tried to get Zoe down for her
late morning nap. But now it's just me as I greet James, releasing
Zoe from the stroller; she has refused her morning nap today.
James emailed me the week before, asking if I wanted to get coffee.
I replied that I hadn't changed my mind since our first meeting, but
that didn't seem to dissuade him.

"I'm already going to be in LA," he explained. "No job offers,
just a wellness check."

But now I can feel the request lingering up his sleeve.

"So, what made you go on Blake's show?" James asks me after
buying my coffee.

"I used to work for Blake," I tell him as I give Zoe an apple squeeze, trying to monitor how tightly she's holding the packet. James watches me with Zoe, and I can feel his grief rise.

He takes a sip of his latte. "I actually went to high school with Blake."

I look up, unable to cover my surprise, "Really? Did you know each other?"

During my years with Blake, I knew all his friends, traveling home to each other's families at the holidays. We would usually spend Thanksgiving with Andrea and Dennis and then Christmas with his parents, having dinner with the high school friends he had stayed close with over the years. But James doesn't look familiar.

"No." James shakes his head, finally returning the latte to the table. "I reconnected with him later, after Rachel's death. I was doing media and ended up on his show." He pauses. "My wife, my ex, we became friends with him and Viki. When we would be in town for press, we'd have dinner." James laughs, taking another quick sip. "It's funny because when we were in high school, I thought he was an asshole, but I think marriage, kids, they were good for him."

I wipe applesauce from Zoe's face, and reply coldly, "That's nice."

"So, you decided if you were going to do any media, your old boss was safe?"

I look up, "My old boss is anything but safe. I . . ."

I stare across the street, watching a family walk into the toy store that sits opposite Starbucks. The father holds the heavy door open for his wife and daughter, a mirror that feels even more cracked in this moment.

I look back over at James, and I share what motivated my call to Yvette. "It's funny, but it was at the briefing, where we ran into each other, I met this woman, Gigi. I had seen her the night of the shooting. And it just hit home, I'm not the only one in this. It's not just my husband I need to honor. But I guess I realized I need to honor him, too."

I sigh before explaining, "I used to be close with Blake's producer and I just felt like, I don't know, they'd let me have my space. I know Blake well enough to understand what drives his show. He gives people the platform to perform."

James asks, "And . . . was it a performance?"

I look down before shaking my head.

"No. No. It was all real, maybe too much. I've just accepted that anger is my default response to this for some reason. Angry that this is now my life. Angry that it's yours."

I pick up Zoe and kiss the top of her head. "I don't know if I would have survived if it was her, James. I don't. I know that maybe that's why it was so important for you to fight. Even for other widows. But my marriage was complicated. I wanted out and I know that sounds fucked up, but I don't know how to talk about what I lost here. Because I don't know what I lost—"

James interrupts me, "Jane, do you know what advocacy is?"

James is nice and kind and his pain is real, but he is also the kind of guy who thinks he knows more than me, simply because he's made more money or sat on more boards or has investment portfolios and a dick. He probably only believes in redemption if the redeemed look like him. I counter, "I've worked the last few years for an advocacy organization, James. I know what it means."

"No." he shakes his head, embarrassed. "I wasn't suggesting that you don't know . . ."

He stops and I feel like his humility is real. It's what makes him likable despite all the reasons that would make me not want to meet him for coffee.

He tries again, "For me, advocacy is where love meets justice. I couldn't deny Rachel's life or my pain, but I also couldn't continue to be angry about it either."

Families United was founded a few years after Columbine, as the assault ban waned and mass shootings became more commonplace. Parents and spouses and friends of the deceased, even some of the shooters' family members, had come together to enact sensible gun laws, yet none had led to a ban on assault weapons. They had prided themselves on being bipartisan, receiving some support from both sides of the aisle, which in an interview in 2014 with Blake, James had described as a near miracle, but that was the problem. They only danced around the miracle; they had yet to achieve it.

It isn't that I'm not impressed or don't understand their work. I just spent the last six years working for a nonprofit, one that also aimed for miracles, helping kids aging out of foster care to find a better life than the ones they were handed. But like with Families United, the miracle always ended up being negotiated down to something far less holy.

"I get it, James." I nod. "And I absolutely appreciate the work." I stop myself before continuing, "Look, I've worked in nonprofits for a while. Ever since I left Blake. I tried to be a part of the solution, but I realized we were only the Band-Aid. Instead of asking people to donate millions and billions to poverty, what if we just redistributed the wealth? Because for every step we took forward, James, poverty took those families two steps back. We love throwing money at the causes, but we refuse the cure."

James interrupts, "I understand, Jane. I do. But we *are* trying to cure the disease."

"That's impossible. What disease, James?" My volume rises and people look in my direction. I know a few have recognized me, even as the memory of the shooting has begun to fade. "Mental health? Is that what you're talking about."

"That is one of the issues," he calmly replies.

"Fuck that," I practically seethe. "Do you know how many people struggle with mental health and don't walk into a bar or a school and do what those men did?"

I hear the words come out of my mouth: *those men.* And so does James.

"I don't think you can get rid of all of us, Jane."

I smile, but only because it's true. I have seen men as the perpetrators, even the good ones, even Theo.

"And that's why nothing changes." I sit back. "Because you're trying to wrestle the ocean, when all you have to do is stop the shark."

"Are you telling me we need to build a bigger boat?"

"Maybe, at the very least, you should get yourself a spear." I quiet down. "Look, I'm not saying I have all the answers . . ."

"You're not?" James laughs as Zoe coos and I hand her back the applesauce, no longer caring if she gets it everywhere.

"I'm not but I know this, we can make the solution complicated and then say, 'aw, fuck, we just couldn't figure it out.' Or we can make it simple and get it done."

We both sit there for a second before James speaks.

"You're not Jewish, are you?" James finally asks me.

"No." I laugh.

"Well, in the Jewish story, which is really all our stories, when the Jews were enslaved in Egypt, all they wanted was to be free.

They realized that more than anything freedom was God's great gift to man. And when we deny people that freedom, we are in direct conflict with God."

"Is that what the Second Amendment people have taught you?" I laugh.

"No, not them. But what I have come to realize is that freedom isn't living the life you want. It's about the ability to fight for what you've lost."

He sets down his drink. "When Rachel died, something in me died with her. But it wasn't the best part of me. It was the part of me that believed I needed to follow someone else's rules to survive. You have momentum now, Jane. Momentum that could drive the change you seek."

I'm not sure James and I know how to secure that change though—I'm not sure if we're both here to advocate for our dead because we failed to show up when they were alive. I almost want to tell James about what happened at the benefit, that I believe there is a space where we can greet them, that they don't have to be lost forever. But then I remember Theo's words, *you can fix this*. But what do I need to fix? Gun laws? Families United? James?

Though Theo's and my marriage wasn't the one either of us deserved, or the one I wanted, maybe this is all family is—an eternal dance between souls who meet here for a brief time, passing along the story like a baton. As I look over at James, so confident and yet visibly cracked, I know we both believe in miracles even if we might define them differently.

I smile. "I understand, James. I've sat on your side of the table so many times, hoping someone would throw their weight behind my organization. But . . ."

"But you don't want to work with us?" James asks.

"I'm just not sure that's where the work gets done. I respect it, I do. I respect what you're doing, but we're running out of time. And I'm not sure we can afford the long way around."

"Unfortunately, there is no shorter way." He looks at his phone and gives me a farewell smile. "I feel like we'll be talking again, Jane. I hope we will." He pauses before adding, "And whatever happened with Blake . . . please don't let that be your obstacle here."

I'm about to argue back, but James has so gently called my bluff, I know it's pointless. Instead, I just nod in agreement.

After saying good-bye to James, I walk Zoe to the toy store across the street and let her pick out a surprise. She finds the aisle with the toy cars, grabbing one of the pickup trucks.

She lifts it up to me and smiles. "Dada."

I breathe in deep, unsure how to respond to any of this, but then I watch my child's eyes go wide, the sudden realization hitting her. "Dada?"

I can see the tears rising. I don't know if it's that she better understands his absence or that she has expected him back by now, the finality of it all emerging as truth. Either way, her whimpers quickly escalate as she begins to cry out, "Dada! Dada!"

I don't know what else to do, so I offer aimless bribes, hoping she will calm. "Do you want the truck? I can get you the truck."

The store is nearly empty on this midweek afternoon; still, I am immediately overwhelmed. I drop the pickup truck on the ground and pick up Zoe in one arm as I push the oversized stroller toward the door, trying not to knock things off the shelves, even as I do. Zoe only screams more, repeating "Dada" over and over again as I apologize to the shop owner and push through the heavy door and out onto the street.

"It's okay, baby. It's okay."

They are the same words that I repeated to Zoe when she was born and was placed shrieking on my chest. "It's okay, baby. It's okay."

I get her back into the stroller then realize I owe her that little truck. I turn us back around as she takes her sippy cup and settles.

I don't apologize to the owner, even though *I'm sorry* lives at the edge of my tongue. Instead, I just buy the stupid pickup and give it to my now smiling child, walking us home along the same route we used to take with Theo ever since moving into this idyllic neighborhood. And though I loved being here as a family, I realize that this town was an always odd fit for Theo and me. We used to joke that we were exotic compared to our neighbors simply because we were the only ones who had ever done hard drugs. I know that Redondo is not my final stop, it never has been, but neither is Montrose.

Zoe and I walk up our street as she fiddles with her new truck, babbling and calling out "Hi!" to whoever walks by, proud of the new words she has been learning in quick succession. I settle into the easiness of our walk, and the small break it provides me from single parenthood.

For so long, I wanted this time with Zoe, but since Andrea has now returned home, not far from the one to which I'll soon be moving, the pendulum has swung in the other direction, with very little space apart. Rose tries to help, which is lovely, but I also feel like I need to figure this out on my own. I need to learn again how to be a mother, creating the kind of routine and order I wished for Zoe, but that Theo struggled to maintain.

I can tell by the quiet from the stroller that Zoe has fallen asleep. I slow down near our house and check to make sure she's comfortable. There she sleeps, full lips settled into a mouthy calm, blonde curls framed around her face as she blissfully clutches the pickup.

I stop to watch her, so grateful that I have her in this, even on the days when it only makes it harder.

I hear a car pull up behind us and am relieved to see Theo's truck, until I see Peter behind the wheel. His face is bloated and red, and I have barely made it to the window when he chokes out the words, "My mom. She's dead. Our mom . . ."

The words hit me as I open the door and Peter steps out and into my arms. I don't need to ask the details. From beyond the grave, Martin Montgomery has just killed someone else.

ELEVEN

We walk back out of St. Sophia's, only months after departing Theo's funeral. The procession is much smaller for Lydia, though there is a flock of heavily perfumed Greek women who all bring dishes of food and dessert, arming George with enough food for a season. Though Peter tried to get him to host a memorial afterward, he asks that we just go home.

I understand. I didn't want my home filled with strangers after Theo's funeral, and in those days after the shooting, everyone felt like a stranger. The hard part is almost everyone still does. As Peter and I drive to George's house, he tries to explain what happened that last day I saw Lydia alive, "She was just so broken. I know my mom didn't mean a lot of what she said to you that day, but she just . . . she wanted someone to blame."

"I understand." I look back to see Zoe sleeping in her car seat. We are in Theo's truck, a reminder of when she used to sleep in this car while her daddy drove. "I do, too—want someone to blame."

"Yeah, I think she saw that. She loved you, Jane."

When we walk in, the house is still dark, the candles still burning among the remaining flowers from Theo's funeral, now over three months old. I carry Zoe in as she sleeps, finding an empty space on the couch between Lydia's pillows and magazines and boxes of tissues. George hasn't wanted to disrupt the room as an altar to his wife. He now stands in the middle of it, and I am so angry again, angry for us both, and for my baby, who has now just lost her grandmother and father, who won't even know the grief that awaits her as she grows up. This is what no one sees from the outside, the places where no one can reach you, where the gauze is simply too thick.

I walk over to George and he grabs me in a hug, I feel the words choke out of me, "I'm so sorr—" before being cut short by George's accented, "Shhhh."

"There was nothing left for her, Janey-Mu. She always loved that boy too much."

I look over his shoulder at the photos of Theo, the pictures from childhood, the Dodgers player card, our wedding, Zoe and her father. I'm not sure whether the value of family is worth the burden. And yet, I know that the love is there, just as Andrea loves me, just as James loved his daughter, just as Lydia loved Peter and Theo, just as I love Zoe. I wonder whether I, too, will disappoint Zoe, whether I will fail to show up or fuck her up so bad she'll never be able to properly stand on her feet. I wonder if I am maiming her even as I work to do my best. And yet, we are contracted to each other, the terms set, the deal done. Just as my love for Theo was inked in something far more utilitarian than I would have ever wanted, so my love for Zoe goes beyond the romantic and into the base, hard units of survival. She is the missing rib made whole. And the same was true for Lydia and Theo.

Zoe wakes up just as Peter finishes heating up dinner, one of the casseroles sent home with us from church. After we eat, George goes back to the living room and returns to the couch where Zoe just slept. I go back in to say good-bye to George, who grabs my hand, as I sit down next to him holding Zoe.

She leans toward him and says, "Papou."

He smiles, even through the sadness. "They both suffered, Janey. Maybe not from the same disease, but they both suffered."

"I know, George," I admit. For so long, it was easier to blame Theo for his disorders than it was to see how hard it was for him to live with them. Because for every bill he couldn't pay, for every email he struggled to send, he suffered. I just wish I could have had more compassion for the suffering when he was alive.

Instead, I sit next to George as he talks to Zoe and hope that I do better by her, that I offer her the compassion I wasn't afforded and that I also failed to give.

"Are you ready?" Peter calls from the kitchen as he puts the food away. Though I told Peter I didn't need to, he was adamant that the two of us go to an AA meeting that evening so I can take my seven-year chip. I told him we could go another night, but he just shook his head: "You know that's what Theo would have wanted, Jane. He would have wanted us to go for him and for mom and for you."

Andrea has agreed to watch Zoe, coming up for the funeral, so we take her home and I pick up my own car as Peter has plans with his new girlfriend later.

"It sounds like it's getting serious," I tell him as we drive to my house, Zoe calling out the word *tree* every time she sees one.

"Yeah, Jen was at the funeral," Peter replies.

"What? You didn't introduce us?"

"Tree!" Zoe yells from the back seat.

"Soon," Peter shrugs. "It just didn't feel like the right time."

"Did I see her?"

"She's older, Korean, really pretty," Peter blushes. He has cheeks that do that easily, and when Zoe was born, I was hoping she might inherit them.

After stopping in to chat with Andrea, Peter and I caravan to the AA meeting. The first night Theo and I hooked up, he had just accepted a birthday cake for seven years at this same meeting, a tradition in Los Angeles AA. The celebrant blows out the candles, hugs all their friends, and then tells the rest of the group how they made it to that moment, light-years away from when they found themselves in their first meeting, unsure of whether their lives were over, or whether they had just begun.

After Theo blew out his seven candles, he shared, "I learned when I was a kid that if you wanted to make it in LA, you had to do more than stay out of the cliques, you had to blow them up with love."

By the time Theo was eighteen, he had emerged from the bullied years of his youth into the type of guy that everyone wanted at their party. He played ball with the pros, dropped acid with the soul surfers, and became best friends with every celeb in LA, not because he cared about them but because they cared about him. And though he was too hyper for most, ultimately exhausting people with his lectures and political tirades, he was the constant in an endless stream of new faces, blowing up those cliques with love.

And here I am, walking up to the same podium, to take the same chip, except Theo isn't here to hold the cake.

"I'm Jane and I'm an alcoholic . . . ," I announce, staring at the seven-year chip in my hand, which Peter has just given me. I don't know that I would have taken this chip without Peter. I haven't been to a meeting in months; I don't want to drink but I also don't know how to be here.

Finally, I admit the only thing I do know, "People keep asking me if I'm okay. And I know I'm supposed to tell you that I'm hanging in there, that I'm staying sober, that I'm so grateful for my recovery and all the fucking tools. But I'm just not sure I know how to pick them up right now."

I look up from the podium into the dizzying audience of faces; I've never been able to focus on just one when speaking at an AA meeting. I usually just focused on my hands. But this time, I try to seek out their eyes, I try to connect. I try to find the same safety that I discovered here years ago, in this awkwardly intimate church basement filled with folding chairs and social anxiety and the old stench of cigarette smoke.

"Sometimes, we're just broken. And there's really no fixing it."

I want to cry and feel the grief that I know would flood me the way the booze used to. I close my eyes. I can sense him now, his weight on top of me, the shots ringing out, the lone scream, the breath that I hoped was his.

After the meeting, people come and give hugs and condolences but unlike Theo's funeral, a part of me wants to accept them. I look over to Peter and I can see the grief across his face. Like George, he has been shattered.

"You hanging in there?" I ask.

He nods no, and we grab each other into a hug.

"I'm so sorry, Peter," I whisper.

"I know," he replies, holding on for a moment longer than usual, the pain between us shared in ways few ever should.

get in my car and don't know where to go. Without thinking, I start to drive toward Silver Lake, and to the apartment I once shared with Theo.

I look up at the large bay window that was in our living room, the pink hibiscus out front, the avocado trees along the side of the building. And then it's like I'm there, right back in the middle of our lives, after we got married but before Zoe was born, during the years when we failed to get pregnant and Theo failed to find work, and I began to feel like the dream I had envisioned with Theo was just as fraudulent as the one I built with Blake.

My husband stood in the doorway as I rushed toward him trying to get out. We had just had another miscarriage and Theo failed to give me the rent again. I told Theo from our first date that I was fine to take care of myself, but I didn't want to take care of him, too. I didn't want to question whether he really loved me or just loved that I paid for every dinner, every vacation and hotel room, every month of rent and the utility bills.

I couldn't help but hear Andrea's voice in my head, "How do you know you're not paying for his love, too?"

"I fucking hate you!" I screamed at Theo across that living room, knowing the words were a lie even as a dash of spittle followed them. Theo blocked me as I tried to move past him. I wanted him to act as terrified of our finances as I was. I wanted him to be a goddamn grown-up and make enough money to give me $500 every month.

"What?" Theo spat, holding me back. "You think you're too good for this. You and your crazy asshole Republican family."

I shoved him, but he didn't move, trapping me as I paced like a caged animal. Theo taking the rare stand against my temper.

"Don't call my family crazy!" I hissed.

"Why? You call mine that all the time. You act like we're all just worthless pieces of shit!"

"You're a fucking worthless piece of shit." I pushed hard this time, punching against his chest, as I moved to the front door.

"Shut the fuck up!" he screamed back at me, grabbing his keys from the dish by our front door. "I'm going."

"Good! You don't belong here anyway. You don't even pay the fucking rent!"

"I pay the fucking rent living with you!" Theo tossed the last Molotov cocktail before moving quickly toward the front door to avoid the effects of its blast.

For so many years of my life, I was known for those types of outbursts. The tears, the screaming, not caring who heard my choking sobs. Boyfriends would follow me down darkened streets until I would collapse onto the cement of a dirty sidewalk, crying about a heart so broken I didn't believe it could be fixed.

But then I got sober and it was.

As I sit in my car outside our old apartment, I wonder whether I can feel the grief because it's just too deep, compounded like sediments of rock and fossil. I wonder if I drill deep enough that I might hit the boom, exploding all the losses at once, my father and Blake and Theo coming out in some gusher of pain that I have disallowed myself. Pretending that not knowing Michael somehow made his loss moot, drinking over Blake to the point where I couldn't remember the night before, let alone the pain, and now Theo is just trapped there beneath both of them. Like me, waiting for the deep breath that might set us all free. And I think about what I said at the meeting. Maybe the drink is the drill.

"You make me feel drunk sometimes," I once told Theo.

"That's just because you like to get high on your anger" was his pat reply.

That hot summer day, I ran out the door after Theo, finding myself barefoot on the street, wearing only pajamas and sweat. The whole city felt like a tinderbox of dried-out succulents and brown grass. I sobbed, hurtling toward the nearest intersection. I didn't know where I was going, and yet a part of me did, drawn to the liquor store down the street from our house.

I walked past the stucco homes and gated windows of the neighborhood where the income levels dipped. I didn't even have my phone. Just a $20 bill that was lying on the table by our front door, waiting for me. I saw the liquor store in the distance and felt like I did years before when the drug dealer would be on his way. My mouth filling with saliva, my pulse quickening as though I was awaiting a long-lost love. And here again I was, my legs pumping down the street, the tears already dry along my face.

Fuck sobriety. Seven years had been long enough. I inhaled sharply, and crossed the street, exhaling as I walked into the liquor store. Coming in from the hot day, the cold blast of the shop air-conditioner was as much of a relief as the booze. I knew exactly what I wanted. Jim Beam. I asked for a pint, before rethinking my choice.

"Actually, give me a fifth."

The older man reached behind him and placed it on the counter.

"And a pack of Marlboros . . ." I added, knowing if I was going to break the lid on liquor, I would need a cigarette to wash it down.

The man leaned down and brought out the pack, before asking, "ID?"

"Oh shit." I hadn't even thought about that.

"No ID, no sale," the man announced.

"I'm thirty-three," I stuttered.

The man shrugged as he put the Beam back.

"No, you don't understand," I tried to argue. "I was born in 1980, I live in the neighborhood."

"Then go get your ID and come back," the man replied.

"I walked here. I'm sober. I won't be back."

The man just stared at me. He looked at my pajamas and slid the cigarettes across the counter.

"You look older than eighteen," he offered, as I gave him my twenty, and settled for a free pack of matches.

It had been years since I packed cigarettes, smacking them awkwardly on my palm. I lit one, took a drag, and tossed it to the ground. Like that, I knew a cigarette or a drink wouldn't fix anything.

Which is why I am surprised that as I drive away from our apartment, I find myself pulling into the parking lot for The Eagle, a gay leather bar down the street, one where I used to drink, hitting their $2 Jäeger Tuesdays. I blink up at the lighted sign and get out of my car. I know this is stupid. I can feel the weight of the seven-year chip in my pocket. I remember a recent conversation with Yvette where she told me about her drinking after Diana died,

"I wasn't that much of a drinker before. Blake was such a mess, and I didn't ever want to be one of his drinking buddies. But I don't know, I didn't even do it to numb me, I did it to make me feel."

I walk into the bar and sit down. It doesn't take long for the leather-clad bartender to come and take my order.

I don't hesitate, "Beam and Coke."

Theo used to say, there is something about a whiskey drinker that can never be changed. We weren't sexy like vodka or classy like gin, not tough like tequila, or chill like rum. We were just stubborn.

"Whiskey drinkers are made for each other," he once joked, but I wasn't entirely sure I agreed. Maybe whiskey drinkers could have fun together, they could fuck or be friends, but could they have children and build a home and do all the things we had attempted to do?

The bartender comes back with my drink but pauses, his eyes narrowing, "Wait. I know you. Your husband was in that shooting in the desert?"

I'm so used to this by now. I nod, looking at the drink. Make me feel, I can hear my silent prayer.

"My husband was killed in San Bernardino," he says.

"What?" I think for a moment I've heard him wrong.

"Yeah, he died trying to save his coworkers."

I am not alone in this. These shootings, they are everywhere, all the time, all around us. And I remember San Bernardino. How we ended up doing active shooter training at the courthouse because it all felt so close to home, because it was close to home, happening only forty minutes from our own government building.

"I'm Jane," I reach out my hand.

"Ryan." The man smiles. "And thank you."

"Fuck, Ryan, I have no idea what I'm doing."

"It doesn't matter." He smiles gently. "We have to stand up for this shit, for them. I tried, too, and I'll be honest, I just couldn't do the dog and pony show of it. I let the horror of it all take over me. I moved here just so I could get away . . ."

He looks away for a moment and I understand. I'm moving, too; in less than a month, I'll be back in Dennis's house, away from this city, away from these memories.

Ryan looks around. "You know, you can't outrun it, no matter where you go, or what you do. I've tried and . . . every time they happen again . . . It never ends, Jane. They never end."

I look down. "I just wanted to be free."

I stop myself. But maybe it wasn't Theo I wanted to be free of. Maybe I just wanted to be free from marriage, free from what happens when you try to domesticate two whiskey drinkers but don't give them enough gentleness to make it work.

Ryan puts his hand on mine. "They're gone now."

I want to tell him they're all gone. So many names I can't even keep track anymore. I can't keep track of the one before or the one after or the one that is yet to come. But something in me shares with Ryan the one truth I know will make this drink impossible, "I'm seven years sober today."

Ryan smiles slowly, reaching his other hand across the bar, and removes the drink in front of me.

"Well, we're not going to let that change here."

"Are you sure?" I ask him, like he knows me, and yet, just like Peter and George and James Toobin and Giselle, I know he does. We have become a part of another secret club, not so different from the one I just left only hours earlier, bonded in our unique grief. We know one another's stories without ever needing to hear them.

leave the bar and get back in my car, and then it hits me, the ground falling out as soon as I close the door. I am back in the saloon. I am trying to catch my breath, but I'm not on the ground. I am standing in the bar and for a moment, I almost think I am in my old apartment because there Theo stands.

There is no one else here, just us. No gunman, no wounded, no one yelling out, "We've got someone over here!"

Just Theo and me, but he feels so far away.

"Theo," I call. "Theo, I'm sorry. I should have stopped him."

Theo smiles and just shakes his head. He starts to walk toward me. "There was nothing you could do, Janey."

But then he stops. He looks at me hard across the room, "But you can do something now."

"What?" I ask, still confused whether I am losing my mind or having a panic attack.

Theo smiles easily, like he's heading out the door to go surfing, and not visiting me in some cold space beyond the veil. It was so hard to hear him when he was alive, but here his message is clear, a directive I can't ignore.

"You need to roar, Jane. And not just for me."

He looks at me from across the room, as handsome as the day I met him, and I can hear my breath as he tells me again, with a slight smile, "You need to roar."

TWELVE

The phone rings at four in the morning, buzzing along the coffee table. I try to grab it before it wakes Zoe. I'm not surprised to see it's Yvette, the one person who would call me at this hour. I'm not sure how I would have navigated the last month without her. From the calls to the media to the daily reminder of the new landscape in which I live, Yvette has been my light. The night I found out about Lydia, she told me, "You know AA isn't the only group in town. They have grief groups, too. Ones for PTSD."

As I've learned, Yvette's wife Diana was as impressive as her. Raised in a wealthy, WASP-y Long Island family who spent their weekends sailing boats and playing tennis at the club, Diana left to study medicine at Johns Hopkins before going to work in West Africa. Though from the pictures, Diana looked like she probably fit into her Glen Cove life, with her pressed button-downs and trim brown bob. And yet, she rejected her family's expectations with aplomb.

"Her family never got it," Yvette told me one night over the phone. "They didn't get why she wouldn't just marry the dick from the estate next door, and get her hair blown out every two days."

Diana returned to America in the early nineties when Hillary Clinton was just beginning to champion healthcare reform. She got on the bus early, livid that her country would make it more difficult for people to access healthcare than in the developing nations where she had just been working.

"Di knew the words *single payer* before the rest of the world was talking about it," Yvette said. "By the time she found me in that lesbian bar in the East Village, she was sowing the first seeds of what would later become the Affordable Care Act. This was years before it happened." When the president began drafting a healthcare plan, Diana was one of his first calls. Over the next year, the president would come to know the doctor well, listening to her arguments for a single-payer system and, later, to her strategies for how his legislation might one day morph into the more egalitarian option.

"You can't keep tossing grenades, Jane, just to disappear again back into your bunker," Yvette lectures me one night. "It's fucking white privilege to start a battle you don't plan to fight."

I nearly laugh. "You're throwing white privilege at me now?"

"I'm not throwing it. I'm telling you that your voice is privileged because it's the one the media is most willing to hear. It's the one that they prioritize."

"But isn't that why they should hear someone else's, Yves? I mean, I think back to that woman Gigi. The one at the urgent care. No one hears her story, no one is asking her to join Families United."

"You don't know that," Yvette presses back.

"Then why isn't she on TV?" I argue.

"Maybe she doesn't want to be," Yvette counters.

"Well, maybe I don't want to be," I say.

"Jesus, Janey. I get what you're saying. I mean, Giselle's Latina, right? So they don't center her. They don't and it's fucked up. But are you going to refuse to step up because of it? You'll just go back to life as normal, whatever that was, because you're scared of what the spotlight might do."

"Yvette, don't you realize? This is what I wanted but what the fuck does it mean if I get it this way? And what the fuck am I supposed to say? I know the story sounds great but the reality . . ."

"Jane, don't you realize, people don't care about the reality. They're connected to the story. They feel connected to you. They want to make it stop. And yes, you are a pretty, white lady. And Theo was a handsome white guy. He was a fucking baseball player, for God's sake. How American can you get?"

"Tragically American," I reply.

"Exactly, people like American tragedies. And they also like American heroes."

"I don't want to be a hero. That's the whole point. I want to earn my place at—"

Yvette interrupts me, "What the fuck do you think you need to go through to have better earned it?"

I sit in the silence of her truth for a moment, knowing how much she is echoing Theo's same words. Yvette continues, "I know you, Jane Ambrose Karras, you have something to say. Stop being so afraid to say it."

"Blake doesn't think so," I can't help but add.

"Blake once groomed you to become him," she tells me, and I can't help but wonder what he has said to her over the years about me. "So become him."

The day after Lydia's funeral, I call James and tell him I'm in the fight. He suggests we start with a letter to the president, but I offer a more direct route.

"How about I call him instead?" I asked, remembering my days as a journalist, and the insufferable mission to always go to the source.

In a way, it reminds me of those days, chasing the story, making the phone calls. I remember when one of the main bosses of the Italian mob was arrested in Sicily and Blake told me to track him down.

"The man's been in hiding for thirty years, Blake. You want me to just call him?" I asked.

"He's not in hiding anymore."

The next morning, I found an intern who spoke Italian and called the *Palermo News*, which led me to his attorney. I had the intern ask how the mob boss was doing.

"*En carcere!*" he replied. He's in prison.

When I told Blake, he just smiled. "Guess you got your story."

It was in the chase that the best stories were born, and not just the story you were looking for, the story of the hunt itself, the anecdote that turned everything into an adventure. As I call Yvette to go to the source, I feel a flicker of what my life was once like, when I woke up every day at 5:00 a.m. ready for battle, strapping on my backpack like armor, heading out into the world not just to tell the story but to find it.

Yvette is right; it is a privilege to access power but also insult to refuse its call.

So, when I get that call at 4:00 a.m., I know something has happened.

"He agreed," Yvette's raspy voice announces over the phone.

"To a call?" I ask.

"To a meeting, actually. He's going to be in LA."

"Shit," I say, rubbing Rocky's head as I speak. I don't know what I would do without the dog that Theo and I used to call canine Xanax. In the nights when I wake up drenched in sweat, praying it was just a dream, I reach out to find Rocky, curling into his thick fur and warm body. Yvette continues her announcement. "He wants to meet tomorrow."

Yvette quickly starts to spew out facts and figures at a rate I can barely decipher at 4:00 a.m. In moments like this, she reminds me of Theo, if Theo had been able to sharpen his intellect on the leather strap of education. She explains that I will be meeting with the president at a private location. I won't be the only survivor, as there are others who also weren't able to meet with the president in July. She explains that a car will get us the next morning.

"Guess, it's time to pull that lightning back out of the bottle," Yvette jokes. But I'm still not sure how I did it the first time.

The next day, a black Suburban arrives at our house. It is pouring rain. I pull out the bright red dress I wore for my organization's gala the year before. It feels persuasive but I'm still not sure what I should be persuading the president to do. All I know is that if anyone has the power to enact change, you'd think it would be the president of the United States. But, in practice, what does that mean? Gun control. An executive order. We're a month away from the presidential election. As my boss at the nonprofit used to say, "Know your ask."

But my ask might be too vague: make it stop.

The black SUV glides across the slick freeways of a rainy Los Angeles. I put my hand on the window and smile at the wedding ring that still sits on my hand. Less than a year after we began dating, and only months after moving in together, Theo asked me what kind of wedding ring I wanted. He had just come in from surfing, leaning his board against the wall in our living room, since we didn't have room for it anywhere else. Whenever I would ask Theo how his surf session went, there were only two answers: "Amazing" or "Made something out of the nothing."

Theo believed that surfing was like alchemy, sometimes you had to make magic on your own, even if nature failed to cooperate. I had just started freelance writing for a few news outlets. Some old friends tried to help me get back in the game, but it felt like all my attempts were half-hearted. I wanted it, yet I couldn't get myself entirely there. I would submit a few pitches, write a few stories, and then it just seemed easier to focus on the day job, and drive to the beach with Theo.

"I'm not saying I'm doing it now," Theo interrupted me as I tried to work on a pitch to LA Weekly. He stood in our living room, looking at me intently. "But if I was going to, what kind of ring would you want?"

Without hesitation, I said, "A rose quartz ring."

Just as Theo and I began dating, I was doing a session at Elissa's house, lying in the middle of the floor for a guided meditation. In it, I had a vision of a pink ring. Afterward, Elissa asked me what happened.

"I think I'm supposed to get a rose quartz ring."

"So, get one," Elissa replied with her usual candor.

One year later, Theo stood in the doorway of our home. He was the first man I ever lived with, the first man to stand before me and promise never to leave.

"Rose quartz?" he asked.

That Christmas, we stumbled into a jewelry store at the mall, and there we found it. It was three carats and shaped like a diamond. It was the most beautiful thing I had ever seen. It was also $3,000, way beyond what Theo was barely bringing in from his odd jobs.

"How will you afford that, Theo?" I asked, even as I knew I was looking at the ring from my vision, now fully emerged into reality.

"Guess I better make something out of nothing," Theo joked.

Over the next six months, Theo pulled an old Honda CB out of his parents' garage and month by month fixed it up until it was back in peak condition. He sold it for $2,400 and had a yard sale to raise the remaining $600, turning metal into gold.

I stare down at the ring as the Suburban pulls into the driveway of the Four Seasons Hotel in Beverly Hills.

The Secret Service leads us into the hotel and through the lobby as people turn in our direction. And then I see her, Gigi stands in a black dress across the room, waiting for us with a toddler in her arms. We smile at each other and quickly hug, and I wonder whether I should have also worn black.

"It's so good to see you," I say as she nervously smooths her hair.

"I didn't want to see the president in July," she explains as we wait for the elevator. "It just seemed too hard."

"I didn't either," I tell her. "We left town. I had to leave town."

She nods, "We're going, we're moving actually, to Mexico next week and when the lady called from the TV show, I realized, I don't know, that maybe this was my last chance."

I start to smile, "Was the lady's name Yvette by chance?"

Gigi nods, "She said the president needed to hear my story."

The elevator arrives as I agree, "He does."

"And who's this?" I ask as the baby hides his face in her neck.

"Junior," she pauses. "He's our first son. We have three girls. Al was . . ."

She goes quiet and we spend the rest of the ride up to the sixteenth floor in silence, exiting out to a long hallway. The carpet is expensive and tan, with a lighter shade of peach scrolling down its middle. An older gentleman steps off from the wall. He has closely cropped white hair, and the muscle memory of a stronger man.

"I'm sorry, but I'm going to have to check all three of you," the agent explains.

The agent waves a wand over Gigi, Junior, and me, before gently patting each of us down as Junior giggles at the wand.

"I wish everybody responded like that," I hear a familiar voice behind us say.

The president walks up. I try to remain calm even as the world goes quiet.

"Mr. President," the older guard interrupts, clearly not finished with his work, but the president silences him with a gentle wave of his hand, which he extends to Gigi and then me.

"Thank you for coming, both of you," he says, his much larger mitt swallowing my own.

"Thank you for having us," I reply.

"You're the president!" Gigi exclaims in shock, and we all start to laugh, our nervousness breaking into excitement. The president is tall and relaxed, like an attractive law professor who understands the power he holds over his female students but is honorable enough not to exploit it.

"I am," he laughs. "And who is this young man?" The president reaches out for Junior. "May I?" he asks.

"If he'll let you." Gigi tries to hand over Junior, but he quickly returns to her neck.

"It's okay. I'm used to it by now. Part of kissing so many babies is that you get used to being rejected by them. Pretty much basic training for the job."

"It's not an easy job," I reply.

"No, it isn't." The president smiles sadly, before brightening up. "Come on, we got some things for Junior."

He leads us into the sprawling Presidential Suite, its large windows a stage for the Hollywood Hills beyond.

"Our staff have made up some snacks for Junior in the kitchen," the president explains to Gigi as she reluctantly hands over her son to a young female staffer who offers him a cookie in return. "And he'll find a few other things he might like."

We stand in the living room alone, just the three of us, save for one Secret Service agent who sits in the corner, quietly reading a magazine.

"So," the president begins. "Let me start by saying, I am truly sorry for both of your losses."

I don't know what else to do but offer him an awkward smile as Gigi and I sit down across from him. He turns to me, "Yvette told me that you used to work for Blake. You were a producer on their show a few years back?"

"I was an associate producer at the time, but yes, that's why I went on the show. The media was unrelenting and I thought that might slow it down."

"Didn't really work out that way?"

"No, I also didn't expect to fall apart like that."

Gigi looks at us both, "You were on TV again?"

"Yeah, after the shooting," I explain. "You know, after the morning they caught me on camera. They wouldn't leave us alone."

"I had one person call me," Gigi says blankly. "From Univision. But I didn't want to do it."

"Your husband worked at the club, right?" the president asks, and I realize I don't know much about Gigi's story or her husband, other than that he took care of them.

"He did the sound system for them," she shares. "I wasn't even supposed to be there, but I had needed the car that night, and I came to pick him up."

She goes quiet. "Our children were in the car."

We look down at the carpeted floor in awkward silence until the president finally speaks, "I've had to do these meetings far more times than I ever expected. They don't prepare you for it, you know. And what I've learned, or seen, is that there's loss and then there's tragic loss. And the tragic, well, it breaks your heart different, breaks my heart different, but also, it changes people. It does.

"And Jane, Theo was a former Dodger, right? For a year?"

"That's part of it. He, uh, struggled a lot after, but also, he cared a lot. About the world. He was incredibly passionate, especially about politics."

"I knew that last part." The president smiles gently. "Facebook. He wasn't a fan."

"At first he was. He was on the wheat pasting crew for your Hope posters here in LA. But you know, things changed."

The president nods as I admit, "One of our first big fights was actually about you. We were driving down to San Diego. We had only been dating a couple weeks."

I can recall the day as though I am still sitting in the driver's seat of my old car, a green Honda Civic. It was a hot April afternoon. We were listening to Neil Young's "Cowgirl in the Sand," taking our first road trip together to San Diego. We decided to do a side trip to Tijuana because it was Easter Sunday, and we wanted to go to church. We thought we were in love.

"My husband could be relentless, but he believed that if you were who we thought you were, you would have ignored the people in power, and executive ordered a better future for all of us."

"Yes." The President smiles, confident in the face of his detractors. "I know the executive order crowd well."

"I told him that you couldn't just executive order everything. We finally made it to the hotel. It was just the beginning, you know. When political fights still ended in bed." I don't know why I'm sharing such a detail with the president, but I want him to know that we were real people.

"Don't worry. I'm married, too."

"So, I heard." I laugh. "But, Mr. President, he was right." I look him in the eye, knowing exactly why I am here. Once again, Theo has given me the idea. "We need an executive order."

I wait as Gigi watches me, but then she echoes my statement, "We do."

The president nods before rising and walking over to a desk near the window. "The Second Amendment is a tricky beast," the president says, leaning against the desk as though he is in the middle of a constitutional law lecture, swiftly adopting the pace and tone of his longer orations. "Had it not been written as a form of protection for the people against tyranny, against their government, democracy or otherwise. Had it been about our protection from one another, it would have been easier. But gun control is a slippery slope."

"Slippery slope? It's an outdated amendment all of you are hiding behind." I stand up, my blood rising above my nerves, the words sharp and fast as they come spitting through my teeth. "With all due respect, Mr. President. You were at Deer Valley. We're not meant to die like that."

The president looks me directly in the eyes, so authentic it hurts. "We're not. I know, Jane. I know. I will die with the images of that school in my heart, those classrooms . . ."

He stops, his eyes wet, the memories still raw. "But that doesn't make changing things any easier."

"Well, it should." Gigi stands up next to me. "That's what you politicians don't understand. You don't see what happens after the shooting. Our whole lives have been destroyed. And we are left to pick up the pieces.

She stops as her voice cracks, "I miss him every day, I wish he was here right now, but what's worse is how I don't know to live without him. We have to move home to my parents in Nogales. My children barely speak Spanish, and now what, they lose their daddy and their home? And we're supposed to be okay with that?"

"No, you're not, Giselle. I understand that, I do. More than you might realize," the president replies.

I feel emboldened by my new partner, adding, "Then help us, Mr. President. We can't get them back. We can't reverse time for us, but we can reverse it for someone else."

I feel desperate, knowing this might be our only shot, "Please, sir, executive order it, the AR-15, all assault rifles. I know it isn't easy—"

"It's more than *not easy*," the president interrupts, transforming into a stern professor finished with entertaining his students' radical views. "It's practically impossible."

The life that once felt so muted in me suddenly roars back into existence. I know that there will never be another opportunity like this, so I tell him with all the force and faith within me, "Nothing is impossible."

As if on cue, we hear Junior crying from another room.

The president smiles, "Except for a toddler."

We all begin to laugh, as Gigi replies, "They are definitely impossible. I'll be right back."

She leaves the room as the president looks back out the window. A slight rainbow has drawn itself across the sky.

"Theo's mother died two weeks ago," I tell him, staring out at the sight.

"I'm so sorry to hear that," the president replies.

"Mr. President, I don't mean to be disrespectful here. I really don't. But as long as we're alive, we have a choice. We have this one little window to do something and your window is way bigger than ours will ever be. You *can* make it stop."

I know I have failed to say the right thing at the right time for too long, been too scared to make the gesture that could change everything. Theo was born without a filter, and it's what made him so scary for people. Not because he was wrong, but because he wasn't afraid to reach across time and space to take the next right action. With that, I take the president's hand.

I haven't held a man's hand since my husband's. The president's fingers feel long and bony in mine, so different from Theo's meaty fist. Los Angeles stretches out in front of us. I love LA for so many reasons, but first and foremost, I understand her. From the outside, she's just another stale and pretty blonde, but once you get to know her, you realize she is a city of revolution, of ordinary people living extraordinary lives.

"I'm moving home next month, too, but it's a different situation," I suddenly announce.

"Do you want to go home?" the president asks, still holding my hand.

"No. But I don't have a lot of other options either. I want to be safe, and I guess, I guess home is safe."

"Depends on your home," the president remarks darkly.

"It does."

The president feels my wedding ring and raises my hand to see the stone.

"That's a beautiful ring," he says, turning it in the light as Gigi comes back into the room holding Junior.

"It was a beautiful marriage," I reply as the president quietly releases my hand.

THIRTEEN

I've always been haunted by the past. Like a soundtrack playing in the background of my waking life, random memories will return—a trip to Macy's with my mother when I was eight, eating ramen on the couch in college watching *Boyz n the Hood*, looking out of the bedroom window of Theo's and my first apartment as the sun set across East Hollywood. Sometimes these recollections would be inextricably linked to other moments, the connection between the two known only to the Mariana Trench of my mind. For years, whenever I did the dishes in our kitchen in Montrose, I would remember walking home the night after leaving Blake's office for the last time. I was wandering down Sixth Avenue, finally ending up in Chelsea.

I found the Rubin Museum, a small gallery on Seventeenth Street that specializes in Eastern arts. The museum was hosting an exhibit from Tibet, a display of modern artists who used aluminum cans to make exotic mandalas. I stared at the displays in the window, knowing I would never understand why the cosmos had to push us to the edge of a scream, how we could wake up in the morning with one version of the universe only to end the day with an entirely different interpretation.

At a certain point, the trauma seems intentional—the car crash, the stage-four cancer, the midnight shooting—none of it feels like an accident. It feels like a contrived plan to make life painful and complicated, but when the cartilage is gone, how can we possibly keep running?

I stand in front of Yvette's apartment building and laugh, discovering that the Rubin Museum is right next door.

"Of course, it is," I remark to Zoe, who sits in my lap, utterly bewildered by the city in which we have just arrived.

Zoe and I are moving to Dennis's in mere weeks, our landlord giving us 60 days to get packed up and prepare to leave the home that Theo and I have been building since we were three months pregnant and moved to the suburbs to give Zoe the life neither of us had. I look out at the streets of New York and wonder what this life might have looked like for us instead. Did the single-family home and middle-class expectations just prove too much for us - or not enough?

I walk up to Yvette's apartment building and exhale. A few days after my meeting with the president, Yvette called me.

"What are you doing next week?" she asked.

But before I could reply, she continued. "Blake is on hiatus next week so we're having guest hosts. I couldn't help but think of you."

"Me? That's crazy."

"What's crazy about it, Jane? You've been all over the news already. You said it yourself; this was what you were meant to do."

"It was, Yves. A long time ago."

"And where the fuck did that woman go? She was one of the sexiest women I knew."

I laughed. "Sexy, huh?"

"Yes, the sexiest motherfucker I had ever met."

I can't help but remember what it was like when Yvette and I worked together—a lion and a tiger ruling over the bear's kingdom.

"When were you thinking?" I asked.

Yvette now opens the door to her penthouse apartment.

"You're here!" she cries, her arms extended wide. I feel myself fall into her embrace though she is so much smaller than me. Zoe squirms between us.

"Come in, come in," Yvette implores. Two small children quickly run in from another room, holding a painted sign, which reads, "Welcom Zo!"

"I made it," Yvette's daughter Ella announces as Zoe waddles over to them, reuniting like old friends, mimicking the bond of their mothers.

I walk into Yvette's apartment and am reminded of how the other one percent live. The penthouse is steeped in opulence, the living area stretching out from a set of back windows overlooking uptown where the Empire State Building arches overhead, partially obscured by a cluster of trees, a friendly reminder that nature still lives here. A spiral staircase stands in the middle, leading to an upstairs floor, and one below.

It's not the first time I've stood in the shadows of wealthier friends. Entrenched by a middle-class existence, I know what life looks like both in the stations above and below me, and though I don't want for wealth, I would like something closer to comfort. Yvette might feel like a peer, but she clearly doesn't worry about how she's going to pay the lease on her Honda CRV.

"I know. It's fucking ridiculous," Yvette replies to my wordless reaction. "Diana wanted it. We'd just bought the apartment below when she was diagnosed. I had just gotten pregnant with Dylan and I . . ."

Yvette stops herself, making sure the children are focused on Zoe and not listening as she grabs my suitcase and sets it against the front door.

Yvette was four months pregnant when Diana died. As Yvette explained during one of our late-night phone calls, "Di had already gone through radiation and chemo when we decided to try again."

My friend's voice quivered as she shared the story. "The tests looked good. Sure, it had gotten into her lymph nodes, but they really thought they'd caught it."

From other conversations, I knew that within weeks Diana went from having trouble breathing to being on a twenty-four-hour morphine drip.

"We had just found out we were having a boy," Yvette told me over the phone one night. "We were so excited."

"We had wanted a boy for our second, too," I shared, lying in bed on the opposite side of the country.

"Maybe it was for the best you only have Zoe," Yvette admitted before blurting out the standard maternal retraction, never wanting to appear ungrateful for the lives she had birthed. "Don't get me wrong, I adore Dylan. He saved me. But no one wants to be pregnant at their wife's funeral . . . And then I still had Ella, who was old enough to understand. She was almost two at the time, close to Zoe's age right now, I think."

"Yeah," I replied, wondering how this period would either be remembered or lost upon my only child.

"I had no choice but to hold it together," Yvette continued. "I was still working with Blake, and I continued like normal. Tried to pretend like I wasn't dying inside. I took maternity leave, but I worked all the way through it. I didn't want to stop. If I stopped . . ."

"You'd have to face it."

"It was easier to focus on the job," she shared as the hour nearly approached dawn in New York. I never trusted people who didn't sleep, but Yvette could run on three or four hours as if she had slept ten.

I missed that feeling, being so challenged by work you could lose yourself in it.

Finally, she admitted, "It wasn't until about a year after Diana's death that I lost my shit."

She didn't say anything else. I was about to ask what happened, remembering her initial email to me, warning me of the consequences of silent grief. But Yvette cut off the call before the conversation could continue. "Oh, fuck it's late. I better get to bed. Kids will be up soon. Talk more this weekend?"

I knew it was a cover-up, but I also knew that as much as Yvette talked, she couldn't be forced to speak.

God, I didn't even finish the story about all that," Yvette admits as we walk into her kitchen, all white marble and glass cabinets. She continues with her story as Ella brings out more toys for Zoe to play with.

"Diana's family and shit. It was a real battle. The idea was that Di and I would add a bottom floor because there's only three bedrooms upstairs, but then her brother wanted the apartment below. I mean, thank God they overturned DOMA, but still, it wasn't fun."

"Are you all okay now?" I ask, as Zoe follows Ella and Dylan to the living room area that overlooks the city. Yvette's décor is a mix of chrome and Lucite. Child-friendly in its soft materials and round corners, but so clean, it looks straight out of a showroom.

Yvette begins to pull out drinks, pouring me a cranberry soda, the kids some orange juice, and herself a tequila on the rocks.

"It's after three," she shrugs, before explaining how the children kept the relationship civil between her and Diana's family.

"Don't get me wrong," Yvette confesses. "There's no great love there. Never was. Diana was their only daughter. They had different dreams for her. Ones she refused to live. At first, they thought I was a passing fancy." She laughs. "I think they liked me better then. Once they realized I was here to stay, that they would have to share their blood and money with me. Well, that's when things got tough."

We carry the orange juice over to the kids. I watch Zoe drink hers, fearful of staining Yvette's perfect living room, but Yvette stops me. "This place is so Scotchgarded, you could murder someone and not leave a stain."

"I love you," I reply. "I'll be honest, when I saw this room, I thought maybe I didn't know you as well as I thought I did."

"'Because it looks like a stuck-up bitch lives here?'"

"Well, at least one that doesn't let her kids spill on the rug. Kids should be able to spill on the rug."

"Adults should be able to spill on the rug," Yvette adds.

I lift my glass. "To messy homes."

"To messy lives!" Yvette retorts, knocking her drink into mine so that they both splash over, leaving barely noticeable stains on the thick white rug.

The next morning, I stand in front of the mirror in Yvette's downstairs guest bathroom, getting ready for the show as Zoe sleeps in a borrowed crib in the next room over. I've been paired with a stand-up comic from New York everyone is hailing as the next big thing. We have our marching orders: election news cycle, discussion on gun control, a few interviews, and an all-female cast.

"This doesn't feel like *The Blake Edwards Show*." I comment as Yvette and I go over the production schedule the night before, knowing Blake's penchant for all-male talent, cohosts, and guests alike. We used to joke that if you saw a woman on set, she was one of Blake's PAs.

"Nope," Yvette replies, clearly relieved. "And I don't want it to be. I don't want it to be like anything else on TV."

We edited the script, making changes to the initial draft with my cohost's notes, creating a genuine riff on paper. As soon as I meet my co-host Krystal, I relax, realizing that we've met before when she performed standup at an event for the nonprofit I didn't know how to leave.

"I used to work for Child Advocates," I tell the now-famous comic as we run through the show.

"No way!" She slaps me on the arm. "In LA?!"

I love when people get excited about coincidences, adding. "I thought you were hysterical. Who knew we'd end up here?"

I try not to sound sad, but it slips through. Krystal brushes it off.

"We got this. Don't worry."

We finish our rehearsal as the cameras are moved into place, finally receiving our last touch-ups, and then three, two, one . . . I was always so nervous being in front of the camera when I worked for Blake, but as the cameras move into position and Krystal and I begin the segment, I realize that it wasn't me, it was Blake. He was there watching, waiting with a set of notes and cruel critiques: I was too blonde or too brash or too much. He was famous for yelling at guests, but I could barely make a wisecrack without him telling me I wasn't testing well. After a few times of trying to be on air, a promise he took years to fulfill, I asked that I go back behind the cameras, writing the scripts and producing the show, but never speaking the words I had written.

Now, it doesn't feel like a performance, some faulty translation of thoughts or ideas or corny jokes. It is pure transmission as Krystal and I find our groove. Once our first guest appears, we are deep in the flow.

When I first began in nonprofits, I loved the work because it felt like there were a million solutions to any given problem. In that sense, it reminded me of broadcasting. For every truth, there were a million ways to tell it. And I loved being a part of the story. It took me years to stop watching the news, noticing which tales they chose to tell, and which ones they ignored. Blake used to remind us, "Find the story no one else is sharing. That's where the real revolution lies."

And I believed in that revolution. I believed in the untold tale, and all the ways that journalism wasn't just some outdated concept that was no longer fit for print.

I knew that our words could change the world, and as Krystal and I swing from hard topics to light-hearted humor, cracking dick jokes and also digging into the power of an executive order, I know there is still a way to engage people, not just through biased op-eds or the sensationalism of a woman soaked in blood, but through the honest rhythms of our humanity.

"We should do this more often," Krystal laughs, as we close out the final interview, and David Bowie begins to run over the closing credits. We get up and begin to dance. And it doesn't feel fake or cheap or easy. It feels earned.

Yvette and I stand in front of a karaoke bar on the Lower East Side. "This place is still here?" I ask. We've been here many times before, back when we would come over late at night to belt out tunes from their music list, which extended way beyond Frank Sinatra and Taylor Swift. It was a broadcasting rite of passage.

Yvette shrugs, "I figured it only made sense we would celebrate with a little song. I mean isn't this where it all started?"

"Back when it was fun."

"Who says it's not still fun?" Yvette asks, swaying slightly after the bottle of wine she drank at dinner. After the show, Yvette and I go out to celebrate. I don't know if Yvette is an alcoholic, and I don't know if it's my place yet to judge. Everyone learns to cope in their own ways.

I take one last drag off my cigarette, tossing it to the ground. "Let's do this."

We walk into the club, and I am transported fifteen years back in time, when Blake would pull me into his arms as soon as my song was complete.

As I look around the club, I realize Blake Edwards was an albatross for us both. Under his direction, there weren't a million ways to tell the story, there was only his way. Yvette orders another drink as I sit down on one of the barstools, still wearing the leather pants from the taping, but with white high-tops and a black turtleneck.

Someone on stage sings "Band of Gold."

"I have an idea," Yvette leans forward, her eyes glassy and flitting in the dark. The sleeveless button-down she wears drapes slightly forward so that I can see the lace of her bra. "What if we pick the most depressing songs we can find?"

"Huh?"

"And we'll see who can sing it sadder!"

"Like a . . . grief-off?" I ask.

"Yeah," Yvette laughs darkly.

"Oh, I got some shit, girl."

"Oh really?" Yvette raises her eyebrows. "You think your straight-girl mourning can best my double-estrogen loss?"

"Hey, I can love like a lesbian."

"You're such a fucking dyke." Yvette nudges me.

"Only when drunk," I reply, which quiets us both for a moment.

Yvette walks off to put in her first song, her tight jeans catching the attention of nearly every man in the place. If Yvette was into men, she could have easily been a rich man's wife. I guess she became a rich woman's wife instead.

"Your turn, motherfucker," she announces, returning from her trip to the DJ.

I try to think of the saddest song I know, remembering back to August, after I returned from my last trip to New York. One morning I was driving Zoe to music class when I hit the wrong button on the steering column, triggering the radio. Phil Collins's eighties classic "Against All Odds" came on.

I left the song on just long enough for it to crack me in half. I pulled off the freeway at the nearest exit and turned off the radio.

I'm not sure if I have the balls to sing it here, but if ever there was a moment when I could laugh at my own pain, this is it. I walk over to the DJ and request the song before returning to Yvette, who has ordered another drink.

"You're never gonna win this one." She smirks at the bar.

"We'll see about that. What's the monte?"

Yvette's face grows serious, as though it's important we establish an appropriate prize. Finally, she folds her arms across her chest, and announces, "A kiss."

The words shoot through my body with an erotic volt.

"We should at least see," Yvette continues, biting her lip again.

"Agreed," I state clearly, as though we're deciding on an automobile purchase, and not a potentially dangerous conflict of interest, one that can't help but remind me of a deal I inadvertently struck years ago.

Yvette hears the first beats of her melody. "Oh shit. That's me."

Before she reaches the stage, I recognize the song, "Girl from the North Country." I expect a straight rendition of it, something heartbreaking and serene, but, instead, Yvette launches into one of the best Dylan impressions I've ever heard, switching seamlessly between Johnny and Bob, like a 1980s impersonator singing "Islands in the Stream" as both Parton and Rogers.

She moves through the saddest lines of the song, still in character, but suddenly it isn't so funny anymore. The audience, who were laughing, now fall serious, as though they misunderstood the joke. I can tell that Yvette is one of those girls who was cutthroat in sports, sliding into first, taking out knees in soccer. I preferred to smoke under the bleachers.

As Yvette hits the final lines, her pain betrays the perfect impression. I can see her pulled over on the side of the road, sobbing in the front seat with her kids in the back. She finishes the song to wide applause, returning to the bar with a gloat.

"Out grieve that, bitch," Yvette swaggers.

"Jesus. Where did you learn to sing like Dylan?"

"I went to college in the nineties. What other music did we have?"

I nod, also graduating into a world of Britney Spears and NSYNC when for four years all we listened to was Dylan, Young, and the Dead. Medeski Martin & Wood if you were nasty.

"Guess you're up," Yvette says, pushing me toward the stage as the first quiet beats of the song begin to play. I walk up to the mic, the words spooling out on the monitor, catching me off guard as I try to get my confidence together.

I close my eyes and try to work my way through the first verses. My voice cracks as I finally land on the chorus. I look up and see Yvette across the room. If grief was life's most personal performance, I am once again making it public. I throw away my concerns about my bad alto, missing the high notes as I belt out Phil Collins at the top of my lungs. The tears come, my body shuddering as I nearly shriek the words to the song.

I stare at Yvette, holding her gaze, revving up before the big drum crescendo. I pull the mic off the stand and move through the crowd. People join in, their voices lifting as they sing along, nearly drowning me out. I'm not sure if the song is personal for everyone, or if with the impending election, our panic has become universal.

I walk back up to the stage as the song comes to an end. I'm tempted to drop the mic, but the last time I did that at a wedding, the DJ got mad. The crowd erupts as I wipe away the tears, eventually giving up and letting them flow.

I head back over to Yvette, who grabs my hand, lifting my arm into the air. She presses her body against mine as I choke back the sobs.

"That was amazing!" Yvette cheers. "Let's get out of here."

We stumble out onto the street and hail a cab back to Yvette's apartment, laughing and crying as Manhattan darts by us in a stream of lights. We get out of the car in front of the Rubin Museum. I start to walk down the street, but Yvette doesn't move.

I turn back. "What's going on?"

Yvette stares at me. "We never decided what you would get if you won."

Her perfect face is caught in the streetlight, her full lips pursed, aware of her power. I know it's against my best interest, but I can't stop myself as the distance between us shrinks and I find myself pushing Yvette up against the window of the Rubin Museum. Our kiss is hungry and dangerous as Yvette cups her hand around my neck, moving us around so my back is now up against the wall. She pushes against me and before I know it, we are in her elevator, and I am unbuttoning her blouse. We stumble into the living room, and, in that moment, I am grateful for Yvette's live-in nanny who has long ago put the kids to bed.

As we make our way to her bedroom, she pulls down my pants, and, before I can say anything, she presses her lips between my legs. I don't say no or protest or think about all the reasons we shouldn't be doing this because everything about her feels so good as my hands tighten in her hair, pulling her mouth closer to me. I finally pull her away, determined to offer the same. She slides down her pants and stands in front of me at the edge of the bed. I sink to my knees and move up between her thighs, pressing my tongue into her body as she leans over the bed, moaning into the pillow. We don't need to pull out any toys because we have mouths and fingers. Although I have been with women before, nothing has prepared me for this. Finally, she comes in my mouth. I move back onto the bed, and we fall into each other's arms.

"What was *that*?" she asks.

"Fuck," I reply, not even knowing what to say as all the protests begin to flood my head—it's only been four months since Theo, we're working together, I don't even know if I want to date a woman—but Yvette falls asleep before we can talk about it.

I get up to move to the guest room where Zoe is still sleeping in the crib. But then I see Yvette's naked body lying there in the dark, somehow all my fears falter, and a desire I haven't felt in years moves up again through my body. I sit back down on the bed and then Yvette reaches over, pulling my underwear to the side and sliding her fingers inside me before I can say anything. Twice in one night I find myself between her legs, our bodes unable to stop it, the chemistry that once felt like friendship exploding into something so big I feel lost between being a mother and a wife and a woman who just remembered how to fuck.

FOURTEEN

As I pack up the life I used to know, the rest of the world is still turning. The presidential election is the next day and I have decided to stay to cast my vote, pulling out my pantsuit and preparing for the election of the first female president. Though I never brought the Bernie sign down from our yard, I am voting for Hillary Clinton simply because there is no way our country would allow for Donald Trump to win.

"My man Donnie is totally going to be the next president," my uncle boasts as I put our remaining family photos in a box. On our last night in the house, Peter and Dennis come over to help with the final packing. Despite my uncle's politics, he and Peter have always had their own camaraderie, cracking jokes together at our wedding and sharing in their uncle duties with Zoe. As Dennis makes his jokes, I see Peter roll his eyes, making me wonder how long their friendship might last should Trump actually win. But then again,

Peter and I don't put much stock in that outcome, believing Dennis is just blowing hot air into a calamitous blimp.

"Not too worried about that," Peter replies as he and I continue to pack up books.

After my uncle helps with the heavy stuff, he heads home. He has a flight out the next day, which I feel he chose so Zoe and I could move in without the stress of another human. It doesn't hurt that he's flying on election night either. After Dennis leaves, I stand in the doorway of our bedroom holding Zoe as Peter looks at Theo's side of the closet.

Zoe has been speaking more since our trip to New York, pointing and noticing things around our house—"my doggy," and "want milk," "love mama" and "where dada?" And I still don't know what to say. That he's here? There are times I catch her looking at an empty space in the room, and I wonder whether she can feel him too.

"You can keep whatever pants you want," I offer. "But if you wouldn't mind boxing up the shirts . . ."

I stop myself. I hold no connection to Theo's jeans, but every T-shirt of his contains a story, pieces of his life that I will one day share with Zoe.

"Sure," Peter replies, trying to appear stronger than he is. He knows them, too—each skateboarding T-shirt, the ones with the political slogans, the old Dodgers jerseys that Theo treated with the same care as the other balled up shirts in the back of the drawer.

Peter looks up in the closet where Theo's baseball caps sit.

"Those too?"

I haven't thought about Theo's quintessential headgear. I bounce Zoe on my hip, planning to give her a bath before bedtime, "No, you can have those. If you want."

After putting Zoe to bed, I join Peter in the bedroom to pack my own remaining clothes into a suitcase. The bed will be donated. The rest of the furniture will be put in storage, until I figure out what's next.

The bedroom is nearly empty, the books and lamps and knick-knacks having already been packed minus our family photos. Those I will be bringing home to Dennis's, including the portraits of Theo and me that have hung on our bedroom walls since we first moved in together. One is a picture of Theo when he was four, riding a pony, wearing a cowboy hat and vest, smiling gleefully for the camera.

I look up at the photo as I fold the last of my clothes.

"That's when they found out about the disabilities," Peter remarks, stopping his own work. Theo's baseball caps are spread out on the bed.

"Huh?" I ask, only half paying attention.

"That photo. He was four, I guess. And they knew he was having trouble talking. He just wasn't like the other kids."

Peter pauses, glancing at the photo of the little boy who was once his big brother. "They got him tested and found out about the dyslexia. The doctors at the time said it was so severe, he might never be able to read or write. The eighties, huh?"

"He never told me that." I stop my own packing, confused that there was a part of Theo's life I hadn't heard about.

"I guess he figured they were wrong, so what was the point?" Peter stands there holding one of Theo's baseball caps in his hand. It is his old worn, Dodgers hat, the one he was given when he joined the team, and that he always wore, a reminder of who he had briefly been.

Peter stares down at the hat. "You know, after Theo got kicked off the team, no one expected much for him. Even me. And I was his biggest fan. If he didn't have baseball, I didn't know what else he would do. I thought he'd just end up living on a beach somewhere. That was the future everyone predicted for him, really."

He looks up at me and asks, "Are you sure you want to do this? Move back there?"

I stop folding my jeans, "No, I don't. It's a terrible idea. But it's the only one I have."

I look around our bedroom, a room I have barely been in since June. "I just, as much as I love LA, I can't heal here. Every street sign, every restaurant. He's everywhere. Our life is . . ."

I can't continue, the sorrow still so overwhelming when it hits like this, standing on the edge of a waterfall. Peter grabs me in his strong arms, and, for a moment, he feels like Theo. A part of me wants to lean in, to let someone share this pain with me. Instead, I pull away as Peter awkwardly remarks, "I can sleep on the floor, so you can have the couch."

"No, no," I reply, the moment breaking before it begins. "You take the couch. I think I'm going to spend tonight here."

I talked to Yvette the night before I pack up to leave, our late-night phone calls turning into daily events. She is confused why I'm moving home, feeling like there are more options on the table than I am willing to see.

"Dude, if you want to pack up your shit and move here, that would make more sense," she tells me. I can tell she's not entirely joking.

"And what would I do there, Yves? I'm not a particularly good stay-at-home wife."

"Well, what are you going to do in Manhattan Beach?"

"It's Redondo."

"Whatever. How about you come to the real Manhattan?"

"You're a very tempting woman, Yvette."

"Am I?" she replies, and I can feel her body across the miles, though our dance is still careful. As much as I wish I could move in with Yvette, blending families and pretending that I'm not months away from the darkest night of my life, I know I can't.

Instead, I pack up the house with Peter, finally closing the door on our now empty closet, wondering when I might see some of these boxes again and what their contents will still mean when I open them on the other side of what is about to be our life.

I look at the bed, untouched since the morning Theo last made it.

Peter nods before giving me a light kiss on the forehead, just as Theo used to do. "Wherever you go, Janey, we'll always be family, okay?"

"We will."

Peter holds up the Dodgers hat, "Can I?"

"Of course." My heart cracks at the sight of the hat that so often crowned Theo's head. Peter begins to collect the rest of the caps.

"Wait." I stop him, pulling out another one of Theo's favorites, the only one of his hats I used to wear. It resembles a sailor's cap, but across the front it reads, "I'd rather be surfing."

"I'll take this one." I put the hat on my head, wondering if it might still smell like him.

Peter smiles. "Fits you."

He nudges down the bill of the hat. "I'll be in the living room if you need me."

Peter walks out of the room as I move slowly to the bed, pulling back the comforter and the decorative pillows. I hope I've protected

Theo's scent. I call for Rocky, who trots into the room and jumps on the bed as he has done for years, happy to return after so many months away. I can't touch the pillows yet, choosing instead to snuggle up behind the dog. Theo and I used to joke that Rocky was the surrogate for our affection. We offered him the attention we should have been giving to each other, but the baby and the job and the stress and the finances and all the shit that stood between us just made the dog easier to love.

"I'm sure that's the case for tons of marriages," I argued at the time.

"But still," Theo remarked, even while spooning Rocky. "We should try to cuddle with each other once in a while."

I remember all the nights that it was Theo and me, in bed with this sweet lab who showed us both that we could take care of someone else together. He prepared us for Zoe.

"We'll never forget you, Rocky," Theo used to tell the dog, never expecting that their life spans would be reversed.

I look up again at the pictures. I am also four in my portrait, which was hand drawn at the county fair in Pomona only a month before my father left. He is somewhere in my view, and I imagine I am looking at him with the same love all four-year-olds bear for their fathers, before he walked out of our lives, and I found out how quickly we can disappear.

I am smiling, with white-blonde bangs and Zoe's ocean eyes and full lips. For years, I positioned the portraits so that mine was looking in Theo's direction, and his in mine.

"We'll never forget you," I whisper into Rocky's fur, before slowly getting up and changing into my pajamas. I walk into the bathroom to brush my teeth and wash my face. I spit out my toothpaste and look up at the mirror. I am afraid to stay, and I am afraid to leave. I know he is here. I can feel him. I look over my shoulder and can see him, brushing his teeth as he used to, both of us vying for the sink, rushing to spit into the basin before the other. I wonder if he'll still be able to find me at Dennis's house. I've already lost him once, and I don't know what it will look like when I'm truly alone, without the memories that swirl around me here, without our laughter echoing, moving in and out of the empty spaces where I wanted to feel more.

I guess it often comes down to this—the decision between faith and fear. The only problem is, I don't which one is pushing me to go.

I look back at myself and ask, "Why couldn't I love you more?"

I'm not even sure if the question is for him or me.

I close my eyes and suddenly I am no longer in the bathroom. I am back at the Mojave Saloon. The place is empty now and it's just me standing alone in the bar.

"Theo?" I whisper. "Theo?"

"Where were you?" he asks as I feel him wrap his arms around me from behind, just like he did when I returned from the show.

"What if I can't feel you anymore?" I ask, worried if these moments will be gone once I am no longer in my home.

"You couldn't feel me before, could you?"

"I wanted to, I wanted to," I admit and for the first time, I realize how much I wished I could have been in love with him. He turns me around and I am afraid to open my eyes.

"Feel me now," he presses his lips against mine and I feel the electricity I longed for when he was alive, the pulsating heat of two people who can't live without each other. He pulls away and whispers in my ear, "There's nothing left to fear."

And then he is gone.

I open my eyes and I am back in the bathroom. I breathe in deep, and I don't know what's real and what's fake anymore, but I know Theo is right. I can't give up now.

I turn off the light in our bathroom for the last time and go into the living room. All of Zoe's toys are boxed up. The books are missing from the bookshelves. The throw pillows and blankets have been donated to Goodwill.

"Night, Pete," I call to my brother-in-law, who is scrolling through Facebook on the couch.

I walk past the vintage record console that we bought when I first got pregnant with Zoe, deciding we needed more music. The records are all packed up. I haven't listened to anything on it in months. Moving my hand lightly over the wood, I realize that maybe.

I walk into our bedroom and close the door. Our bedside lamps are already gone, so as I switch off the overhead light, the room is draped in nightfall.

I edge toward my side of the bed, then stop, moving back over to where Theo used to sleep, closer to the door. I slip into the bed. Turning my head into his pillow, my hands clutch at the soft cotton of the pillowcase, and I breathe in deep. It smells like a warm fire as I inhale the last faulty memory of my husband's flesh and release the great unrelenting "why" I have refused myself ever since that night when I lay under his warm body, praying to hear his breath.

At first, I try to muffle the pain, but then I can't hold it anymore, exploding right there, willing to abandon Zoe and Rocky and be absorbed by my husband's sweet and cedar scent. "Why?!" I scream into the pillow, unafraid if I am going to wake Zoe, unafraid if

Peter is going to hear me, or the neighbors, or the whole of this heartbreaking world. I don't want to be okay. I don't want to be strong. I just want him home. I am so exhausted from not grieving like this, from damming up the pain so I can hold my shit together. I don't want to march in line to this grief, walking back into my childhood because I have no other choice. Like Yvette said, I can't keep swallowing the pain and not expect to be choked by that shit. There are no more rules applied to our love, there is nothing left to fear, including this pain, which rises up like the face of a terrifying wave. Tonight, finally, gratefully, I let myself drown.

After breakfast, the movers arrive to distribute the contents of our life into two categories: storage and trash. Peter offers to stay behind to manage the movers while Zoe and I go to cast our vote for the first female president. Zoe doesn't know we're making history, and I'm not sure what lies beyond this day. If change can ever be possible, or whether hope will always be diluted. But I put my ballot in the slot, take my picture with Zoe, and hope that tomorrow offers more promise.

When I get back to the house, Peter is working with the movers to load up the last boxes. Rocky runs up to greet Zoe and me, and then Zoe starts rolling around in her little pink car, which will be left out on the street when we leave.

"You must be Jane," a voice announces, and I turn around to see a woman sitting on our back patio. A twelve-year-old boy stands on a skateboard, and I know immediately this must be Peter's girlfriend.

"I'm Jennifer." She reaches out her hand. She is Korean and a little older than us, but still cool with her punk rock tattoos and side-shaved head. She is a perfect match for Peter.

"I hope you don't mind. They came by to help." Peter walks up.

"Not at all." I reach out to her and we hug. "We're family."

Her son Harrison does a kickflip on his board, and I recognize it immediately as Theo's.

"He just wanted to play with it," Peter interjects.

"No, he can have it," I offer. "I mean, as long as you don't want it."

"Naw, that work for you, Harrison?" Harrison shrugs nonchalantly like all twelve-year-old kids on a skateboard.

Jennifer sits down to play with Zoe as Peter and I go through the house and garage. Everything is quietly empty. We walk back outside where Jennifer is now pushing Zoe in her little car. Zoe squeals, delightfully unaware of what is about to happen. Peter throws the tennis ball for Rocky as he launches himself into the air for the throw.

"Air Bud!" Peter yells before turning to me.

"Hey, Peter." I hug him. "Thank you."

I say good-bye to Peter's girlfriend and her son as they head to Peter's truck out front. Peter strolls to the front yard to watch as the storage company closes the back of the truck. I throw the ball for Rocky as he races across the yard where Theo and I planned to hold summer barbecues. We talked about adding a second fridge to the garage, where the kids could hang and play Ping-Pong, sneaking beers and first kisses before heading off to college and having families of their own. We would settle into our Big Sur retirement, proud of the beautiful lives we had led. If only we would have made it that far.

"Are you sure you don't want me to wait for you?" Peter comes back through the gate, startling me as I stare into a future that is no longer there.

"No. I think I need to do this alone."

"You know, Janey, no one ends up being who they think they're going to be. You still have the chance to surprise yourself, okay?"

He tosses the ball in his hand, "Fuckin' Theo, man."

"Fuckin' Theo," I reply as Peter finally releases the ball, throwing it across the yard for Rocky.

Zoe pulls at my slacks, wanting to be picked up.

Peter musses Zoe's hair before he starts to leave, stopping to share with a grin, "Nice pantsuit."

I stand in the backyard with Zoe, alone in our house for the last time.

The drive to Redondo Beach doesn't take as long as I anticipate, though it's 4:00 p.m. I realize everyone is home or with their loved ones, watching the election results. Dennis is on a red-eye to Boston and the last person I want to watch the results with is Andrea, who has already expressed her passive support of Donald Trump. As she told me the weekend before, "I don't like the man, but I like what he stands for."

If the South Bay could be described in one quote, that might be it.

So, instead, I call Maggie, having made plans for her to come over the next day to help me move in.

"Hey Mags." I tickle Zoe's legs in the back seat while I drive. "We're heading your way and I wanted to see if you and William wanted some In-N-Out."

"Sure," Maggie replies, as I hear video games in the background. "I've been trying to avoid this election madness. I'm not looking forward to tonight."

"What do you mean?" I ask naïvely. "I mean, I don't love Clinton, but we're about to get our first female president."

"I wouldn't be so sure about that," Maggie warns.

Zoe and I bring over the In-N-Out. William is excited to see Zoe, bringing out some of his old toys to entertain her as Maggie and I turn on the TV. Maggie has described herself as apolitical, but I think it's her own form of rebellion against her parents' stead-fast commitment to the Democratic Party. When I told her that I was meeting with the president, she was nonplussed. "My parents have met him dozens of times."

And she acts no different throughout dinner, until the announce-ment comes through, the floor dropping out as the commentator reports, "Donald Trump is now expected to take Florida and Ohio. He has a clear path to victory."

We look at each other and I see the horror in her eyes. It was one thing to joke about it, but the nightmare has become real. Zoe begins to fuss and so we go home to Dennis's house, driving down the I-405, on what has become an eerily quiet night. The usually packed highway feels empty, everyone now standing in front of their TVs, shocked by what we should have seen coming, but truly didn't believe would transpire. The moment feels as big as 9/11, Watergate, the assasination of JFK, a moment in history so big it leaves its own personal scar. It's late by the time we get to my uncle's so I just bring in our overnight bag, leaving the rest of the luggage in the car until the morning.

I walk into the three-bedroom bachelor pad that has been my tempest in so many storms, saving me throughout my childhood and until now. But as I move through the house of the uncle I love, the one who also voted for Trump, I don't even know if I can turn on the TV, putting Zoe in my uncle's bathtub instead.

I am sitting in the bathroom, washing Zoe when the ping comes through, "Donald Trump is expected to win the US Presidency."

The tears burst out like a broken dam, unable to contain my shock. I find myself against the back of the tub, hiding my face from Zoe as she pleads, "Mama? What's wrong?"

I am no longer just afraid for our world but for hers. For the future we have just assigned them to with the election of this man, who at best is a simpleton, and at worst is a monster who is ready to lead the masses through the streets, inciting violence and hate against anyone who doesn't look like him.

And like that, I feel the blast again. The room is dark and I am spinning, and the world has been sent off its axis, hurtling through galaxies of darkness, and we are all lost. I don't know who to call and so I call out to Theo . . . Theo . . . Theo. Oh why isn't he here to protect us, to make it safe? And now I am truly alone in this world, alone with Zoe, standing in the exact moment in history when everything changed.

FIFTEEN

Theo was a loser!" my mother hisses across Dennis's living room as I sit with Zoe in my lap. I can only hope Zoe doesn't understand Andrea's words even as I rise against them. I stare at my mother, her face drawn tight over her fillers. Though Dennis cooked a beautiful dinner, the tension running underneath it made the meal hard to enjoy. Then again, tension on Thanksgiving has been a side dish in our family for so long, you'd think we'd be used to it by now. My father was never a part of our Thanksgiving tradition, and once Dennis moved to town and got a job working for American Airlines, he would host the turkey feast, inviting over friends and family and coworkers.

But then 1992 happened. I was twelve years old. We didn't find out until we made it home from Dennis's house, when the police arrived at the door and Andrea took the news, unmoving in the threshold of the small condominium where she still lives, the one in which she raised me. Later, I would hear the tears echoing from her bathroom, even as I struggled to know how I was supposed to feel, having long grieved the idea of him without ever really knowing the person.

In the years that followed, we would still go to Dennis's for Thanksgiving, but it was different. A quiet would hang in the air around us as though everyone knew, the anniversary marked in pencil on their calendars, when it felt inked into ours. But now here we all are, standing in the living room as though it is a standoff, my mother's words hanging there as I hold Zoe. My uncle enters the room knowing some unspoken truth has just been detonated.

"What's going on?" Dennis asks, holding a dish towel from cleaning up in the kitchen, and likely drinking the rest of the bottle of wine.

"You can't stay out of work forever," Andrea continues, ignoring Dennis and trying to act as though this was never about Theo. Then again, I'm not sure it ever was. Zoe begins to cry in my arms, and I wonder whether I should jump in my car and leave right now.

"It's only been five months," I argue back. "And I just did an appearance on TV. I'm doing things."

"It's not like you got paid for it, Jane," my mom spits, suspicious of my friendship with Yvette and of her motives, too.

I try to stay calm as I bounce Zoe against my hip. "I'm sorry but I'm just not going to take whatever job comes my way because I'm scared. I'm not going to keep living small and meek and ordinary."

It has only been two weeks since the presidential election, and this new president epitomizes my mother's life, bellowing the belief that salvation is to be found in submission.

With both Andrea and Dennis voting for Trump, I feel like I am living behind enemy lines. My move away from them was partially political. New York, and later LA, were rejections of their belief systems, one in which my dreams and ambitions were secondary to the allegiance to a nine-to-five job, to the violent belief that capitalism was going to save us.

Though Dennis has been the outspoken Trump supporter in the family, Andrea feels like the more dangerous one, quietly supporting the man who resembles her own boss when I was young. I know she sees it, too, not wanting to call it out, trying to ignore the decade during which a philandering narcissist controlled every part of our lives, from where we went on vacation to where I went to college.

"Oh God. Jane, you have a child, and you don't have a husband. It's time to get over these stupid dreams already. Grow up."

"Grow up?" my voice begins to rise as Zoe begins to fuss again. "Zoe, shhh," I plead.

Dennis reaches out and takes Zoe, who quickly clings to him. Since arriving in Redondo, Dennis has been staying in town, trying to help me out. After my father died, Dennis stepped in. And now, he is taking on the mantle of grandfather as he learns to watch Zoe on his own.

"She wants me to start temping," I explain. "If I was going to temp, I could have stayed home, in our house."

Andrea cries out, "With what money?"

"The fundraiser," I begin.

"Please, Jane," Andrea waves her head dismissively.

"I don't need to defend myself to you. I've been on my own for years. Theo and I built that life . . ."

Andrea rolls her eyes again, which only incites the anger that had just begun to subside. "We did. He gave more than you did. You—"

"Watch it there, Janey," Dennis interrupts. "You're right. You don't need to take a temp job. It's why you're here. So, you can take a break, so you can breathe. And then in a few months, maybe you can look for something, something you like."

"Dennis," I smile softly, taking Zoe from his arms. "I'm not staying here. I mean, I agree, I'll stay a few months, but then Zoe and Rocky and I, we're going to go somewhere else."

Andrea starts to get upset again, "Where will you go? Your family is here."

"Theo was my family," I reply calmly.

"Family? He left you with nothing. The life insurance . . ."

Her words trail off, the resentments failing to fade even in death.

"I need to put my daughter to bed," I say, punching out each word like I'm repeating lines from a play, because I've had this conversation too many times. It's why I didn't want to do Thanksgiving, only reminding me of how Theo and I re-created the holiday. When we began dating, we decided to start our own Thanksgiving traditions. Theo told me he didn't really didn't do the holiday in his family.

"It took my parents a few years to even understand what the day was for," he told me. I used to joke that the only thing I knew how to cook was a seven-course Thanksgiving dinner. Peter would usually bring a girlfriend and Theo and I would invite any orphans we knew, usually newcomers from AA who needed a safe place to eat turkey. Lydia and George would be there, along with Andrea and even Dennis.

But it was our holiday. We dictated the music and the games, we made the dinner and created the guest list, and we didn't allow for any family traumas. The only Thanksgiving spat we had was when Peter challenged Theo to a wrestling match, and they ended up breaking a chair. But no one stood in the middle of the living room, ready to fight or flight because some old nasty business was calling them to task. As I carry Zoe into the bathroom, the memory walks in with us, Theo standing behind me at the kitchen sink after our first Thanksgiving, knowing it wouldn't be our last.

"We're good at this," Theo whispered into my ear. And though I knew by then that Theo struggled to hold down a job, that he couldn't help with the bills, that there was a chance that the financial responsibility of our lives might always be on my shoulders, I also knew that we were good at building a family, probably because we could never quite trust our own.

I send Yvette an SOS text though I know she is in the thick of it at work: "Andrea went after me. Wants me to get a temp job answering phones and wearing Republican pantyhose."

It only takes a few minutes for Yvette to reply: "Maybe someone will grab your pussy."

I know I can rely on Yvette to remind me how to laugh.

Since our night in New York, our late-night chats have quickly evolved into pillow talk, and though I have done this before, building something bigger than a friendship but deeper than a fuck, I'm not exactly sure what our relationship means.

"I've never considered myself a lesbian," I tell her one night.

"Maybe you're queer," she tells me.

I laugh. "I thought I was too old to be queer."

"You're never too old to be who you really are, Janey."

I lean back against the wall of my uncle's bathroom as Zoe plays in the tub, wishing Yvette could answer her phone now but imagining she's likely in a late-night meeting with Blake, so strange to suddenly be so close to him once again. And that is what I miss. I miss the energy of the conversation, of spitting out ideas like we were tossing around a ball. As much as Blake went on to break my heart, he had created a space where youthful passion was allowed to fuel the message. We didn't just tell the news—how boring would that have been, Blake used to say—we painted a dream where there was justice, where we fought back. And I can only imagine the conversation they are having now, weeks after the election. I ache to be a part of it. Instead, all I can do is reply to Yvette's text with the two words we have been repeating since the election: "Fuck Trump."

It takes a moment for Yvette's reply: "Fuck Trump."

I take Zoe into the guest bedroom where we have set up her pack and play, using it as a crib for now. Even though so much about our lives has changed, Zoe's bedtime has remained untouched. I read her the same book that Theo bought for her on the day she was born, before singing her "Forever Young," and laying her down in the crib. I step out of the room, slowly closing the door behind me before grabbing my bag and heading outside. I sit down and light my cigarette, looking out over my uncle's backyard, the setting for so much of my childhood—birthday parties, visits with Blake when we would come to California together, and, later, Christmases spent here with Theo. The lighted pool and the jacuzzi where I used to drink beers and smoke joints with Dennis.

I take my first drag and wonder if my mother is right.

Not about Theo. The truth is she has always been right there. By all outdated notions of success and masculinity, Theo did lose; he lost a lot. His ADHD led him to addiction and his addiction stole his dreams. Maybe there was a version of his story where he got it back, returned to baseball, won a championship, but without the structure of school and club sports, his ADHD was too unmanageable for him to make that kind of comeback. So much of our struggle had been over his refusal to take any of the medications that did make it manageable, starting and stopping in rays of hope that ultimately left me feeling betrayed and him resentful. After a while, he stopped coming up with excuses for why he forgot to take his pill, and I stopped believing that he ever would. We had already watched the same dance with his mother, and I saw what Theo's dad had been through because of it.

I knew how our story would end.

I loved him but I also felt like every boss who had ever fired him, wishing it was different, even as they sat him down and said, "We hate to do this, Theo . . ."

Because he was a good person, so confident in himself that he wasn't afraid to love anyone, the opposite of our new president. And those words ring truer than any other insult being levelled against him. Andrea's judgments aren't about Theo though. They are and have always been about me. I am the real loser. I hear the back door open as my mom steps outside. She sits down next to me and removes a cigarette from my pack, lighting one herself.

"You're not the only one that has been hurt by this," she tries to explain.

"Really? You could have fooled me."

My mother sighs as I turn to her. "I'm not getting a temp job."

My mother sighs again, which is almost as bad as calling my dead husband a loser. "Jane, I guess I just see you starting your life again."

"My life didn't end, Mom."

But I know she doesn't mean my life since Theo's death. She is still speaking of an earlier time when I was someone she could brag about.

"I know," Andrea hesitates before adding, "I just think if you were working, you might start to meet people."

"People?" I ask incredulously, knowing where this is going. "Like some rich lawyer?"

"That's not what I'm saying."

"That's the solution though, right? Meet a rich man and somehow everything will be fine."

"I'm not—"

"Because that's where you screwed up, right? You married some dude who just left us in the middle of the night. I mean, when you think about it, Dad killed himself because where else could he possibly go? Once he lost all his money, what purpose could he possibly serve?"

I know my words hurt her, but I don't care anymore. I know Michael wasn't a good man. I know he walked out on us (and that was before he chose the more permanent departure), but Andrea played a part, too, refusing to let him back in when he had nothing left. Though she might have taken on the role of grieving widow when he died, I knew it was an act.

The year after my dad died, an editor at *Rolling Stone* approached my mother for an interview about the aftermath of the 1980s, how greed and drugs had destroyed a generation. Andrea chain-smoked her way through it and came off sounding like a callous bitch who was happy her husband had died. I was only thirteen so, even though I met the reporter, I wasn't interviewed. When I decided I wanted to go into journalism, Andrea pulled out the piece, reminding me of the man who was then running his own show at a major news network: Blake Edwards.

Though my mother said she didn't appreciate Blake's depiction, I thought it was spot-on. Blake saw through her act, which I would later learn was what made him so successful. He could call bullshit unless it was on his own. But maybe that's why I have been so afraid to wear the role of widow. I can't imagine repeating Andrea's fraud, or worse, telling a similar truth. I know in this moment that my mother probably agrees with me: I should have never come back here.

"Janey," my mother interrupts. "It's not that I want you to forget Theo, but I also . . . I don't want you to have to make it on your own."

"Why not?" I ask, as though women don't make it on their own every day across the world, as though she wasn't one of them. "I need the time to be sad. And not sad because I'm back in Redondo, depressed that I'm settling for some temp job away from Zoe, I'm sad because my best friend was killed, and the life we were supposed to share died with him."

What does it mean to settle? I remember Maggie once telling me, there was no such thing as settling. There was only settling down. And I wanted to believe that was what Theo and I were doing. I wanted to believe that Theo was going to figure it out and that he would be okay driving to work every day to be a drug counselor and I would accept being a grant writer and the promotions and slight raises and comfortable benefits would be enough. But with every job Theo lost, with every day I got out of my car at the courthouse, we both wanted more.

We just didn't know how to get it.

"Jane," my mom turns to me with tears in her eyes. "I know Theo loved you, I know you were doing your best, but I'm your mother, and I didn't want to see your life be so hard."

"I know, Mom." I flick the ash off my cigarette. "It's just, Theo, with all his flaws, he looked at me and saw everything I could become. He believed in all the dreams I had yet to achieve, and he didn't care about the ones I had fucked up."

"I know," Andrea replies quietly, still embarrassed by her outburst after dinner.

"Theo knew who I was supposed to be."

"Who's that, honey?" Andrea asks as honestly as she can.

I pause, knowing I don't know how to answer that yet, pivoting instead, "Look, I know you voted for Trump."

"Oh, Jane, what does that have to do with anything?" My mother rolls her eyes at the mention of Trump's name, frustrated by my enduring belief, the one that bonded me to Theo, that politics were personal. They were the reason my father chose suicide over prison time in the face of the S&L crisis. They were the reason children ended up in foster care. They were the reason Martin Montgomery legally purchased an AR-15 and killed eleven people.

"It has to do with everything, Mom. It has to do with the type of world you believe in, and the type of world I believe in. It has to do with the world I want for Zoe."

"And what kind of world is that?" she asks, the exasperation returning.

I stand up. "One that doesn't make me feel like this."

I never wanted to be the prodigal daughter. I didn't leave home planning to one day return, becoming the woman my mother hoped for me to be. I left so that I could finally become me. I put out the remains of my cigarette before heading back inside, leaving my mother to sit by herself, staring at the lighted pool.

SIXTEEN

The driver pulls the car in front of the Hyatt in Tampa Bay as I look down at the strange outfit I have chosen for this trip, taking Andrea's suggestion to look professional. Ironically, it's the same pantsuit I wore the day I voted for Hillary Clinton. "I'll have to tell the president that," I say to myself with a laugh.

I get out of the car and a member of the Hyatt's staff quickly takes my bag. I walk into the hotel where I am scheduled to meet with James Toobin, and, later, Blake and Yvette. A few days after Thanksgiving, James called me to let me know that Blake had pitched him a story idea, and that James suggested I join.

A few days later, Yvette texted me, "You wanna meet in Tampa?" But it was James who explained the plan. After my meeting with the president, the advocacy groups had taken over, trying to negotiate a final executive order.

"The president is making one of his last public addresses," James shared, explaining the invite over the phone one morning. "It's going to be at MacDill Air Force Base. Blake had scheduled to do a sit-down interview with him and then thought it might be a nice addition to invite me.

"When he told me about adding the gun control piece to the interview, I, of course, mentioned you," James adds. I was tempted to tell James what happened the last time Blake and I met, but I figure it can wait until after our reunion in Tampa.

After signing in at the front desk, I walk through the Hyatt. It's big and corporate and reminds me of the type of hotel I used to stay in with Blake. I notice the bay through the back windows, walking over to see the water. I look out at the ocean and then down at the picture Dennis sent me that morning: Andrea feeding my now eighteen-month-old her morning oatmeal. And though watching Theo do it while I walked out the door to a job I didn't want had always inspired frustration, I know I am here for another reason. For the first time in years, I am here for me.

"You got here early?" I hear a familiar voice behind me. I turn to see James, already dressed for the event as well, the pinstripe suit and blue tie, the classic brown shoes and clean white pocket square. I have been searching for father figures all my life, and it doesn't take me long to find them. Yet still, there is a temptation here as James looks out at the bay, his eyes closing briefly to feel the sunrise.

"My flight got in early." I say, leaning against the railing of the patio after him, feeling the warm sea breeze. "I've always loved Florida."

He laughs. "Me too. Cynthia, my ex, and I used to have a house in Naples. We came all the time with the girls."

I've never heard him mention another child. "You have two daughters?"

He nods, without saying anything.

"Is she in Austin?" I ask.

He leans against the railing, alongside me, "I'm not sure. Sara . . . she has her issues. It was hard." He pauses before adding, "She got into drugs and well, I think it's safe to say, she doesn't want to talk to me . . ."

I nod. "Theo and I were sober. I mean, I still am, but . . . There were times I couldn't talk to my mom. I was either ashamed or pissed at her for all the things she did. Sometimes, I was just too messed up to call."

"I think you and Sara would probably like each other." He laughs.

"Addicts usually do."

He stands up straight again, clearly not comfortable with the word. He looks at his Cartier watch, beveled and sharp on his wrist.

"I'm going to refresh upstairs for a moment before we head out. You go up to your room yet?"

I pull my key card and look at it. "Shit. I'm on the top floor. Fancy."

James laughs, the crinkle kicking in again. "You want to head up together?"

I slip the card back into my pocket. "Not yet. I think I need another minute."

I wait for him to leave before I pull out a cigarette, getting in a smoke before I am back on set, thrust into the spotlight of Blake and James and the president of the United States of America. I honestly just want to stand here and be wrapped up in the humid Florida heat.

After I go upstairs to wash off the smoke scent, I meet James at the front door of the building. He ushers me into the waiting Escalade, touching my back gently to help me into the car. It's an innocent gesture, but it still feels intimate. I am professional, coiffed, and even perfumed to cover up my Marlboro Mediums, though they don't call them that anymore, changing the brand during the years when I was no longer a smoker. We are the perfect picture of the future Andrea has been plotting for me my whole life, and likely why she loaned me her own old Cartier for this trip, the one she got when she left the mortgage company.

I get in next to James and comment, "It's been a while since I've been on an air base."

"You've been on one before?"

"With Blake. We . . ." I don't know whether I should say. That we saw the world together? Or just that it was simply my job? "There was a lot of travel."

James shifts a bit in his seat, "I don't want you to think this is weird, but I was doing some research and I found the piece Blake wrote." He pauses. "About your father."

I nod and look out the window. "Yeah, he knew about me before I knew about him."

"Odd coincidence," James remarks.

"The world is made of odd coincidences," I tell him. "Besides, as I'm sure you know, that's kind of a Blake thing. Six degrees of Blake Edwards. He gets around."

I sit back in my seat, getting a better view of James. "Let me guess, you were the popular quarterback, and he was the geek that ran the newspaper."

James throws his hands up. "Guilty as charged. Like I said, we didn't really know each other back then."

"But then you both became rich and powerful men and had something in common," I nudge.

The crinkle returns to James's face, but there is something sad about it. "And I'd say a shared passion. Blake understands my mission."

"Blake understands how your mission drives his numbers," I reply, tired of pretending it's something more noble.

"Do you think?" James asks, as though he is naïve to the world in which we live.

"I'm sure you're friends, James. But Blake is someone who . . ."

I hesitate. What do I say? The affair was consensual but being blacklisted wasn't. Blake didn't just have sex with me, he didn't just promise me a life he failed to deliver, he blocked me from getting the one I had earned, not at night in his bed, but during the years I wrote and produced and created the programming for which he won awards while I was told I wasn't senior enough to walk the red carpet. They never knew I was there, and when it came time for me to cash in my chips, I found out they were worthless.

"I was a young girl, probably not much older than your daughter now, and Blake, he made a lot of promises to that young girl. It wasn't just that he screwed me; I could've forgiven that. It was just he knew how much the work meant to me, and when he took that away, I didn't just lose a job, I lost me. And I didn't know who I was anymore. I know it sounds strange, but I think I'm just finally getting myself back."

I know James doesn't expect this confession. He's not the type that usually receives them.

I look out the window, immediately ashamed. "I'm sorry."

"No." James's voice is stronger than my resolve. "Don't be sorry. I wondered as much after our coffee. I don't know, I could just feel that something happened there. Look, I don't know much about Blake's personal life or what he does or how he conducts himself . . ." He thinks about it for a moment before continuing. "But that's not right. What he did, it's not right."

I don't know why the tears come, but hearing this clean-cut man in his pinstripe suit honor the truth that so many others have denied breaks me a little. It was what made me fall in love with Theo on that first morning, the comfort that came from knowing I wasn't crazy in my grief, that what Blake did to me was wrong. I nod as we pull into the air force base and I bend down into my purse to get my ID, batting away the tears before we pull through the security gates.

I see Yvette first, but I can tell immediately something is wrong. I am expecting a happy reunion as we haven't seen each other since New York, but she gives me a brief hug and peck, offering James the same, before leading us to the press table so we can get our credentials for the speech. It's still hard to believe that Martin Montgomery was once a part of these ranks, standing in line with the rest of the uniformed soldiers who are now quietly filing into the ominous hangar, a blue curtain hanging behind the podium surrounded by American flags. I don't even see Blake as he approaches, hugging James warmly before offering me a similar embrace. "You look great, Janey," he says loudly.

I look to Yvette for a hint on his attitude, but she is ignoring my glances, pretending to be busy. I know there is something she needs to tell me. I send her a text, "What is going on?" but then a murmur passes through the crowd as the first general steps out to approach the podium, introducing the president before he emerges.

I know that most in the room would oppose the executive order we are about to propose to the president, but I also believe that none of us want to see our children massacred or our husbands slaughtered. No one wants to keep a piece of their loved one's skull in a jewelry box next to birthday presents and Mother's Day gifts that haven't been worn in years. No one wants to walk into a bar or a church or a school and hear the loud clap of a gun, the screams, the silence. No one wants to be encrusted in gore, tasting the metal of someone else's blood in their mouth, wondering if they had only done something else, made another choice, the outcome would be different.

As soon as the speeches and handshakes end, Blake and Yvette lead us backstage to a small greenroom that has been set up for the interviews. The president approaches us, greeting Blake like an old friend.

"Blake, thanks for making the trip, though I doubt any of us can complain about this weather." The president shakes Blake's hand with both of his own, before offering the same to James. "James, nice to see you again."

I'm not sure how many meetings James has had with the president, and I wonder for a moment if they were as intimate as my own: if he has cried, begging him to make the changes that would have saved his daughter's life four years before.

Blake introduces the president to Yvette, who I realize has never met him before, despite her wife's own relationship.

"You were married to Diana Wells, right?" the president asks as they shake hands.

Yvette smiles. "I was. She respected you immensely."

The president doesn't let go of her hand. "The feeling was mutual."

Finally, he turns to me.

"Jane," the president says, his voice dropping. He leans in to hug me, gently kissing my cheek like a kind uncle. "You finally got Families United on the executive order bandwagon, I hear."

I laugh and all the tension I felt moments before feels cut by the president's easy response. Maybe these are just people after all, not theories or motives or political positions.

"They're working on it at least."

"You and those executive orders."

"It was Theo's idea, really," I reply, feeling Blake stiffen for a moment at the mention of my husband's name.

The president nods and turns to James. "Is it something you think I can sign?"

"You're going to have to be the judge of that," James replies.

The president nods again. "Well, you know what I'm up against there."

"I do," James replies, as though they are speaking a secret language.

I feel a flash of anger surge through me that reminds me of my husband's temper more than my own. I feel like I am standing outside my body, but instead of staying silent and thinking of all the things I wish I would have said, I say them here.

"I thought that was the whole point of an executive order," I interrupt. "I'm sorry, really, I am, but they can keep their fucking handguns and shotguns. Civilians just shouldn't be allowed to have weapons of mass destruction. How simple is that? Or is the whole point just to watch us shout into a vacuum, knowing our demands are worthless? That our lives mean nothing against their guns."

They're all standing there staring at me. I can tell James is shocked that I am speaking like this in front of the president, and

Blake looks like he's about to laugh, shaking his head as he says, "Jane, I don't know how you ended up in that back-ass nonprofit writing grants."

I feel the sting but know in his own way, he means it as a compliment.

I smirk. "You know why."

Blake's face sours as he changes the conversation before anyone else can see it, but Yvette sees it, tossing a knowing glance in my direction. She asks the president, "Shall we start the interview before they whisk you back to DC?"

"Let's do it," the president replies, hugging me again as he leaves. He tells me, "I'll do what I can."

It's not a guarantee, but it offers the one thing the president has promised: hope. James and I go back out of the room and wait on two folding chairs in the hallway.

"You know what I used to do professionally? Before all this." James asks.

"I've done my research, too, James. You ran a law firm. Corporate litigation. You're still involved, right?"

"I don't manage it anymore but, yes, my name's still on the wall."

"But you're still a lawyer," I reply. "I mean, you believe this can be settled out of court, that it can be negotiated out."

"I don't think there is ever a true win, no." He looks down. "We're up against a lot of powerful forces, people who don't want to lose their supporters, their funding . . ."

"Their power?"

"That, too," James admits.

"But how can change ever happen if no one is willing to surrender their power? If no one is offended by it. I mean, what happened to Theo and Rachel. *That's* offensive. That is what we're up against.

"James . . ." I grab his arm, pleading with him, hoping that the raw place in him, the heartbreak he flashes like a business card hears my own. "We can make it stop. I believe that."

He nods and the tears come to his eyes, just as they did on that first day when he attended Theo's funeral and showed me the pain seeping beneath the surface. We wait for Blake and Yvette to come out before we go on set.

The cameras and lights are waiting for us as Blake prepares for our interview, doing the same warm-up routine he used to undergo every time he was on location, as though he needed extra vocal rehearsal when he wasn't on his own soundstage. Then the cameras are rolling, and Blake is smiling his famous half-smile, the one everyone loves to see in their living rooms at night. He turns to us like we all just met and asks, "So, how did you two come together?"

At first, James leads us through the conversation, not treating our initial meeting as the formal interview it was but, rather, two people coming together in a shared grief.

"And Jane," Blake focuses on me. "Are you part of Families United now?"

I laugh. "Not officially, but I agree with what they want to do. You know, at one of our FBI briefings, an agent told us that with a handgun, it's a murder. With a semiautomatic, it's a massacre. If our leaders can't stop their own people from being massacred, who will?"

James agrees, breaking in, "It's not just victims or survivors either. Martin Montgomery's mother has joined us, parents are begging for help. People don't want to see their loved ones on either side of an AR-15. We all agree that we need to make it stop."

The interview wraps as Yvette calls cut and the grips pull the lights and the boom, and a part of me relaxes for the first time all day. It's already evening.

"I think you two have something you need to discuss?" Blake asks Yvette, motioning to me.

"We do?" I ask.

He leans in to hug me again, like an old friend. "I can't wait to hear what you think, Jane." Blake turns to James. "You free?"

"Sure. I could use a bite." He shrugs.

"Great. Come with me. Yves, you want to catch a ride in Jane's car?"

"Sure." Yvette takes me by the arm, leading me out through the now empty hangar before I have the chance to say good-bye to either man. As we get back in the Escalade, I see that it's 10:00 p.m.

"Oh shit." I pull out my phone. "I need to call Zoe."

"Made that call myself while you guys were taping," Yvette shares, lying back in the seat and closing her eyes while I check in on my mother and daughter, saying good night and giving kisses through FaceTime before Andrea puts Zoe down. After I hang up, I lean my own head back. I am exhausted by the day, but also the old me feels alive again, illuminated even in my fatigue.

"What's going on, Yves?" I ask her.

"I need a drink," Yvette replies, refusing to tell me.

"I need a cigarette."

"Good. We'll sit outside."

When we arrive at the hotel, we find a table out on the patio. It's a quiet corner where we can hear the waves lapping in the warm night. I breathe in the humid and heavy air and tell Yvette, "I think I might move here."

"Really?" Yvette looks around. "To Tampa?"

"No, not Tampa. Miami maybe? Key West? I always loved the Keys."

"You gonna be one of those women wearing palm tree dresses and lots of beaded jewelry?"

"I was thinking more like Hemingway."

"Hemingway shot himself. You know that," Yvette replies as the waiter shows up with our drinks. She practically snatches her glass of wine from the waiter, drinking down half of it.

"Life is a funny motherfucker." I exhale the drag of my cigarette as I see James inside the restaurant. He is sitting down with Blake, whose back is to me. He is watching me, and I smile in his direction. Yvette follows my gaze.

"He's handsome," she comments.

"He is. And he is also exactly what I have been trying to avoid for the last ten years of my life."

"Success?" Yvette asks.

"No," and I suddenly realize why I chose Theo. "Powerful men."

You were a girl then," Yvette interrupts. "But you're not anymore. You're a grown woman. And maybe it's time you get over it. All of it." She takes a deep sip of her drink before continuing, "Jesus, Janey. You've got Families United writing an executive order for the president, something they have failed to do since they started. You've had one of the biggest trending hashtags of the year, and, with one interview, you fucking changed the landscape James Toobin has been courting for years."

I feel the truth of her words, yet they're still hard to accept.

"You cannot continue to be an asshole." She grabs my cigarettes and lights one.

I crack up laughing. "An asshole?"

"Yeah, an asshole, move to Florida, Key West of all fucking places, wear muumuus."

"I never mentioned muumuus . . . "

"You don't want to live in Florida, Jane."

"Then where else can I afford to go?"

Yvette eyes me warily. "What about returning to New York?"

"I said, afford. Honestly, Yvette, what am I going to do there?"

"Work for us," Yvette announces. She pauses, bracing for impact as her words move across the table. "But as talent, not in production."

Suddenly, everything comes into perfect focus: the water lapping against the side of the building, the chatter from the bar, the sound of Yvette's fingers rubbing the edge of the menu.

"Blake is launching a new program, a roundtable," she continues. "He's looking for some new blood, and he liked what you did with Krystal. He wants to have you on."

"Oh." I try to find a reply. "Like, for an episode?"

Yvette smiles. "No, for, *like*, the series. It wouldn't be every night, but you can negotiate an episode minimum. Something that would make it worth the flight . . . or the move."

I laugh. "The move?"

"New York."

I sit back, in shock. "To work with Blake?"

Yvette smiles, but it's a sad smile. "And me."

"Yves, if it was just you, I'd say of course, but is Blake the way? I feel like if I asked Theo, he would say no."

"Theo's not here."

I suck in my breath; I don't know how to explain this. Or if I should.

"But he is."

She looks at me and I can tell she's wondering just how many drinks she had.

LIVE THROUGH THIS

211

"Not, like, in a Patrick Swayze kind of way."

"Phew," Yvette laughs. "I was going to start singing 'Unchained Melody.'"

"But when I close my eyes, sometimes, it's like I can visit him. I go back to the bar, the Mojave, and I find him there and . . ."

I can see her getting worried again but then she sees my tears.

"And we talk."

I smile. "I know it's weird, but he's told me not to give up, and I know he's right, but wouldn't going back to Blake be giving up?"

"It's not going back to Blake. It's a starting point, Jane. You said it yourself, this is your do-over."

"And I also said, I have to do it right this time. Jesus, Yvette. It wasn't just the affair. I couldn't get work anywhere. You remember that, you told me yourself, it was just a matter of time—"

"It was," Yvette interrupts me. "But you went home and gave up. And now, you're giving up again."

"I'm not giving up. Fuck, Yvette. I came home and was a mess. And sorry if I didn't feel like ponying back up to the table. I was sick of it all."

"But you loved it!" Yvette practically yells and I see she's had more to drink than I realized.

I reply, quietly, "I did, I still do. But how can I work for Blake Edwards, Yvette? After everything."

"What other choices do you have?" she asks me, and I realize she's not wrong. I hear my mother's words echoing about temp jobs and nonprofits, and I know I can't go back to that either.

Yvette leans forward, the wine whetting her tongue. "Look, Blake's a terrible fucking person. He is. But we've helped shape the message and not just some weird corner of it. The entire fucking thing. And it's terrifying because, really, we're just a bunch of idiots, but I care about this shitty world and if any idiot is going to do it, I'm glad it's me . . ."

Yvette puts out the half-smoked butt she has bummed from me, standing unsteadily. I see her face shift, something foreign and odd shadowing her face, and I realize it's anger.

"Yves, where are you going? What's going on?"

"There's one other thing I need to tell you. Blake knows about us. I don't know how. He made me sign this crazy clause this week. Basically, I can't have intimate relationships with anyone on staff."

"What?" I ask, shaking my head.

"That's ridiculous, Yves. Then done, I'm not going to take it."

She shakes her head angrily at me. "Jane, no. We'll figure it out. Maybe not now, but one day, and, honestly, one day when you're ready. But if you want change, if you want to have a voice, if you want to fight for Theo, *this* is your fucking chance." She sways for a moment, as I get up to help her. She puts her hand on my shoulder like we're just two old pals, but her eyes say something else. "I just want you to know I was really looking forward to seeing you tonight."

I feel a pain I haven't felt in years, not grief, but heartbreak, acute and deep, like she's scooped out a part of my chest. "I haven't even said yes to the job."

"You will. You better. I'll call you tomorrow, okay?"

"Okay." I stand there, wanting to say no to the job, wanting to grab her hand and offer her the one thing she deserves, but I can see the same resigned look in her eyes that for such a long time lived in mine. As powerful as Yvette Morales is in the world, her constraints don't look so different than mine did, knowing we can do more but undermined by Blake's whims. Yvette deserves her freedom; it's just her reward has become too big for her to see any other way.

She starts to walk away before turning around to say, "You did really good today, Janey. Remember that."

Finally, I head inside, passing the bar. I notice the back of James Toobin, who sits alone. I hesitate but know there is nothing I can say, and I've already watched one drunk friend stumble to their room. I take the elevator up, leaning against the wall as the exhaustion hits. My flight leaves early the next morning, and I am now heading toward a twenty-four-hour day. I arrive at my floor and start to walk down the hallway when I hear the elevator ding behind me, the door sliding open.

I know someone has followed me, and I half expect to see Blake step off the elevator, never one to miss an opportunity at a hotel, but instead I am surprised to see James Toobin stumbling gently toward me.

"James?" I ask, walking toward him, thinking he might be lost.

"I remembered what you said," he slurs as he reaches me, holding out his hand to steady himself. I take it, worried that he needs help.

"What?"

"That you're staying on the top floor."

And then I realize he isn't lost at all.

"It wasn't right what Blake did to you," he starts to share, his eyes crinkling up at the corner again. "I would never do that to you."

"James, you've been drinking. You need to go to your room. Do you remember your room number?"

"Can you take me there?" he asks, moving closer to me.

There was a time when I might have said yes to this pathetic display, but Yvette is right, I have grown up. "James, please. You don't want to do this. You want to go back to your room."

Though he's drunk, he can still compute the rejection. He straightens a bit, acting as though he arrived here on accident.

"I'll just find my room then." He starts to back up, letting go of my hand, and feeling for the wall.

"Are you okay?" I ask again.

"Nope, angel." He shakes his head and turns around, hitting the down button to the elevator. "Haven't been for a long time."

SEVENTEEN

I stand in Maggie's bedroom looking at a full-length mirror. "We look like escorts."

Maggie ignores my comment, turning me back around to streak cat-shaped eyeliner across my lids, adding just enough red lipstick to make me look French. I can't imagine spending New Year's Eve without Zoe, so Maggie has negotiated this night out instead, making plans for us to get dinner and drinks at the Ritz-Carlton.

"I've been invited back to New York," I tell her as she continues with my makeup.

"For Blake's show again?" she asks.

"In a way . . . it would be a new show. I mean, Blake would be on it, but I would be a regular guest. Like, I would move there."

Maggie pauses while applying my lipstick, "Is that what you want?"

"Honestly? Yes. I mean, a part of me does. I want to be part of the conservation, and now more than ever, that conversation needs to change. I don't know. There is so much about it that feels like a solution but not the right one."

"Because of Blake?" she asks, returning to my makeup. "I was there for all of it. I hate Blake Edwards, too, but fuck, Janey, if you can get your career back, why let him stop you?"

"Well, there's a hook. I can't be with Yvette if I do."

"You gonna date girls now?" she asks as she heats up a curling iron for my hair. Maggie's directness throws me off. I know she doesn't consider me gay, only knowing me with men since we were in high school.

"I've fucked women before."

"Yeah, but have you been in love with one?"

"I don't think I could be in love with anyone right now. I'm still in love with Theo." I can tell by Maggie's look she doesn't believe that either.

"I am. Jesus, Maggie, it was just six months . . ." I stop, remembering that day, sitting in Dennis's house, shocked that only half a year had passed since the day Theo died. And as I sit here now, I can't help but feel guilty that I'm betraying him just by getting dressed up and going to the bar. That if I closed my eyes and went to the saloon, he would be there with a sad look in his eyes, the one he only reserved for me when I had gone too far in one of our fights. "Shit, I don't even know why we're going out like this tonight."

Maggie kneels in front of me, "You don't have to run off with anyone, Janey. Okay? You deserve to have fun. You need some fun."

"So do you." I smile.

"I know! So let's get out of here!"

It's almost been five years since Maggie's divorce was finalized. Last year, Chris remarried, settling down with a twenty-six-year-old law student. She had a son from a previous marriage who Maggie's own son immediately befriended. William now prefers to spend weekends at his dad's with his stepmom and "brother," leaving Maggie more alone time than she can likely bear. Her solitude has become her armor, but it is also her heartbreak.

Maggie smiles. "We all get to decide what we need to heal, Janey. You can do it however you want to, whatever is right for you."

She pulls out a plunging burgundy lace dress that narrows into a V just below my solar plexus, reminding me of something a Kardashian might wear. It's still in a dry cleaning bag from 2010, so I can tell she hasn't brought it out since the divorce, back when she and Chris would go out on the town. I slip on a pair of Maggie's Louboutins as she quickly polishes my nails, so I don't "have hands like a goddamn farmer." I feel sexy for the first time in years.

A few days after I returned home from Tampa, I received an email from James. It wasn't long, but it said what it needed to:

Dear Jane,

I cannot begin to say how embarrassed I have been over what transpired in Tampa. I have truly respected working with you, and I recognize how crude my actions might have felt. I want you to know that is not the kind of person I am. But I also want you to know that my intentions were not untrue. I know you are nowhere near where you would need to be to consider any romance right now. I understand you are still deep in grief, but when the time comes, know that my admiration for you goes beyond the professional. I am not afraid to say that, and you can take it as you will. I thank you for your work with Families United. You have pushed us further than we thought we could go, and I know that our work is far from over. I hope you can forgive my behavior and continue this fight together.

Sincerely,

James

It was businesslike and kind and so James Toobin, innocent even in its insult. Everyone gets drunk and does stupid shit, but I also know that had I said yes, had I agreed to James's drunken proposition, the respectful email would likely not have been sent afterward. It's in my denial that I have won James's admiration, which makes his feelings even more suspect.

I slept with Theo the first night we ever hooked up. I tried not to, playing coy and saying no, but then the intensity of our chemistry took over and I was ultimately the one to unzip my jeans and move on top of him. The next day, Theo treated me like his girlfriend, but men with power frequently play a different game, using consent as a sign of conquest. Maybe James is different, but I doubt it. I hit reply but kept it brief.

Dear James,

We all have rough nights. I look forward to continuing our work and thank you for the apology.

Speak soon,

Jane

I closed Safari and then I saw it, December 27th, two days after Christmas and six months since the shooting they now refer to as Mojave Saloon. I don't want to go back there, but then again, where else do I have to go? Instead, I see the icon on my computer for the Photos app. I have avoided it for months, trying not to look too far into my computer's memory. I opened it up and quickly scrolled through the photos of the last few months, going farther back, watching the years tick by like a clock in reverse: 2015, 2014, 2013, 2012.

2012.

I heard my breath catch. I knew I shouldn't open it. But then the photos began, the great download of our life, lined up like a firing squad. I sat in my uncle's kitchen, the sun glistening on the pool outside as I watched the photos unspool. Of course, they showed the best of our adventures, not the fights and financial fears. But then the computer froze, landing on a photo of me standing alone, posing naked on the final day of our honeymoon. We didn't ask for cooking sets or serving plates for our wedding. We just asked for money so we could travel, going to Europe to visit Paris and Italy and Greece. On our last few days in Italy, we traveled to the southern town of Matera. I remembered Blake once recommending the stop, saying that everyone should see Matera once. We decided to take the long way down, flying into Pisa, making our way across the less traveled Southern Italy, listening to Bob Marley who we preserved like jam, listening to him only on road trips and vacations.

"Keynes believed, like Marx actually, that the goal wasn't the four-hour workweek, but rather the twenty-four-hour," I said as we drove through the mountainous roads of Southern Italy. "That way, people could explore what they were really put on earth to do."

"Yeah, but they would never let that happen," Theo argued, ever the believer in the invisible "they." "Then we'd have time to revolt."

I laughed. "Yeah, that was the idea, too. If we had equity, we'd create art. If we didn't . . ."

"We'd create revolution," Theo offered.

"They'd rather keep us overworked and exhausted," I said, looking out at the grey sky.

By the time we made it to Matera, the clouds had turned into sheets of rain. Theo navigated our small car across the narrow twists and turns of the mountain roads, finally bringing us to the ancient town that was the goal of our pilgrimage. Matera was carved out of the belly of a mountain, limestone walls and curving paths, buildings sloping their way down impossible inclines. At once cruel and mysterious, at other turns touched by the sacred, only God's hands could have carved Matera, and then like a master builder frightened by his own talent, he abandoned it before finishing the job.

The year I got sober, I remembered watching this one episode of *The Sopranos* where Carmela goes to Paris with a friend. The friend just wants to shop and flirt with the waitstaff, but Carmela has a different experience. As she stands in a set of ruins near St. Germain, she realizes the fleeting mortality of our history, telling her friend, "We worry so much sometimes, it's like that's all we do. But in the end, it just gets washed away. It all gets washed away."

But Matera, in all its unfinished perfection, was a reminder that some things remain.

We went down to swim in the hotel's pool, which was built into an underground cave, the sounds of the rainforest drifting through

the hotel's sound system. In a rare moment, our chatter-filled relationship felt quiet, expanding horizontally across the surface and
into the deep end. We made love upstairs before heading out into the
city. In all our years together, we were never so solid, so immutable,
so made of skin and bone and muscle and heart and dreams and
fears and the knowledge that this, was just the beginning.

We walked down the carved granite steps of Matera, led on by
the unexpected sound of a thrashing guitar. Deep within the limestone crevasses of the millennia-old city, someone was playing psy-
chedelic surf rock from California.

"It's like a Tarantino film," I laughed.

Theo was quiet for a moment. "It's like home."

We followed the sounds to a small bar carved into the side of a
wall as foreign and familiar collided before continuing our adventure. The town was empty, already abandoned by most tourists in
October. We walked alone, sharing the sights with a handful of
feral cats who ran as we approached, prancing along the roofs of
the stone-carved buildings as though the city was built for their
small feet alone.

Though the music was long-gone, Theo stopped, and in a rare
move, he pulled me into his arms, as we began to dance. We weren't
a couple who slow-danced. Our whole relationship moved too fast
for it, filled with conversations and adventure and fights and the
deep and unreliable overwhelm of Theo's disorders and my inability to ignore them. But there we were, alone in this ancient city,
knowing even then that we would be the only people to share this
memory, to ever know this moment. And so, I leaned into Theo's
chest and in that limestone square, he didn't feel like the burden-
some brother he would become, he felt like my partner, my husband, my love.

We danced back to the hotel room where he undressed me in the moonlight and fell on top of me in the small twin bed of our tiny room as we laughed and made love and believed that yes, darling, we might just make it after all.

The next morning, Theo took a photo of me. I had just gotten bangs, finally far enough from Andrea's judgment to chop a thick line right above my brow. I was standing naked in front of our hotel window, the light streaming in behind me. The limestone hills and houses of Matera framed my body, a *Mona Lisa* smile on my face, slightly shy and unquestionably bold.

I sat in my uncle's kitchen and stared at the picture. What surprised me the most was how little I had changed. Same belly, same breasts, same hair. Though I was now working with an entirely different operating system, the shell hadn't changed.

M aggie and I head out to the Ritz-Carlton at Laguna Niguel, sitting at the bar like two working girls in our red-soled heels. Maggie drinks a glass of champagne as I sip on a cranberry and soda. I notice David as soon as he walks into the hotel bar. As though she can see me watching someone, Maggie turns around on her barstool, offering David and his friend Brandon an inviting glance at the low-slung back of her dress, the fabric draping only an inch above her ass.

It doesn't take long for Maggie's dangerous smile to draw them to our side of the bar. They are both Black and handsome and as soon as they sit down, I can tell Brandon is the bolder of the two. David is the wingman. The men quickly offer to buy drinks and are amused when I don't accept the offer.

"You pregnant?" Brandon asks me.

Maggie views me cautiously, like a teacher overseeing a test. She's skilled at this flirtation, knowing how to say just the right thing at just the right time with just the right voice and an easy cock of her head.

"No, just sober." I try to keep my answers short, sensing Maggie's judgment as the master quickly takes over the conversation, turning the attention to Brandon and David, asking why they're there (business), where they're from (Chicago), and if they want to buy a bottle of champagne for the three of them.

"Don't worry," Maggie assures our new friends. "Janey here doesn't drink, but she still knows how to have a good time. One of the best dancers I've ever met . . . and she does it stone-cold sober."

"Really?" David finally turns to me. "Girl can dance?"

"Like my life depends on it."

"So, tell me what sober means?" He leans in as I get a better view of his face. He looks like a movie star, tall and built, with high cheekbones and eyelashes that curl up along the edge.

"It means I hit my quota too early."

"Ah." David sits back, leaning against the bar. "So, you're an alcoholic?"

I'm surprised he gets the reference so quickly. I wonder whether he's also sober, which would be like hitting the jackpot. Before responding, I check to see if Maggie is listening, knowing she'd be mad if I go there in the first five minutes.

"I am. And you?"

"Me? Naw. I know how to have a good time, but I keep my shit together."

He stops, looking at me as though he had just realized something. I'm not sure if he recognizes my face or if my voice is triggering the memory, but I can tell he is trying to place me. To his credit, he doesn't say anything.

"But we do share one thing in common." He smiles.

"What's that?"

"We love to dance."

"I'd say that's a pretty good start." I feel bold in this tight and plunging dress, crossing my legs so he looks down at my calves, the light sculpting out the shadows of my ankles.

A smile creeps from the corner of his mouth as he replies, "It is."

The night progresses with easy small talk, some light politics, and, finally, where the party should move to next.

Since both David and Brandon have rooms at the hotel, it's a simple enough progression to head upstairs. Maggie and Brandon finish the bottle of champagne, the booze making their fingers bold as they get closer to one another on the couch in Brandon's suite. David has only had one drink the whole night, staying sober next to me.

It's clear Maggie and Brandon want space, so David and I excuse ourselves.

"Don't worry about me," Maggie calls. "I'll just catch an Uber."

As we leave Brandon's room, I reach into my bag to find my valet ticket.

David stops me, following my hand into the purse, holding it gently. "Don't do that."

"David, you're lovely. Really, you are." I pause, knowing I can't unload the truth on him right here. "But my situation . . . it's difficult."

"I know it is," David says, lowering his voice to practically a whisper. I pray he doesn't say what we have both been thinking for the last two hours—I am that woman whose husband was killed in the shooting last summer. Instead, he just smiles, an open and friendly gesture. And in his offering, I appreciate the anonymity that I have struggled to find elsewhere. I just want someone to not know me, to not tell me what I'm supposed to do, or who I'm supposed to be. I want someone who just wants to be with me without all the heavy lifting of what happened in a past that I still don't know how to explain.

"Anyway," David adds. "We haven't danced yet. Come to my room. At least do that."

Here I stand, in yet another hotel hallway, but David's request isn't a drunken plea; it is a sobering request. And I get to make the choice that so many times before didn't feel was mine to make. That woman I once was—hungry and free—rises to the surface, buoyant even in her grief.

"I'll give you that," I say with a smile, leaning into David as he leads us to his room. Once there, he doesn't break his promise, plugging his phone into the stereo, and putting on some Billie Holiday. I confess to parenthood for the first time all night. "My daughter's middle name is Holiday. We named her after Billie."

I feel a dull stab in my gut, thinking of my sweet baby at home, the little girl who still feels so lost in all of this, even as she acclimates to Dennis's house and frolics in Kindermusic and twirls my hair with her fingers in the morning while we lie in bed, and I thank whatever energy controls this mess for her life.

David smartly ignores the "we" pronoun, perhaps feeling my distraction, the fault line in every mother's consciousness between the life she has with her child and the one she desperately tries to protect for herself. Instead, he pulls me against his tall frame and dances with me, just as Theo and I did that one night in Matera but failed to ever do much of again.

It doesn't take long for David's lips to find my neck, quietly kissing his way up to my face. Our kiss is so passionate and tender it takes me by surprise. Even from my first kiss with Theo, our chemistry always felt safe, but as my hands begin to move across David's chest, as his fingers began to inch up my skirt, I am reminded of how much I love having sex with a stranger. No backstories or easy friendships. No future to worry about or fantasies to indulge. Just the pure, present moment of the fuck.

And he's not Yvette either; he doesn't quite feel like home, but there is something here that feels so simple, no strings, no conflicts. I'm moving up and down on David's body, groaning into his shoulder, as he grabs me in all the right places. He bites at my breasts, his cock full and deep in me as I arch back and hear him moan. My body shakes and I slump down on top of him, both of us out of breath and laughing.

David wraps his arms around me, taking care of the condom with barely an interruption. He is so kind and gentle and warm. I fear I will quickly regret this rash decision but to my surprise, I am asleep in minutes.

I wake with a start. Though it's still dark outside, I can feel daylight creeping across the sky. I reach for my phone, which is dead. Then I remember there is a man sleeping next to me. And he is not Theo.

I get up quietly, removing myself from David's embrace. Pulling on the tight dress from the night before, I am reminded of countless other mornings where this was my life, slipping out of Blake's bed to go home and change my clothes before work and, later, when I was hitting bottom in Redondo, random men whose names I can barely now list. But for so many years, I woke up to the same warm body, untouched by that unnecessary spike of shame.

It's already 6:00 a.m. I don't even look in the bathroom mirror as I grab my purse and creep toward the front door.

"I'm sorry, Jane," David announces as I open the door. "About what happened. Your husband."

I stand there frozen, trapped between the fantasy we created the night before, and the reality in which I have once again awoken. I don't say anything, knowing that if one word slips from my mouth, it will crack my resolve like stone against glass. I just nod my head and close the door behind me.

I get in the car and plug in my phone, calling Maggie to see if she wants a ride. She texts me back that she's staying for breakfast. I drive out of the hotel garage, and begin to sob. I don't know my way around this area, trying to distinguish streets and signs. Finally, my phone turns on. I pull over, wiping at my eyes before calling Dennis.

"Is Zoe awake?" I ask, afraid my baby is crying for me.

"No, she's still asleep, honey. We're all good here. Are you okay?"

I'm not sure if it's my tone, or simply that Dennis has had enough one-night stands to know where I'm coming from.

"I'm fine," I lie. "I was just worried about Zoe."

"Don't worry, honey. I got her." My uncle is confident in his skills now.

I hang up the phone and try to breathe. I close my eyes, searching in the dark for the Mojave Saloon, trying to find Theo. I want to go home, back to the safety of our old bed, the comfort of our home, the boredom that I once felt suffocated by. I just want my husband back. I miss my friend, the person I could turn to and say,

"What the fuck am I doing?" But I find nothing but darkness. I hear my phone ring and open my eyes. It's Yvette. She doesn't even say hello. "You have a minute?"

"Technically." I put the car in reverse. "I'm about to start driving."

"Don't. Wait one second."

Yvette puts me on hold, as she clicks over to the other line. I look out to see if any cops are coming, hoping my hazards are enough.

Finally, Yvette clicks back over. "Are we all here?"

"Jane?" a familiar voice asks. I quickly try to compose myself as I reply, "Hello, Mr. President."

"I'm so glad we got you on the line," the president begins. "Though I wish my call was under better circumstances."

"Better circumstances?"

"Well, we've been working on that executive order. I've had my people on it the last few weeks." He pauses before explaining, "But Jane, as I said when we met, it just isn't that easy."

I nod numbly. I feel like I am back in that exit interview when the HR person offered me the deal I never should have taken. The powerful working to protect the more powerful.

"Really?" I reply.

The president sighs. "You should know we tried everything we could, but we have a new administration to contend with, and, the truth is, we just don't know where things are going at this point. But Jane, I want you to know I did try."

I watch as people begin to make their way across a parking lot, heading to work. I wonder if anyone really gets the power a bullet can command.

Finally, I reply, "Thank you, Mr. President."

"Good luck, Jane. Maybe we'll meet again out there."

"I hope so, Mr. President," I reply, unsure what *out there* might look like for us both.

"Jane, are you still on?" I hear Yvette's voice ask as the president hangs up.

I'm quiet for a moment because I don't know how to tell Yvette the answer I know is the right one.

She continues, hearing my breath, "We can fight this, Jane. We'll get you on the show, we'll tell them—"

"I can't Yvette."

"What?"

"I can't do the show with Blake. I love that you want me on it, I wish I could but . . . "

"Jane, no, you can't keep doing this. You can't keep giving up."

"I'm not, Yves. I promise you, I'm not. But Blake is not the way."

"Who says? Your ghost husband?"

We're both silent for a second and I want to laugh but also, I want to say yes. Yes. I can't keep betraying him and I can't pretend what happened ten years ago didn't occur just because that same man is now offering me the one thing that I wanted the whole time. There is the form of harassment when someone denies you a job if you won't fuck them, but it is also harassment when they deny you the job because they're done fucking you.

"I'm sorry," Yvette stutters, and I'm more shocked by her apology. "I know the Blake thing is weird, but I just don't want to see you trapped out there. You've done that for long enough."

"I get it, Yves, but I feel like everyone wants to tell me what I need to do—James has his plan, you have yours, Andrea's laying out the pantyhose as we speak."

"You know, I grew up with a mother who was abused and used and spit out by a boss that might as well have been Blake Edwards, fuck, he might as well as have been Donald Trump—"

"Blake isn't Donald Trump," Yvette interrupts.

"Isn't he, though? I realize he talks about the powerless and caring for people, but he's a predator, too, Yvette, in his own way, and I'm not going to let my own daughter watch me surrender just because I can't come up with a better way to take care of her."

"Sometimes we don't have a choice," Yvette replies, and I can tell she takes my statement personally.

"Oh, Yvette, we do though." I smile as I pull into the parking lot of a local strip mall. "And it doesn't mean we have to carry their guilt but there has to be a space where we stand up, right? Where we say no. But I've got to figure it out on my own. Or at least I need to figure it out without Blake at my back. I need to figure it out knowing that Theo would agree. Ghost husband or not, I am finally getting the chance to get it right. I owe him that, Yves. I owe Zoe that."

Back when I was seventeen and had just graduated from high school, I went on a date with a high school dropout who had already spent time in rehab. Nick Palermo had a six-pack and a sleeve of tattoos long before they were commonplace. I helped him get his GED and motivated him to find a real job, something beyond dealing weed out of his dad's apartment. On our first date, I asked him to take me to a tattoo parlor around the corner from my uncle's house where, using a fake ID a friend had given me, I had three small stars inked on my left boob. It was the first and only tattoo I ever got.

For years, I threatened to get others: "Los Angeles" on the inside of my left arm and the maligned last lines from Keats's *Ode on a*

Grecian Urn ("Beauty is truth, truth beauty") upon my hip, but I was always stopped by a naysayer—Andrea, my uncle, even Theo, who told me to wait until I was sure. I decide to add one more, "Live Through This," scrolling down my arm.

"How many can I get at once?" I ask the tatted receptionist behind the desk. Ever since the election, it's hard not to judge whether you think someone has voted for Trump. Fairly or not, I look at the woman's over-bleached hair and Harley-Davidson T-shirt and assume she did.

"Depends what you're doing," she replies, barely looking at me.

I smile, a *Mona Lisa* smile, the kind one adopts when the only thing they have left is who they really are.

EIGHTEEN

I wait in the coffee shop in downtown Los Angeles, less than a
mile from my old office, sipping on coffee, waiting for James
Toobin, who has scheduled my appearance at the Women's
March today. I invited Rose along because she was planning to go
anyway. Also, I'm not quite comfortable meeting with James alone
after our last experience. Though I appreciated the apology, it feels
like a safe correction to bring a friend.

"Is this what you want to do?" Rose asks me, as I leaf through
the speech.

"I want to get up at the podium," I stop. "Theo wants me to get
up at that podium."

I close the speech and smile. "Remember what a great speaker
he was?"

Rose and I used to love when Theo shared at AA meetings, his
honesty resonating with everyone in the room but also his rawness.

He never looked down, staring straight out into the crowd like he feared nothing.

"Fuckin' Theo, man," Rose remembers.

"Fuckin' Theo, man," I reply. "I want to give a Theo speech. I do. I want them to know what we lose every time we don't stand up. I want them to know how much we've already lost."

Yvette is also concerned about me doing a speech written by Families United.

"We don't know what these marches are going to look like yet," Yvette tells me over the phone. "And fuck, if you're going to speak at one, come to DC."

But DC terrifies me. And LA feels safer. LA is home.

I know Yvette is annoyed by the outcome from the president, and not just on this issue. She has friends in DC. She knows how every decision made by his administration is now vulnerable, and the people coming in are bullies. They prey on vulnerability. But her bigger concern these days has been the new show.

"What's Blake planning to do about the new president?" I ask.

She hesitates, which is weird for Yvette.

"What's up, Yves?"

"I'm looking to leave."

I take a deep breath. Though someone like Yvette should have left years ago, I also know that being Blake Edwards's producer came with a cache that was hard to top. Who else could she possibly work for?

"Some of the streamers are looking to have their own news shows. It's a new era, whether we wanted it this way or not, the conversation is changing, Jane."

"That's amazing."

"Yeah." She laughs. "I mean, you'd think I wouldn't be terrified, but I guess I'm more like my parents than I thought. Working in the same kitchen at the same restaurant for thirty years, just watching opportunity pass by."

"Yvette," I beg her. "Please, for me, do not let go of this one. You can be doing so much more than working for Blake Edwards."

"Yeah, the crazy part though is that if he finds out before I secure a deal, I fear I won't get one."

"God, is he still that powerful?" I ask.

"No, just that vindictive."

I wonder again if I am making the right decision working as the spokesperson for Families United.

Yvette doesn't make the choice any easier, offering before hang up, "I'm not saying Families United isn't legitimate. I respect their work, I do. But you should be out there sharing *your* message, not theirs."

I have written grants with words like *equity* and *resiliency* and *empowerment* so many times, but I could never say whether people were more equitable or resilient or empowered by the work. At a certain point the language of change gets snuffed out, losing its meaning and its power. And this idea of advocacy, of the ways in which we move from A to B, whether we rewrite the laws, bring down or rebuild the system, find some justice in this world, can just as quickly became a copy and paste job, and not real impact.

James walks in and I can tell he is thrown by the friend sitting next to me. But then he gives me a game-day smile, hugging me like a coach before the big scrimmage as he exclaims, "I knew you could do this."

As though that moment in the hallway and his follow-up email never occurred, we return to the warm, platonic relationship we had begun to establish. I know that, before anything, James is a businessman who sees me as an asset to his brand. I get that they have been waiting for someone who can amplify the message that keeps being forgotten as soon as the echoes of the last shooting fade. But I'm still not sure I'm the right person.

Andrea is oddly hesitant about this appearance, and I wonder if this is the source of my own confusion. My mother never seems to know what she wants for me, and despite all the ways in which we see the world differently, there is still a part of me that wants her to be proud.

"You don't want to be connected to this forever," she warns. "At some point, you want to be able to move beyond the shooting."

James reminds me of my mom: coiffed, professional, unblemished. I'm sure he fell apart after his daughter died, but he's sewn himself back together now with presidential meetings and mission-driven suits.

I look at his nails. They're short and clean, but he can't hide the shredded cuticles around the edges. I notice the tan line where a wedding band once lived. I try my best to smile, to offer him the Gen X cheerleader he hoped I would be, young enough for the kids, but mature enough for my fellow suburban moms. "I guess we have to find some piece of normal now, right?" I ask.

"You do eventually." His voice drops. "But it's always there, Jane. It will always be there."

He pulls a binder from his briefcase because he carries a briefcase, placing it in front of me. "Your speech."

But I have my speech," I reply, looking down at this new draft. It is all carefully scripted. I know this is what Yvette was worried about.

It's easy enough. It holds our politicians accountable. It addresses the NRA. It asks that we be heard. But it is also mechanical. It is the same speech that gun control advocates have been giving since the Brady Bill. It sizes up the height of the mountain but fails to move it.

"This isn't the draft you sent me last week? The one we worked on?"

"Our communications team spent a lot of time on it." He scrolls down a few pages. "We added in there, 'make it stop,' you know, like you said."

"Oh," I reply as if this makes the speech more exciting.

People think less loopholes will stop stop an AR-15. But I know what an assault rifle can do. And I'm just not sure that civility can remain the response.

"Is this the speech you want?" Rose asks and I can tell James is annoyed I brought her.

"I hate to say it, Jane," he interrupts. "But you agreed to the speech we approved."

I shrug, knowing I can't make many changes at this point. "It works."

James eyes me warily. "Jane, it's very important that you follow what's been laid out here. I understand you were just speaking for yourself on Blake's show, but today, you're representing the movement. Today, you're speaking for all families."

I'm wearing the leather pants I wore in New York with the one item I saved from Theo's drawer. Though I hate message T-shirts, I am wearing Theo's bedtime shirt, the one line repeating itself down the front: "Stop the bully. Stop the bully. Stop the bully."

He softens. "I know this is strange. It's weird to lose something so personal, so intimate, and then find yourself with a new career because of it."

"I just want to make sure that I am doing it in a way that honors Theo."

"I understand that." I see the flash of pain on James's face. His loss cuts with a different blade. He lost his baby. And though Theo and everything that disappeared with him feels irreplaceable, I still have my child.

I breathe in deep. My child.

That's also why I'm here. Because she has to know I spoke up. She has to know I didn't watch her father die only to fade back into the crowd.

"I'm ready," I announce. We both stand and James hugs me again. He holds on to me a little longer, as though I am the child he lost. For a moment, I know he asked me here not just because he thinks I can bring the movement something, but because he hopes it brings me something, too.

We take a car over to the Women's March where the Families United team has convened near the stage. The crowds are thick, and traffic is rerouted around the site.

James, Rose, and I are ushered to the stage as people throng around us. I've been to enough protests to know the rush of a crowd, but usually they have been in foreign lands. Americans don't usually do this; for a country that is always at war, we're still not quite sure how to fight. Instead, we make signs, knit hats, and believe that someone will help us if we're nice and say please.

That is what my script advises. Be nice, say please, and maybe they'll make it stop.

James and I are brought backstage and then I see him.

Blake stands slightly off-stage, surrounded by a group of female producers and assistants, huddled around their famous boss as though he might keep them warm. He looks up and sees me. A strange look crosses his face, as though he was waiting for this moment. He walks away from his flock and up to me.

"Janey." He smiles at me with his eyes, and I know Yvette has told him that I turned down the offer. A part of me wonders if he knows about James's request at the hotel, feeling sick that I might have been part of some locker room talk. "You too big for me now?"

I shake my head. "That's not what this is about, Blake."

Blake looks bloated again, like he did back in September. He leans in and I can smell the evidence on his breath as he nearly hisses, "Just remember, Janey, don't act. When you act, you come off as fake."

"I'm not sure that's true anymore." I bat away his insult even as I'm suddenly unsure of the script again, knowing that Blake will see right through it, knowing that it's exactly what he would have expected from me. He wants me to lose my resolve, he always has.

"Well, you know yourself best," he replies, and I remember exactly what it was like to work for him, the kindness just a disguise for his criticism. "But fear smells like fraud."

"Really, Blake?" I smirk. "Because I'm pretty sure fear smells like three martinis before breakfast."

He smiles, refusing to be pierced by the dig. I hear them announcing my name, as James returns to my elbow, greeting Blake with a friendly handshake as my introduction begins. The bio is short. The fact that I worked as a fundraiser or an associate producer for the alcoholic narcissist that is Blake Edwards is meaningless in the face of why I am here.

I am here because Theo is dead.

I walk out on the stage. There is a sea of people in front of me. I clutch the papers provided by James and walk up to the podium. I move the lectern down to meet my lips and close my eyes. I try to pretend I am at an AA meeting, just giving a share. A well-prepared, legal-reviewed share. I look down at the words and begin to speak. "My name is Jane Karras, and on June 27, 2016, my husband was killed in a mass shooting."

I stop there. I slide my hand in my pocket and feel for the one totem I refused to leave behind. I pull out the sliver of Theo's skull that has stayed with me since the shooting. After talking to Yvette, I knew that if I was going to keep begging for the truth, I needed to be able to stand on my own, no matter what it cost me. Though I respect Families United, though I respect James and his pain, I know that I'm not just tired of looking down, I am tired of looking out at the long arc of history, waiting for it to bend. It's time for it to break.

"This is my husband's skull." I place it on the podium in front of me. I can hear James whisper my name from the side of the stage. I close the speech, and stare at the small piece of bone, the only remnant left of this living, breathing, loving life that wanted nothing more than for all of us to stand here and demand something better than what we've been given, but especially for those who have been given the least. I look up at the crowd and begin.

"When I was twelve years old, my father killed himself. He was an alcoholic, he was in debt, and he put a gun, *a gun*, to his head and pulled the trigger . . . Because this is America."

"Jane." I hear my name whispered again. I look at the last piece of Theo as I continue.

"But my mom and I survived. For twenty years, she worked for a boss who sexually harassed her the entire time. When she finally left the company, he gave her a fucking watch.

"And yet, her sacrifice gave me a 'better life.' I am privileged. And I am here in front of you right now because of it. I went to private schools. I had choices many of us do not. Because this is America."

James has stopped trying to silence me, and a similar lull falls over the crowd. I can see Blake from the corner of my eye, the women standing a few feet behind him as he watches from the edge of the stage.

"And when I was twenty-two years old, I got a job working for one of the most famous men in New York. I spent five years fucking him and when he was done fucking me, I, quite literally, never worked in that town again. But what can you say? This is America."

A murmur runs through the crowd. I know there is a legal document I have just violated—a promise to never mention our relationship in return for six months' pay—and I can feel Blake just feet from me, his anger palpable from the sidelines.

"The thing is, for a long time, I didn't believe I should be on a stage like this. I thought, *who the fuck am I?* Just another anonymous woman paying her bills, fighting with her husband, trying to raise a child, always in debt, frustrated by the things that didn't work out.

"When Theo, my husband, and I first began dating, we used to have that famed Margaret Mead quote on our fridge, 'Never doubt that a small group of thoughtful, committed citizens can change the world. Indeed, it is the only thing that ever has.'

"But when Theo died, I realized something, we can't change the world by staying silent. We have to speak up against the powerful, against the performative acts of change, and against the ultimate perpetrator, the one that put a hole in my father's head and eleven holes in my husband's body. It's the one that almost left our one-year-old baby with no parents of her own. It's the one that takes away daddies and mommies and children and friends. And in this country, it's not just a meme or a trend or breaking news on fucking CNN, it is state-sanctioned murder. Because, this is America."

I pause as the audience cheers and screams, knowing that changing the world feels bigger than any plans I've had in a while, when most of my goals were around getting a raise at work and finding a preschool that felt safe for Zoe, but as I stand there, I realize that this is the window. Because if we don't stand up, if we don't tell the truth, if we don't bear witness to what has happened to us, the arc will just keep spooling out in front of us, justice forever out of reach. I think back to Theo, I close my eyes, I am alone in the saloon, and he is on the stage, and he is staring right at me. He whispers to me from across the room, "Roar."

"And I'm not sure we can stop an assault rifle with a knitting needle . . ." My eyes narrow as I utter the words, "But we can certainly take out an eye.

"Because I am tired of asking for people to make it stop. We are going to make it stop. We are going to show them that this is *our* America," I nearly snarl into the microphone.

"So let's take our anger and our power and begin to deny them. Deny them when they ask for our money. Deny them when they ask for our taxes. Deny them when they ask for our bodies and our minds and our pleases and thank yous. Because we are the light, we are the eternal spark, we are the tempest. But we are also the mother fucking storm.

"And we are going to roar."

The crowd roars in response as I pick up my husband's bone and the speech that James gave me. I am about to leave the stage when I hear the thunder from the crowd. I turn to face them as the wave of applause hits me. The tears are now wet and heavy on my face. I walk off to where James stands. I hand him the speech.

Though the tears have stopped, my voice still quakes. "I'm sorry but I can't keep lying."

I walk up to Blake who is already dialing someone. Knowing him as I do, I center myself and lean in. "When you talk to your lawyer, Blake, why don't you ask him what the truth smells like?"

I don't stay to hear his reply. Rose is at my elbow as she leads me out through the backstage, and out on the streets of Los Angeles, the city that has been my home, the place where I married Theo and birthed Zoe, the city that healed me.

She laughs as we make our way through the crowd, "Fuckin' Jane, man, fuckin' Jane."

NINETEEN

I walk outside into the California night. It is unseasonably warm, feeling more like summer. I carry Zoe to the car, wearing my pajamas with a coat too heavy for this balmy night. She won't sleep. I'm not sure if it's her molars or her personality or all the stress of the last month, bombarded by posts and comments and media attention. It's only a couple days later when I get the first call: "We're going to tear you down, you fucking cunt," an angry voice growls.

I shouldn't be shocked by death threats anymore, yet my face grows red, not from anger but from embarrassment. It's a pedestrian form of humiliation like my credit card was just declined. I'm not sure if it's my emotion or Andrea's shame that I am carrying. Then again, I've been carrying my mother's shame my whole life.

Since the Women's March, Andrea has been staying with us at Dennis's, fearing, unrealistically or not, for her life.

"They have my address," she says, glaring at me. I feel bad. Although I don't believe any of the threats, the last thing I want is for my mother to be scared.

Maybe that's why more people don't stand up. You become vulnerable when you kneel on the field, when you raise your right fist, when you stand apart from the easy opinions and scripted material. It's safer to compartmentalize the truth, and I am seeing first-hand the fear that happens when you attempt to disrupt it. It comes in the form of internet comments and posts and memes. It comes in the form of phone calls and awkward looks at the grocery store. It comes in the form of someone coming up to me at the playground and telling me that I'm too angry to be a mother. It comes in a million different voices and armchair discussions and opinion pieces about what is too much.

"We can't advocate for violence," talking heads say on various talk shows.

I wonder if they're as tired as I am of treating anger like a default setting, pretending it's stress or work or life. We idle in it and then wonder why we can't progress.

The night before, I finally spoke with James on the phone. He thanked me for my honesty, but explained gently that I wasn't a good fit for their organization.

"We've been doing this a long time, Jane," he told me with his usual calm. "And we know that change is slow and hard, but it takes a certain level of patience."

"We've practiced patience, James. And your daughter and my husband are still dead."

Despite the waves of people who disagree with my speech, there are many more asking for my voice. I receive daily offers for interviews and panels and presentations. For every death threat or cruel comment on Twitter, my name also shows up in kinder posts.

It only takes a matter of days before the lawsuit arrives from Blake Edwards. I have broken my NDA. They are suing for my severance plus $1,000,000 in damages. I laugh as I read the document.

My mother does not. "What's going to happen now?"

She shakes as I look at the lawsuit, overwhelmed yet somehow, not afraid.

"I've always told you," she continues. "You keep your mouth shut, you keep quiet. You don't know what these people can do."

"What are you talking about?" I look around like I've just entered another dimension. "I just lost my husband to what people can do. Mom, you can live in your denial, but I can't."

"And what—we're just supposed to take care of you while you bring this down on us?"

"I never asked for you to take care of me."

"Well, someone has to," Andrea clicks her nails against the kitchen counter.

"You know, Mom, sometimes I think the most revolutionary thing I've ever done was to marry Theo Karras."

"It wasn't revolution, Janey," she shakes her head. "It was just you rebelling."

I can't help but smile at her belief that any request for power is a symbol of adolescence. "Rebelling? Why? Because he didn't care about money or staying silent or playing some stupid fucking game? Because he believed in doing the right thing?"

"I think we have very different versions of what that means," my mother admits.

Dennis finally interjects, "Come on, you two. We have enough here to deal with."

He takes the lawsuit from my hands.

"What a creep," he says as he reads through the suit. "All right, time for a lawyer."

A few days later, Maggie and I take Zoe to South Coast Plaza; I am scheduled for three interviews next week on various news programs, announcing the new organization I have become a part of creating. The week after the Women's March, some of the women involved in its creation asked me about helping them launch a new advocacy group. Something more radical than Families United, uniting mothers who are especially determined to see the laws changed, just as mothers did with MADD, taking down drunk driving.

It took us one conference call to agree on a name: Mothers Organized for Change.

"MO-Fuck?" Maggie asks me as we drive to the mall.

"I prefer Motherfucker." I laugh. "But yes, close enough."

"So, you got a job? Andrea happy?" Maggie smiles like it's a nudge.

"It's not what she would have imagined, but yeah, she feels like it's going to give me 'lots of new opportunities.'"

I sigh but Maggie knows me too well to let it ago. "You're not profiting off him, Jane."

"I know. I mean, it's good work. It's great work. It's what I would have wanted whether he was alive or not."

"Then what?"

"Maybe I'm just not ready to be happy yet."

"Mmm-hmmm." Maggie looks out the window.

"What?" I can sense her judgment.

"You think you're ever gonna be ready to be happy?"

"I've been happy!" I argue, knowing that I wanted to be happy but after a while, I gave up, and then no matter what I did, I just stopped seeing the wonder. I couldn't see it in my job, in my marriage, even in my love for Zoe. I raged at Theo but really, I saved my sourest resentments for myself.

"Janey, just because you thought you'd be better without Theo doesn't mean you can't be better without Theo."

I catch my breath, unable to process the truths I still hide from. Maggie continues like an overbearing mother, as though I don't already have one of those. "Have you called David?"

Maggie and Brandon have continued to date long-distance though Maggie doesn't think it will go anywhere, which is why bringing up David feels hypocritical.

"No. How are things going with Brandon?"

"Don't change the subject," she replies though she is also changing the subject.

David texted me a couple times since that night, but as I finally explained to him, I think I only have one night in me.

"Zoe's my focus now . . ." I hesitate. "And figuring out what to do next."

I smile at Zoe in the rearview mirror, and she giggles, "Mama."

She is talking more and more now, moving from a baby into her own little toddler personality, making us laugh and chase her around. And she inherited Theo's and my shared trait of stubbornness. I know my work will take me away, but I also know that I won't sacrifice Zoe for it. I will fight to be her mother, every morning and every day of her life. I will fight to show her wonder.

"Has Andrea been helping?" Maggie asks.

"Of course," I admit, grateful for how much my mother has shown up for me in these last few months. "I mean, it still comes with a price."

"Everything comes with a price," Maggie replies. "She's probably bummed you didn't get that life insurance. You could have bought the condo next to hers," Maggie adds.

I laugh, both at the truth of her comment and how well she knows my family. We were raised in each other's homes practically. I know her parents as well as she knows Andrea and Dennis.

"Anyway," Maggie continues, "no matter what you do—the organization, this media tour, your revolution—at least we're gonna make you look good for it."

The whole point of our mall expedition is that Maggie is tired of my "worn-out mom look."

"You look tired," she chastised me a couple days before.

"I *am* tired."

"So is everyone. Doesn't mean you have to look it."

We go to Nordstrom where Maggie pushes the makeup girl aside. Finding just the right eyeliner and mascara and lipstick, she starts applying the makeup like she runs the place. When she finally swivels me around, even Zoe squeals, "Happy!" her one-word expression for pleasure. After months of looking like someone whose husband has died, I actually look like me. My hair has grown out and it's wild and wavy again. My lips are full and my eyes are clear. But most of all, I don't look angry.

Tears come to my eyes, and Maggie smiles. "Makeup is magic."

I hug my oldest friend. "No. *You* are magic."

We take Zoe to the toy store where she gets blind bags of *My Little Pony* and *Peppa Pig*, her favorite TV shows. Between her choice in programming and her love of princess gowns, I might be raising myself a Maggie.

As we drive home, the sky begins to deepen as though a storm is gathering.

"So stop dodging the question? What's going on with Brandon?"

A sly smile crosses Maggie's face. "I don't know. He's coming to town next weekend."

"He's coming to town?"

"For work," she replies, pulling out her phone.

"Do you feel like there's something there? I mean, do you like him?"

Maggie looks out the window, so guarded even now, "I might."

"Maggie, it's okay, you can let yourself get hurt again."

She pauses before shaking her head. "I don't know that I can."

I look down a lonely suburban street, the homes all uniform in shape and size, their landscaping mimicking each other as well. I remember growing up here, knowing the floorplan to every home.

"You can't avoid it, Mags. None of us can. And I don't know. Sometimes getting hurt is just the price we pay for living more interesting lives."

Maggie puts down her phone. "Janey, not every life has to be spectacular."

"I didn't say *spectacular*," I begin to argue. The storm clouds threaten as I drive Maggie back to her place in Costa Mesa. "We don't have to stay the same person, you know. I remember this Viktor Frankl quote, 'The last of the human freedoms is to choose one's own way.' You are free to choose whatever way you want. We're all free to change."

"Jesus, Janey. I don't know."

Maggie looks down at her manicured nails as I try to find parking on her street. Zoe has finally fallen asleep in the back. "I guess I've just gotten good at being alone. Because here's the thing, I get to be me when I'm by myself, and I never got to be me with anyone else before. I had to be some perfect thing all the time and now, I'm a woman who doesn't need a man to be her mirror. I don't want to be someone else's façade, Janey."

I wonder if Theo was just that, a reflection of myself, but one that blinded me to the real Jane. Maybe I was able to look the other way during our relationship, too, as I gave up on my dreams, taking a job I hated because someone had to be counted on to pay the bills, settling into the sacred mediocrity that was our life.

In a way, marriage always requires that you disappear a little. In becoming one with someone else, parts of you must be discarded, even if they're some of the best ones.

I pull up to my uncle's ranch-style home, with his modern urban landscape, the hedges lined up in synch with his neighbors. Zoe is still asleep in the back after dropping Maggie off at her house. At first, I don't notice anyone at the house until after I've put the car in park, but then I see where Yvette sits on the front step. I roll down the windows and get out of the car, leaving Zoe to nap in the back. I walk up and hug my friend, so grateful to see her again.

"I'm sorry I didn't call before coming," she says, returning the embrace.

"What are you doing here?"

"I don't know," she looks lost in a way I've never seen her before, even years ago when she was new to the work and just learning the ropes, her assuredness felt unbreakable.

After my performance at the Women's March, the floodgates on Blake's behavior broke. In fact, had it only been one or two other women, everyone could have said, "Things happen in the heat of the moment, long hours, nights at the bar . . ." But as the news was beginning to report, Blake had sexual affairs with almost every assistant on his staff at one point, often with the carrot of career advancement dangled before it. My departure finally makes sense in ways it didn't before—the NDA, the way I was rushed from the scene of the crime. There were so many women, so many silenced complaints, so many damaged careers. When bad behavior is endemic, its coverup can only be conspiratorial. My sad, little story was quickly becoming just one page of a very thick file.

Yvette sits down on the step and confesses, "I just quit."

"Good for you," I reply, joining my friend on the step.

"I feel like I should have done this so long ago," Yvette admitted, her sad gaze filled with the same regret that has flogged my life for the last decade. "It wasn't just the money, we had built something here, Janey."

"I know you did, Yvette. I was there, too, remember? And we did build something."

"But does it count if it was all lies?" Yvette asks me, and I realize she is trying to figure out how much power she had in the situation herself.

"Did you know?" I ask, even though I know there was no way she couldn't.

"I knew there were affairs, of course. It's not like it ended with you, but my God, fucking everyone had affairs. There was so much drinking and travel, and you know, it was Blake.

"But no, I didn't realize what happened to them after they left. I was tracking their careers. Fuck, my wife was sick and then she wasn't dying and then I had two kids and a huge job, and I spent a lot of my time with Blake alone. And some did continue to work. I would see them at functions as they moved up the ranks. A lot of people do unacceptable things."

I look at my friend and I think about all the dreams both of us have had. We came to this work wanting to do the right thing, to expose the predators, to give voice to the silenced, and yet somehow, we both became a part of the machine—only amplifying the voice of the predator and becoming silenced ourselves.

"I thought I would be able to fix it," Yvette admits. "I thought that if I got my own show, I could reverse the years of feeling that I worked in his shadow. And I know I should have left earlier, I know I should have paid more attention, but I became a part of it, too. That apartment, our lifestyle, I couldn't just quit."

"Yvette, you're not Blake Edwards."

"In some ways, no, I know that. But also, I can't help but feel I'm on a spectrum, here. I know it's what you've struggled with, too. We want things to be different, we feel maybe we're the right people to make them different, but does that necessarily make us good people? I know it's easy to call someone a monster, but it's harder to see where you might be one, too."

I sit back and look across this suburban neighborhood that my uncle and I have called home for so long. The rows of tract homes and nine-to-five jobs, the Priuses and Hondas in the driveways, the simple pleasures and still hard times of modern American life.

"I don't know, Yves. I guess you were right when you said, whether we like it or not, we've become a part of history. We either chose to be on that stage or we got pushed on it, but we're here. And this shit ain't gonna get better, we know that. You want to keep quiet now or do you want to get out there and make some noise?"

"But isn't it just more drama?" she asks. "That's what I'm finding out. I thought I was doing the good work and it was all someone else's fucking soap opera."

I grab her hands. "But if we disappear, we just give them a bigger role."

I stop and I can feel her energy, the cracks in her armor only making her more beautiful, more human. Who knows what draws some people together and others apart? What scent of attraction or old history tells us this is the person we must meet, we must fuck, we must marry, with whom we must mate. The strange call from across the room that carries us into someone else's arms, the echo that keeps us there.

I know I don't have to say it, and yet I also know I do, confessing to Yvette, "I fucked someone."

She just laughs, "Well, I hope you didn't call all his potential bosses and prevent him from pursuing a career."

"No, I just felt like, I don't know, that you should know."

"Jane, we're friends and I don't know, maybe there is something here. I'll admit, I would love for something to be here. But look, I remember those days after Diana died. I was drinking and I would wake up in beds wondering how the fuck I ended up there. Grief does that.

She squeezes my hand in return. "I believe in you. I do. You're one of the reasons I started to have those conversations. Because I believed we could create the programming we used to talk about. We could Trojan horse a revolution."

In that moment, I can feel what it would have been like if Yvette and I got together, a power couple transforming the medium of television. I can feel the awards programs and red carpets. I can feel what our future might hold.

She shakes her head. "The fucked-up part was that I had been talking to a streamer about launching my own show. After you said no to *The Blake Edwards Hour . . .*"

"Was that what they were going to call it?" I start to laugh.

"Yes," she replied. "Horrible, I know."

"But no one will call me back now," Yvette continues. "I can't imagine after all those years, I'm now the one blacklisted. I guess it's a common side effect working for Blake."

"It shouldn't be," I reply. "Fuck, Yvette. We shouldn't continue to be punished by his behaviors. We have to find a way to get ourselves free."

I watch Yvette look out at my car where we can see Zoe still asleep in the back.

"We've got to feed them somehow, right?" she asks and I know that even with all her wealth, Yvette is still a single mother, still the only person on whom her children depend.

"We will." I grab hold of her hand. "We will."

Hours later, I pull out of my uncle's neighborhood in the middle of the night after fighting with Zoe to go to sleep. These are the hardest moments now, the ones where I used to have a partner I could turn to and ask, "What should we do?"

Theo and I never had to drive Zoe around. Between the two of us, we were always able to get her down, but now it's just me, and I am out of ideas.

Andrea returned to her condo last week, feeling safe again since the internet has found another focus - the new president's issuance of an executive order banning immigrants from predominantly Muslim countries.

I don't know what else to do as I head toward Palos Verdes, where Maggie and I went to high school, where we used to party with Chris's friends. I could have moved here, married the lawyer, strolled my kids to the local park, driving my Lexus SUV and carrying my Louis Vuitton Neverfull into Neiman's to buy some makeup and a pair of earrings for the gala fundraiser. I could have done all that, but I know I wouldn't have been any happier.

I keep driving, passing the bars and hotels where we used to drink and do drugs, thinking that we were on top of the world at twenty-three.

Now, I'm thirty-six. As I dropped Maggie off that day, I confessed to her, "I thought I could be safe or happy—but not both. It was either a staid life living here in Redondo or being married to Theo, or some crazy existence where I might be on a red carpet or I might be dead."

"Janey, it doesn't have to be one or the other. You can find quiet and still be happy."

"I'm not sure," I replied. "I know that we all have our choices to make, but I don't think it's about making the right choices. It's about making the choices that feel right to us."

"We're getting there." Maggie smiled, gathering her things.

"I leaned over to hug my oldest friend, before watching her walk back to her townhouse, a scaled-down version of the life she thought she wanted but ended up being the right one all along.

As I turn down the PCH, I think back to what Maggie said about Andrea, that she just wanted me to be happy. I see her high-rise condominium jutting up along the highway in the distance. I pull into a visitor's spot in the parking lot and get out of the car quietly, not wanting to wake Zoe as I lift her from the car seat and carry her into my mom's building. The security guard waves us up. Though I have keys, I knock on the door. Andrea is half-asleep but she immediately reaches out to me, worried. "Are you okay?"

"I'm fine," I reply, and for the first time since the shooting, I mean it. "Zoe couldn't sleep."

"Come in, come in," my mom welcomes us. I put Zoe in my mother's bed as I hear my mom putting on the water kettle. When I was in high school and she would come home late from work, we would meet in the kitchen for tea. I walk in to find her taking out two cups.

I stand there in silence for a moment.

"There is a part of me that wants to leave this relationship," I finally tell her.

She turns around and I can see the panic in her eyes.

"You can't leave your family," Andrea argues.

"Yes, you can. Mom, I can't separate who you are from what you believe, any more than you can do that to me. I am what I believe."

"Janey, it's just politics," she shakes her head, unable to see the divide that politics has always created, even as the fissure is quickly becoming a canyon.

"Politics just killed my husband, Mom. It killed him while he lay on top of me."

"Sweetheart," she moves forward and grabs my hands. "I understand that. I do. I saw you, too, you know. I saw you and I thought, Jesus Christ, what happened to my baby? But that doesn't mean you have to go out there and air our dirty laundry. Tell people we're traumatized or something."

"No, Mom. It's to show how traumatized we all are. Look, I don't know how to be your daughter if you can't see what I'm doing here, why I'm willing to sacrifice our safety. I mean, Mom, imagine it had been Zoe that night. Imagine I didn't walk out."

She shakes her head as she pours the water into our teacups, "But you did."

"Exactly. I survived. And you're right, you saw what they did."

"What *he* did."

"Who? Martin Montgomery or Theo Karras? Because that's it, isn't it? You just don't want me championing him. And yeah, the marriage? It was a rebellion but Theo stood in contrast to all this bullshit—the parking tickets and the taxes and the ways you and me and everyone are forced to pay for people who couldn't care less about us."

"We pay because it's our responsibility. It's about *being* responsible."

"To who, Mom? To people who let guys like Martin Montgomery buy that gun? Responsible so Blake can do what he did? Or so Michael can blow his brains out because he didn't want to go to jail over, what, money? Money is the thing? That's what we're responsible for?"

"Yes," my mother replies with every ounce of her being.

"Then what about love?" I ask. "Theo loved me, Mom. He loved me unconditionally, something I had never felt before, except maybe from Dennis. And he showed me how to offer that love to Zoe. How to love her without condition."

"I loved you that way too, Janey. My whole life."

"Loved. And you did, as long as I agreed with you. As long as I wanted the same things, but I don't want to sacrifice love for my vision of how I am supposed to live my life. And I did that, I did that with Theo. I regurgitated all these lies to him—about responsibility and money and yes, we had to pay the bills, but I didn't have to hate him because he couldn't. And you don't have to hate him either."

"I didn't hate him, Janey," she looks down into her tea. "I just wanted someone to take care of you."

"But he did. Just not in the ways you think a woman should be taken care of, but you didn't have that, Grandma didn't have that. Maybe we just don't need it. Maybe we are just too damn good at taking care of ourselves."

"It's exhausting, though." My mom slams down her teacup. Suddenly, she looks so small. This woman has spent so many years alone, the demands and joys of partnership are an unknown language, one she's heard before but can't decipher. And as she gets older, the loneliness has settled into her high cheekbones and deep-set eyes, raising the bar so high for everyone around her, no one can pass, including me.

"It doesn't have to be, Mom. That's what I'm trying to say, what I'm trying to do. And I want to be your daughter, but I'll tell you right now, if you can't have any compassion, or connection, to who I am, then why pretend?"

"But I do love you, Janey," she practically whispers, her eyes wet. "So much."

"I know but I need you to be able me to trust me, too."

I can tell there is a part of her that wants to say, yes, I do. But she doesn't know how to let go of the system on which she has built her whole life.

I push away my teacup, "I can sleep out here."

"No, no," my mom replies. "Go sleep with Zoe. I'll stay on the couch."

I pause, not wanting to let my mother help me, not wanting to feel like I owe her anything, when the interest is so high.

"She's your baby." My mom looks down into her tea. "She needs her mama."

I just nod my head and go to sleep next to the little girl for whom my love knows no bounds, and I pray it never learns.

TWENTY

I turn off the 210 onto Rocky Peak Road, driving through the mountains that surround Box Canyon. Woven into their rocks are deep and large caves where some of the Manson family once hid, lending an eerie quality to the large brown boulders heaped up into the sky. The Santa Susana mountains feel like they are out of the American Southwest with barely a tree dotting the landscape of the bedrock plate. They were a part of the trading crossroads between Tataviam, Tongva, and Chumash people, stretching west to the sea, and inland to the Angeles Forest, which was right above our former home, a reminder of the length and legacy of the great land on which we have all attempted to live.

For years, Elissa's house, a meandering Spanish villa with work trucks and a teepee in the front yard, was my temple. In the little room where Elissa held her sessions, I emerged from my family's anxious cocoon. It was there that I accepted I would never be a well-coiffed executive in a corporate office building, becoming instead the type of woman who believed in magic and rocks and alchemy. And because of that, my life choices would be rooted in a different code, one where the problems of the world couldn't be ignored or absolved by its luxuries.

"Have you ever been to the Manson caves?" Rose asks, sitting quietly in the passenger seat as Zoe sleeps in the back.

"Theo and I tried to find it once after a sweat, but we never did," I explain as I pull off into Elissa's neighborhood, houses perched at the base of the mountains, the large rocks looming overhead. Rose and I have been here together during happier times, but she is coming with her own wound today.

"You would think I could walk into a venue without flinching . . ." Rose has been trying to get back into music again, but she struggles at the shows. She looks out the window.

"It's just not fun anymore, I guess. And I don't want to do something if it's not fun."

Instead, she has been hanging out with us in the South Bay, helping with Zoe as I begin to spend more time working on MOFC, even if that doesn't feel quite right either.

We park in Elissa's yard, which doubles as a parking lot, and get out. I look around the property that I have visited so many times— before Theo, with him, and now after. Elissa once introduced me to the life beyond this veil, showing that if we were willing to trust the journey, we could find our truths in the dark.

A group of women stand around an open fire, already cooking the rocks for the sweat. I see Elissa from across the yard, and smile as she sees me, too.

The week before, I called Elissa, having failed to return any of her calls after Theo's death. "I don't know what to do," I finally choked over the phone. "I just know I don't know how to do this. I don't know how to do any of this."

The last few weeks have felt like years, as time rushed by, every day another allegation stacking against Blake Edwards as everyone in his sphere ran for safety. The one thing that protected Yvette in the end was that, much like with me, she didn't know what the inside of Blake's life looked like. From the outside, it looked like a consensual affair, instead of the abuse of power that left so many women like me without a career.

Yvette called to tell me the bad news, "The streamers aren't calling my agents back. They say it isn't looking good."

"I don't understand." I try to make sense of it. I know Yvette doesn't want to blame me. My voice catches in my throat, worried that I stepped out too hastily, if in all my anger, I couldn't see my own privilege. Straight, white women have a history of perpetuating these cruelties, thinking they are fighting for equality but only to their own advantage, and yet, this is what Yvette has been asking me to do this whole time.

And yet I can't help but wonder whether I've fucked it all up again. Just like I did in New York a decade earlier, I pulled out the wrong Jenga piece, making the whole structure fall. If only I had played nice, gone along with the plan, I would have gotten what I wanted. More importantly, I wouldn't have lost the thing I loved.

I am trying to throw myself into the advocacy of Mothers Organized for Change. I am back in the thick of fundraising and program building and looking at data to determine whether the great and brilliant plans we seek are legislatively possible. But the series of meetings ahead of us don't feel very different from the job I just left.

As I tell Rose along our drive, "I feel like I am going back to the same world, writing the grants, making the asks, doing the thank-you letters. I don't know, Rose. I haven't done all this just to end up back where I started."

Andrea is hopeful that I will find something stable out of the organization, but I know even as I begin to meet with other women who have lost husbands and brothers and sisters and wives and children to these horrible shootings that I am tired of pretending our tragedies are enough to solve this.

"I can't do this alone, Elissa," I whisper to this woman who years before helped to save my life and who now holds me in a firm embrace in her yard, her hugs an artform.

I've always had a troubled relationship with faith. Although, I'm not sure there is any other kind. I had tried and rejected so many religions throughout my childhood: Catholics, Baptists, Methodists, Episcopalians. I even went to the Scientology Center, hoping to find some easy relief in their personality tests and informational videos but as Elissa told me when we first met, faith is in the seeking. I believed her when she said that our flesh was but an envelope. That the light within was the truth. And in Elissa's sweat lodge, I found my church, a place of dark and peaceful worship where I made prayers for everything I wanted when I was newly sober and finally believing in life again: a husband, a child, a family who cherished my light.

When Elissa invited me to the sweat, she asked me if I wanted to bring my own people, those other women like me, the ones who shared my grief. I reached out to the quickly burgeoning numbers in Mothers Organized for Change, along with Rose, who I know needs her own healing now, each of us wearing our survivor's guilt in different shades, but in this moment, they all feel like the same color.

The world is teetering, and we can all feel it, the furniture is sliding across the room, and we are hanging on to the doorframe. Everything we thought we knew and loved about this country feels uprooted, tossed about by a horrible tornado called politics, but also something far more subtle and hostile, fear. And everywhere around us, we feel it. We feel it in the quick succession of executive orders being issued from the new presidential office, and with each one, I feel the failure of the one we put forth.

I once told Theo that I got into nonprofits believing that for every problem, there were a million solutions. He shook his head. "There is only one solution. A million solutions just mean there is none."

And his one solution was that everything needed to change.

I step into the teepee where the women do their prayers before the sweat, immediately recognizing a few women from the organization. We all hug each other, as Zoe runs around the large structure, squealing before falling into one of the beanbags that are scattered about for guests. The women all agree to take turns watching Zoe.

Finally, Elissa joins the group, opening the ceremony with a few clear shakes of her rattle, which we pass around as we share why we are there, what we hope to experience.

She smiles deeply, "I've been thinking a lot about this sweat all week. And I want you all to know that it takes enormous courage to face the totality of life without withdrawing from it, without trying to shield ourselves.'"

Elissa finally catches my eye. "The question is, how can we embrace tragedy on its own terms? How can we find that affirmation of life that comes when we have been broken by it?"

This is what I owe Zoe—I need to show her that she doesn't need to be afraid of the dark. Even as the bullets echo, even if I can smell the dust and beer on the ground, the scent of gunpowder and Theo's flesh, we cannot hide from the tragedy of this world at the cost of its beauty. I want the passion to flow so freely through Zoe's blood that she never has to question herself. I wonder whether healing from trauma isn't about resiliency at all. We will break. But rather, true healing is about generosity. When we no longer live in fear of the world around us, we can truly become a part of it, we can love from the most generous space, the place I wasn't able to offer Theo in the real world, but that I am learning to offer him now.

Elissa slowly beats her leather-bound drum, singing quietly while alternately pouring water over the rocks, which hiss and steam into the blackness as the women release their pain and stress and frustration through guttural noises. Some cry, some scream, some laugh, others stay silent.

I lie in the dark and remember my first sweat lodge with Theo. We had found each other hot and sweaty in the dark during the third round. As people howled around us, Theo kissed the tears from my face and I licked the sweat from his neck; animals in the dark, we clung to each other. After that first sweat together, we took a hike in Box Canyon, catching glimpses of the Santa Susana Mountains as we made our way through the hilly path, trying to find those elusive Manson caves.

"I sometimes think it would be nice to live up here," I told Theo.

"Chatsworth?" Theo asked.

"No, just away from everyone. Close enough to visit but like, you're in the middle of nowhere. A place where you can create your own life, by your own rules."

"We could get married here," Theo added, coming up behind me, kissing the base of my neck, sliding his hand around my waist.

"Married?" I laughed. "We're getting married now?"

"Yeah." Theo turned me around, so we were looking at each other. "Not now, but someday. We'll get married."

"You seem pretty sure about that . . ." I tried to act like I hadn't been thinking the same thing.

"You're not?" Theo asked, as he walked me backward to a grassy patch off the trail pulling off my dress as he helped me gently to the ground. I wrapped my arms around him and squeezed my eyes shut, blocking out the sun, which stared right down on us. I guess that was what Theo was trying to give me the whole time. Like a Japanese sculpture, he was filling my cracks in with gold. And even though I knew it, I couldn't see it until now. But it was also time I gave him the same, that I saw in him all the glory that he found in me.

I close my eyes and there I am, there we are. The saloon is empty, and I am standing in the middle of the dance floor. Theo sits across from me on the stage. He looks up, like he's been waiting for me.

"Hey buddy." He smiles, and before I know it, I am running across the room, and I am in his arms and everything that stopped us from having this moment when he was alive is gone. He lifts me up and my lips fall on his and I kiss him in a way I never knew how. I feel my whole body melt into his and he holds me, and the tears fall from my face as I finally tell him, "I loved you, I loved all of you but I didn't know how to let go of everything out there.

"And I let go of you. But I loved you, Theo. I loved all of you."

He pushes the hair back from my forehead, and as his strong and handsome face leans over mine, he slowly dances with me as though there is phantom music playing. I remember every detail of his sunburnt eyes and his strong cheekbones. He leans his mouth down to my ears, "You were my everything."

I feel him fading. I've never been in the journey this long, and I pull back to see him walking away.

"Theo," I call, and he turns around. "I'm going to fight."

"I know." He smiles. "Never give up, Janey. Never. Give. Up."

And then he stops. He stares off for a moment and I see the crack, even beyond the veil, the losses we can never stave. He turns to me, "Tell Zoe, tell her I'll always be with her, okay?"

I feel my body shake as he smiles that great, big Theo Karras smile and walks out of the back door of the saloon, the same one Martin Montgomery entered months before, the one that brought us here to this space beyond time, allowing Theo and me to finally find the love that alluded us in life.

When I was one year sober, I woke up every morning and meditated, breathing in faith, and breathing out fear. It was a simple enough technique, but simple techniques frequently bring enormous change. Every day, I confronted life with a deep belief that things were happening as they should. Even when I rear-ended someone on my way to work, even when a boy I liked failed to call. Faith gave me a bird's eye view. I was just one of the pieces being moved across the board by a far more skillful player.

The day after the sweat lodge, Dennis and I take Zoe and Rocky to the park near his house. Every day since the inauguration has become more difficult for me to understand this man I love so much. Because Dennis is both my deepest connection to kindness and everything I believe is wrong with the world. And I'm not sure what choices I am supposed to make in the face of that conflict. Can I raise my right fist from a podium and yet still love this man so much? Am I now required to hate him or is that, in fact, what people like Donald Trump want? They want me to make him a monster so that they can have him completely, so they can strip him of his kindness and tolerance and make him believe that I am the enemy.

"Almost every woman I know has been sexually assaulted," I explain to him as we walk. "In high school, a guy tried to rape me, shoved my hand down his pants. In college, I hooked up with a guy, and said no to sex. Two hours later, I woke up to find him on top of me."

Is this progress? That I can now tell my Republican uncle the definition of date rape. That he can know that sexual assault is a rite of passage and that I have experienced it.

"Jesus, Janey."

"That's who your friend Donnie is to me, Uncle Dennis. He's the guy who gets on top of you after you say that's not what you want."

Finally, we make our way down to a little man-made pond in Dennis's neighborhood. I pull Zoe from her stroller as Dennis sits with Rocky. We show Zoe a family of ducks glistening across the water, so natural in this industrialized place.

"Ducky," Zoe calls out, pointing to the birds. Though Dennis is right there, I close my eyes. I inhale faith, and then as my breath catches in my throat, I exhale fear. It feels awkward at first. I don't know how to find faith in this new life.

"Ducky!" Zoe calls again.

I open my eyes as my daughter turns to me. In slow motion, Zoe comes into view. Her blonde hair, her perfect profile, her soft lips and Theo's eyes. Her voice filled with laughter and hope and faith. And now, we start again. Always, we start again. And with each rising sun, we find that there never was an end to the tale, there was only a different beginning, one we rewrite each day. I reach out for my daughter as the tears emerge, an easy reaction now.

"Mama, no cry," she says, finally beginning to find her words.

I pull the baby into me as she looks out to the ducks. Dennis turns around from watching them.

"Janey, you're going to be fine," he states with a confidence that would unnerve me in anyone else but in him I trust. "You're a survivor."

I smile. "I don't want to be a survivor, Dennis. I want to live in a world where we don't have to survive. And that isn't going to happen if we keep arming hate."

"Jane, you know how I feel . . ."

"I do, and you need to understand that how you feel is only going to kill more people. Dennis, please, I love you so much. I don't want to see you with blood on your hands, too."

He looks at me, and I don't know that we're ever capable of changing each other, but then again, Theo changed me. Dennis ruffles my hair, "I love you, Janey. Nothing will ever change that."

I spent my whole life seeking family outside the one I was given. I knew I couldn't trust Andrea, and so I tried to find other parents and siblings, I tried to find people I could trust, and then I feared trusting them. But there way always Dennis, there, waiting. And he is now also the enemy. I look at him and know that his life has not always been easy, and yet, he doesn't realize and might never know just how easy it has been. He's like a golden retriever bouncing through the grass, ignorant of all the ways in which the world can be cruel and harsh. And I don't know how to reconcile this man who can be so loving and kind and who has been friends with Black women and gay men and who used to play poker with his Islamic neighbor, and who now thinks that Donald Trump is his savior.

I'm not sure if he even understands his own cognitive dissonance. I feel my phone buzz in my back pocket.

At first, I ignore it. But then it buzzes again. I see it's Yvette, she's called a few times.

"Give me a second," I tell my uncle, answering the phone. "What's up, Yves?"

"I got it."

"What?" I ask, not even sure what she means.

"The show . . . the streamer that went cold, they came back fucking hot."

"What happened?"

"I don't know, but apparently, they're still interested. They want the show."

"Jesus, Yvette, you did it."

"We did it," she says, as I look over to where Dennis and Zoe feed the ducks as Rocky tries to steal the bread.

"I'm coming back to LA," Yvette adds. "We need to talk."

That night, Andrea and Maggie come over and Dennis cooks the same lamb chops I have loved since I was a kid. When Theo and I started dating, he took me to a Greek restaurant for one of our first dates; I joked that I would marry any man who could feed me that much lamb. At our wedding, they served lamb chops, the small kind you eat with your fingers, and in some box somewhere, there is a picture of me in my wedding dress and Theo in his suit, both with a chop between our teeth, fingers dirty from the meat.

Sometimes, I still think about the fact that Rose wasn't supposed to come to Zoe's party. Had I not moved it to Saturday to have Peanut, she wouldn't have attended, she wouldn't have told us about John Thomas. We wouldn't have gone to the saloon that night and Theo would still be here.

One of our last fights was the day after Zoe's birthday party. Andrea was at the house, along with Theo, who was supposed to be at work that day but was now going to be returning to his job as an Uber driver, the backup that felt like failure. We were in our bedroom as I was getting dressed, pulling on my wool slacks and slipping on my two-inch heels.

"I don't know what you want me to do," Theo snapped at me after I complained that he would be hanging out all day while I went to work. "We agreed that one of us needed to be home with Zoe."

"I want you to be a grown-up," I hissed, hoping Andrea couldn't overhear us, though she was likely listening at the door.

"I am doing the best I can, Jane," he pleaded, which only made me angrier. "Maybe you just need to accept that it's not that bad. Our life is good. Why can't you see that?"

"All I see is that I am the one making it happen," I told him, ignoring that for most of Zoe's first year, it had been Theo who had taken care of her, it is Theo who would help to rock her at night, it is Theo who would hop up to change diapers or make a bottle or get her a snack.

Theo looked wounded. "I don't think that's it, Jane. I think you know you want more than this. And that has nothing to do with me."

As I turned to see myself in the mirror, dressed in another woman's uniform, the hair, the heels, a far cry from someone they once nicknamed the hunter, I didn't know how to tell him he was right.

So, you're gonna be a big-time star reporter now?" Maggie jokes as my uncle passes the food around. Yvette didn't share much with me, except they were looking for hosts for the show, and my name topped the list.

"I don't know. I don't really know what's going on. Yvette will be here this weekend and then she'll let me know. She's still getting it all confirmed herself."

"Is it going to be funny, like when you did the show with the comedian?" Maggie asks.

"I don't think there's a comedian."

"Oh, well then, forget the comedy," Maggie jokes.

"Hey, I'm funny," I push back and Maggie laughs.

"Getting there. You used to be hysterical."

I realize that over the years with Theo, I began to lose my sense of humor, caught up in the frustrations of domestic life and universal disappointment. I guess that's just the consequence of low-grade trauma, of the daily onslaught of small frustrations, of bottles that won't open and cereal boxes that rip, of overdraft fees and money that doesn't come through on time because the bank is holding it, traffic jams and fix-it tickets and waiting in line and running out of baby formula and post-partum depression and dead fathers and mass shootings and presidents who are accused of rape and the unending hostilities that even in the best of circumstances, even with white skin and some money in the account and an NYU degree gathering dust in some storage unit in Torrance, I simply forgot how to be funny.

I want to be funny again.

"Look, lady," I reply. "I've had a lot on my plate."

Maggie laughs and Dennis even follows, though I can tell Andrea still doesn't know how to respond. She is happy for me and yet she can't help but be scared. I don't know what the future holds for me and these people who raised me, who sacrificed for me, people who are now on the other side of enemy lines. I'm not sure how long love will hold us in place.

"Mom." She looks up. "I'm going to be fine."

Because though the Mojave was the match to light the fuse, I have been filling the barrel with dynamite my whole Goddamn life.

TWENTY-ONE

After nearly ten years of unending drought, Los Angeles is consumed with rain. Despite the downpour, Zoe and I make our way to the airport, to pick up Yvette.

I wait with Zoe by the baggage claim for Yvette to emerge. As soon as she does, we don't hold back, rushing into each other's arms. The energy we had in New York is still there, still burning through the friendship that started so many years before when we were just starry-eyed kids who knew about broken hearts but not shattered ones. The final FBI briefing is the next day. I asked if she would join Peter and me.

"Thanks for doing this with me," I murmur into Yvette's ear.

"Of course." She flashes me a sigh. "And we're also doing it for the show."

"The show?"

"We have a lot to discuss." She takes Zoe from my arms, "Get over here Zoe-bo, tell me what's been up in your world."

That night, we go out dinner at the Sunset Tower, where she has booked a suite for the weekend, one of those swanky hotels on the Sunset Strip where celebrities and fancy media people like Yvette hang out. After we sit down, I finally ask Yvette the question she has yet to answer, "So what happened after Diana died?"

Yvette looks at her menu, refusing to lift her gaze. "What do you mean?"

"You said you could have lost the kids. What happened?"

Yvette looks up at me. "I tried to kill myself."

She sighs, like it was all just a bad dream, "It was right after Dylan's first birthday. I don't know. All those memories. Thinking back to what it was like when Ella turned one, how happy we were."

Yvette stops, "I knew how dangerous it was. If Diana's parents had found out, they would have taken the kids in a heartbeat. I got into therapy, started going to a grief group, all the things you're supposed to do."

She pauses and looks at me. "The things you should start doing."

"Did it work though?" I ask, thinking of all the things I haven't done, knowing that I have barely begun to heal, living in the adrenaline of vengence, and not in the quiet spaces where grief has the space to grow but also to mend.

"I just keep thinking there's some end date in sight, but then some days I wake up, and I'm right back at the beginning."

"Grief isn't linear, Jane. It just shows up when it wants to, however it wants to, those memories, those moments."

Yvette smiles. "I mean, you know as well as I do that nothing will ever work, exactly? You can get everything you want, and something will always be missing."

She looks off a bit and I realize that there might be another reason Yvette hasn't felt a need to rush anything between us. She is still in love with Diana, still connected to the woman she married, the mother to her children. And maybe moving on isn't such a victory after all. Maybe holding on offers its own rewards.

I reach for my iced tea, looking back down at the menu, as Yvette changes subjects.

"So . . . the show, it's going to be fresh. The idea is that we do a deep dive on a different topic every year, but we want there to be a community organizing component, too. We want to create forums and marches and take the media to the streets, like literally. We want to use it as a way not just to inform or educate but to mobilize."

"Yves! That's amazing."

"I'll be in charge of everything, developing content, and as I just negotiated in my deal, hiring the hosts . . ."

"You should just hire yourself," I tell her, confused why Yvette won't take her rightful place in front of the camera.

"You know who I want to hire."

I don't know how the roads led Yvette and me back to each other and I don't understand why we've had to lose what we lost to get here, but there is no doubt, we were meant to intersect. We nod at each other from across the table as it begins to hit me. "My life is about to change, isn't it?"

"Forever, if you want it to."

And just as I did years before standing in a white dress at a Greek Orthodox church at the corner of Normandie and Pico in Los Angeles, I say, "I do."

"I want the first year to be about gun control, but I want it from all sides. I want to dig deep, and I want people to become a part of it. I want—"

"A revolution," I reply. "Look, Yvette, if we're going to do this, I want us to tell the truth. The real truth, the kind that can actually liberate people. Because we do have a chance to do it right this time, and not just us, personally. We have a chance to avenge all of this, even our own wrongdoings, and I don't mean by power or punishment or any of that fucking shit, but through love and ambition and generosity. And I cannot back down from that fight again."

"I'm not hiring you to surrender," Yvette leans back with the kind of confidence I once had but am now beginning to rebuild.

"I got nothing left to fear, Yves. And neither do you."

Though more details are to be hammered out, the offer is simple. Over the summer, I'll will be hired for a twelve-episode season.

"If by fall, the numbers are tracking, we'll look at a year contract."

"So, it's like an extended audition?" I ask, raised to doubt every good deal.

"Yeah, in a way. Look, of course you can fuck it up. But are you gonna fuck it up?"

"I'll do my best." I laugh.

"Good, because you're right. I don't just want to burn it down. I want to build it, too. I want to stop the bully."

I lean forward, stating as clearly as I can, "With a roar."

Yvette takes a sip from her glass. "See, I knew you'd do fine."

I sit back, as overwhelmed as if I'd just been given bad news, because trauma can cut both ways. Our reaction to the best in life mimicking our reaction to the worst.

Yvette smiles. "You know the one thing Di and Theo had in common? They weren't afraid to speak their mind. To anyone, they just said what they felt. And if nothing else, we learned that from them."

I smile softly at the comparison of our spouses. "So, I won't be exploiting Theo?"

"No, honey. You'll be making him proud."

I look across the table at this woman who is everything I have wanted in a person, kind and ambitious, bold and persistent. She is the mirror I was seeking, but more than that, she is the partner I wanted.

I smile gently as I hold up my glass. "To messy lives."

Yvette meets my toast. "The best kind."

A re you ready to do this?" my brother-in-law asks as we make our way east to the desert. Yvette sits in the back seat with a cameraman she hired to capture footage of the day, planning to use it in the series.

Peter's girlfriend doesn't join us, but as we get onto the I-10, he tells me they're moving in with each other at the end of the month.

"That's amazing," I smile, mussing his dark thick hair that reminds me so much of Theo's. "You planning to pop the question?"

· Peter taps the steering wheel and smiles. "Feels like it. I want my own family. And Jennifer and Harrison, they're my family."

Yvette stares out the window as we move along the I-10. The city turns to desert and the wind turbines emerge, welcoming us to Coachella Valley. I am reminded of that final trip with Theo, irritated by the traffic and his tardiness, worried that we would be late, that we would miss our reservation and not be able to get into the show.

"When do you think it gets easier?" Theo asked.

"What?" I replied, watching the blades cut across the sky. "Parenthood?"

"Parenthood? Life? All of it?"

"When we die?" I laughed lightly, not even remembering the joke until now. "I don't know—if we have a second kid, do it all again, maybe six years. I think it gets easier when they turn five."

"Really?" Theo asked. "But then aren't there a whole bunch of other things to worry about?"

"There's always something to worry about." I rolled down the window to feel the heat outside. "I guess that's the thing about parenthood. You're given this one gift that if you lost it, you don't even know if you could survive, and then you have to send them out into the world every day and have faith that they're going to come home. It's a crazy concept, really. I don't know who came up with it."

"Kind of like marriage, huh?" he laughed, remembering our conversation from the week earlier as we were driving back to the house for Zoe's birthday, the one where I told him that marriage was just too hard to make sense anymore.

"None of it's easy." I looked over at him. "That's why we build families, I guess. Better than going it alone."

Peter exits the freeway to San Bernardino, heading to the Convention Center, where the final briefing is being held. There is a main presentation, PowerPoint slides describing Montgomery's plan in bureaucratic detail, documenting everything he used to undertake it. At the end, they show pictures of the crime scene, except this time, they don't leave out the pictures of the bodies. We see our loved ones stretched out, slumped over, caught in the camera's lens, like people sleeping under unsuspected surveillance. And they show us the dead and mutilated body of Martin Montgomery. Unlike Theo, at the end of that long two minutes and twenty-eight seconds, Montgomery no longer had a face. What more was there to say?

I sit down with the other families, while Yvette captures the conversations. Some come up to me, saying how much they appreciate what I've done. Others eye me warily, believing in their rights to hold whatever gun they please even after burying a sister, a father, a son. In an adjacent room, all the evidence is laid out for victims and their families to see, including the AR-15 that killed eleven people that night. Comparatively speaking, it was a small shooting. More will follow, we all know that. But what happened that night in the Mojave felt like an intimate affair, the shooter moving in front of the small bar—we, his captive audience.

At the break, I walk into the evidence room and stand over the gun. This is who I blame. It wasn't the hard life of a human, complicated by grief and anger and trauma. The gun was a symptom, but our leaders had ushered in a pandemic of violence. The fact that the solution was so simple made the problem all that more cruel. The fight was about offering all of us a softer place to land, a place where we could find pause from the grief and anger and trauma that affected us in varying impact. We were standing at the crossroads of history, and we were responsible for how it bowed. I look up only to see Giselle standing on the other side of the display.

"Hey," I say. She smiles, and we meet each other in the middle of the evidence tables.

"I was hoping I'd see you here," she says after we hug.

"I tried to call you," I explain. "I was doing this interview, I left you a message."

She shakes her head, "Yeah, that's not for me. You did good though. You're good at this."

"It was my job . . . once."

"Mmmm," I can tell that Gigi might like me, but she still sees me as one of them, someone with resources and power, and though I might have felt poor and powerless over the last few years, my privilege cannot be ignored.

"Where are you living?" I ask.

"Mexico, Nogales. It's okay. Kids aren't in school, their Spanish isn't there yet, and I can't afford private." She shakes her head. "It's kind of messed up."

"Look, I know you don't like the speeches and the politics." I reach into my bag and pull out my MOFC business card. I don't know how long it will apply to me, but I wonder whether it might mean more for Gigi. "They're just starting, and I don't know what you do for work, but I bet they could use you."

Gigi doesn't take the card at first, just looks at it.

"I can figure it out, you know. I don't need help," she replies.

"I know. But we need yours." She reaches out and takes the card.

Peter walks up, "Come on, they're starting back up."

Gigi and I hug and I don't know that she'll ever call but together, we become the Trojan Horse they never expected.

Peter and I walk back into the conference center where Yvette and Ted, the DP, wait. I sit back down and try to ignore the camera trained on us. Though everything Martin left in his wake was messy and confusing, the crime itself was as simple as they come. After the presentation is over, there is a Q&A, where Yvette's crew will film us asking the usual questions—knowing there is only one good answer.

I am walking down the hallway when I hear someone call my name; I know who it is before I turn around.

James approaches as I smile. "Man, you love these things."

He laughs quietly. "I don't really. It's my job."

"You have a shitty job."

He pulls me in for a hug that feels too intimate and yet is exactly what I need.

"So, I ran into Yvette," he shares. "She said you're working on a show together."

I laugh. "She is the worst at secrets."

"No reason to hide that, Jane. You deserve it, you do."

"It's what I wanted, you know? Just feels like a steep price."

The tears come before I can stop them.

"No, sweetheart. We might not have always done right by them when they were here, but we get to do that now."

He puts his hand against my face, much like Theo used to do, "And I promise you, he is so very proud of of you."

I draw myself up on my toes to press my lips against his. It's not sexual but his lips feel warm and right and I'm pretty sure we've helped each other. I come back down and James smiles. "We're gonna make it stop, Jane. I believe that."

"Me too," I reply. "See you soon, James."

I raise my right fist to which James laughs. He's probably never raised a right fist in his life, but he does now, as he offers, "See you soon."

I turn around and walk out of the hall.

The next day, I pick up Rose to give her the good news. Despite all the changes that have happened over the year, Rose has remained the same, her wild curls framing her 1940s face. She is my constant sidekick, the Robin to my Batman.

Rose reaches over the back of her seat to see Zoe. "There's my Zozo girl!"

"Hiiieee," Zoe squeals.

"Hasn't lost her cool, I see?" Rose leans over and we hug. "How you doing, kid?"

"It's been a ride," I reply. The show is preparing my contract and my job is to find an agent to negotiate it. Yvette instructs me to pick one I believe will stick with me in sickness and in health. I look over at Rose and remember the first time we met in high school. It was no different than the first time I saw Theo, knowing immediately he would forever be a part of my life. I saw her across the room, and I knew this lifetime had brought us back together for another round.

"Once you've met with the agents, what happens next?" Rose asks, as we move through East Hollywood, passing Thai Town and Jumbo's Clown Room, the strip club where Courtney Love is rumored to have gotten her start.

"Yvette said that we're supposed to start shooting the first week of June," I explain the plan to Rose. "They'll work out my deal, and then I'll move to New York."

Rose doesn't reply, just shakes her head, adjusting her seat so she can recline a bit.

"Assuming they figure out my contract, I'll need to be there by next month."

"Shit, that's fast. Do you have a place?"

"Apparently, the network has an apartment in Murray Hill I can use. It's ridiculous but it has a garden for Rocky, and I thought, for Bowie, too."

"Bowie?" Rose asks, confused why I am mentioning her dog. A small smile begins to grow across her face.

"I don't want to do this alone, Rose. And I get if you want to stay here, but I just thought, maybe it would be a good change for both of us. I mean, you are a Julliard dropout? I'm pretty sure there's a revolving door for returnees."

Rose presses her hand against the window as Hollywood passes by, laughing, "We bringing Maggie too?"

"I wish." And this is where the bitter meets the sweet because I am actually free to go. I've asked Rose to come with me to the beach, to do the one thing I have been unable to do since Theo's death. We make our way to the water without saying much. It is a cloudy but beautiful day, the usual smog feels cleared by the rains.

Rose doesn't have to ask where we are going as I finally put on my blinker and turn in to the parking lot for Topanga Beach.

On one of our first dates, Theo and I drove out to Topanga so I could watch him surf. Topanga was initially settled by the native Tongva tribe, who gave the region its name, meaning "a place above." It was the western border of their territory, butting up against the more famous Chumash to the north. Before we began dating, I had only been to the area a few times, though I had long known of its mythologies, stories of Neil Diamond and Neil Young and the Topanga Corral echoing across LA's modern history. But for Theo, Topanga was a second home, its rocky point break his favorite place to surf, garnering him a spot in the lineup even among the territorial locals.

At the time of our first date, Theo was selling flea market art, screen prints that he made in his garage of famous icons: Presley, Brando, Monroe, and lesser-known legends like the surfer Bunker Spreckels and the blues man Robert Johnson.

I had gone by the Melrose Trading Post to pick him up on our way out to the beach. As Theo counted the twenties and tens he had made that day, I realized that the small bundle accounted for his weekly earnings. Otherwise, he did odd jobs when they came, bartering on his name and former Dodgers status when he could.

But that day as we drove across LA, I was just beginning to understand the inner workings of Theo Karras. How for his lack of money, he had cultivated a personality that was absolutely abundant.

"When we were kids, Petra and I would ride the bus all over town," Theo explained, as we inched along US 101, heading north. "The RTD. Rough, tumble, and dirty. We didn't even know where were going. Just wanted to get out of the house."

At the time, I still had a tape deck in my car, and as we made our way through the Valley and into the wooded, hippie community of Topanga, Theo found my lone cassette, the single for Iggy Pop's 1990 classic, "Candy."

"Iggy Pops!" Theo rejoiced, adding an *s* to the singer's last name.

"It was my favorite song in middle school," I said. "I've had the tape since then."

Theo popped in the tape. We began to talk about past loves, our relationship so natural from its first day, as though we had known each forever. Perhaps that was the hardest part of our marriage—how we threatened the friendship that stood at its center. He told me about his ex-girlfriends, and I told him the whole and unabridged story of Blake Edwards as Topanga Canyon passed outside the window.

"Sounds like an asshole," Theo replied.

"Yeah, he was. And yet, I still believe, I still know, we were in love."

"That's what makes him an asshole." Theo grabbed my hand, awkward still in our new romance. "Being in love shouldn't be something you can walk away from."

"Really?" I asked, as Theo rewound the song, playing it again from the start. "You think love can actually last forever?"

"Of course," Theo's confidence was firm. "My parents, they didn't even love each other in the beginning, but now, they would never want to be away from one another."

"Yeah, but they sleep in different beds."

"I think love changes."

"I believe in love, don't get me wrong," I paused before continuing, aware that we were stepping onto the ice of a new relationship. "I just don't know how good I am at forever."

remember my words as I pull into the Topanga parking lot, recognizing some of the surfers and skaters hanging out by the staircase, old stoners who Theo knew for years, using with them back in the day, and later, helping some get sober, even if only a few of them stayed. I hold Zoe as Rose and I make our way down to the beach. It has been a long time since we've been here, almost a year since the last time Theo and I brought our then baby to the beach, Zoe sitting in the sand while Daddy went out to surf. Zoe becomes instantly obsessed with the small palm trees that line Topanga's shore.

"It's funny—we didn't come here that often with Zoe," I remark as I kneel with my daughter. Rose remains standing, making circles in the sand with her toe.

"Really?" Rose asks. "I would have thought you guys would have brought her all the time. Theo thinking she was a surf prodigy and all."

"Yeah," I look out at the surfers along the water. "I guess we figured we would do that more when she was older . . ."

Rose sits down as Zoe crawls into my lap.

"Are you okay with this?" Rose asks quietly.

"With what?"

"Fame? Fortune? Whatever is next?"

"Hell, I don't know," I reply, kissing the top of Zoe's head. I look back out to the sea, "I just wish Theo got to see it."

But then I remember that last time I saw him in the saloon, the last time he held me. After years of being with someone who couldn't remember or figure out who she was, he was holding the right woman. And Theo got to meet her. He waited around just so he could.

I don't know how to explain this to Rose, that Theo was here, that he didn't leave right away, and that if I look hard enough, I know I'll still be able to find him. I smile. "I guess in the end, though, he did."

As though she can read my mind, Rose leans over. "Janey. People might die. But after we go, love is all that's left."

I watch the surfers out at sea and realize that might have been what made loving Theo so hard. He was always himself, always so sure of his abilities even when I could only see his flaws. I had been raised to demand perfection, and I forgot that the biggest adventures were born from mistakes and accidents. I'm still not sure why a wedding band changed us so much, why the responsibilities of parenthood made it so we couldn't see the magic anymore, but I feel it now. I know the magic was there, that it's still here. I look up and out at the sea. And then I see him, a surfer on the water, paddling into a set.

Smiling, I raise my hand and wave.

I drop Rose off at her apartment in Silver Lake before heading back to the Sunset Tower to meet Yvette for dinner. I don't even think about it as I drive north away from Rose's apartment and into Montrose. I pull the car up across the street from our house. The new tenants have installed slatted blinds across the living room windows, blocking out the main view of the home, but as I get out of the car, pulling Zoe from her car seat, I get a clear shot of what was once Zoe's room. They've repainted it charcoal gray, so different from Zoe's happy mint walls. Gone even is the rose bush that grew outside Zoe's window, a perfect pink rose sprouting every few months.

"Zoe's rose," Theo would remark.

Zoe and I walk up the street a bit to a neighbor's house, which has a display of fairies and angels in the yard, an assortment of small pebbles for the children to collect. While Zoe plays, I look down the street. The bougainvillea is alive again, the trees draping along our street in verdant repose. After a day of thick clouds, the sun begins to break through, casting a long bright shadow across the Verdugo Mountains in the distance.

"We were happy here," I say out loud, as Zoe picks up the little blue stones in our neighbor's yard, quickly putting them in her pockets.

"Happy," she repeats, smiling up at me.

Maybe that's all revolution is—it's reincarnation. And we'll return again and again and again until we get it right. So, it's okay if I fuck it up. I'm not giving up.

Never. Give. Up.

Down the street, I can see two girls playing in their front yard. Theo and their father were friends, at one point shaping a surfboard together in the man's garage. The girls' laughter drifts up the street. I know this is all gone now. I will raise Zoe as a single mother. I will learn to be someone else, in the great act of becoming, cells dissolving to reunite as a new element altogether, and together, they rise.

I bend down and pick up my daughter. "Come on, Zo. We better get going."

Together, we walk back to the car. For a moment, I allow myself to pretend that Theo is still alive, hanging out at the house as Zoe and I return from a walk, playing ball with Rocky in the backyard. I put Zoe in her car seat and get behind the wheel of my old CRV. I look back at our house. The past forever playing on repeat as the sun begins to set. I start the car, and drive out of the life that once was, and into the one that is just beginning.

ACKNOWLEDGMENTS

This was a long journey, as writing usually is. And there were so many people who helped me along the road: readers, editors, friends, and workshops. I want to thank many of you: Tamela Gordon, Gina Frangello, Ellen Bass, Diana Wagman, Jennifer Pastiloff, Roxan McDonald, Jamie Lou, Sarah Blake, Carrie Howland, Katya Lidsky, and Cassie Mannes Murray. This book has seen many twists and turns over the years, and I thank you for your inspiration and guidance along the road.

To my husband and little loves—thank you for giving mommy the space to write this book. I started it with a one-year old baby and am ending it with a seven and four-year-old. Things take time, but I wouldn't have had the time without their grace to pursue this dream.

To my family—who still don't understand why I'm a writer. I wrote this for us, for the unspoken debates about who we are and who we should be in this world, and the gaps between both. I believe we all can still cross them.

And finally, for anyone who has been impacted by gun violence. Every morning, I kiss my kids hoping to see them again at the end of the day. I pray for all of us that we find a way to remove that reality from our lives and the lives of our children. We can make it stop.

ABOUT THE AUTHOR

KRISTEN MCGUINESS is the bestselling author of 51/50: The Magical Adventures of a Single Life. She has appeared on the "Today Show," in USA Today, and in Marie Claire, and has written for numerous publications, including Rolling Stone, Marie Claire, Salon, Psychology Today, and Shondaland, among others. In addition, Kristen is the founder and publisher of Rise Books, as well as the co-founder of Row House Publishing.

Kristen began her career working in publicity for St. Martin's Press before joining the editorial departments of Simon & Schuster, Free Press, and Judith Regan at Harper Collins. She also spent time in film development before leaving the entertainment industry to become a fundraising professional for non-profits.

Kristen received her Bachelor's degree from Hamilton College and a Master's degree from the American University of Paris. She lives in Ojai, CA with her husband, two children, and a dog named Peter.